LORENA

LORENA

Frank G. Slaughter

Doubleday & Company, Inc.
Garden City, New York

Except for a few historic personages, readily identifiable as such, the characters and events of this novel are entirely fictional. It is a coincidence if any person, living or dead, is mentioned by name.

LORENA

Book One

Mist from the bottoms had obscured the turnpike during the last hour of Dr. Yancey's journey. It was lifting rapidly, now that evening had dwindled into night. The cold November stars were clear above the pine barrens to the north.

Flicking his whip above the ears of the ancient gelding that drew his gig, the plantation doctor hardly welcomed the promise of better weather. Rain and mist had been a blessing while the false Indian summer lingered over Georgia. Bad roads and swollen streams had kept the Yankees within the perimeter of occupied Atlanta. Once the bad weather ended, they would surely be on the move again. Would their next strike take them southeast, toward Savannah? Or would they first secure their flank by moving on Macon by way of Indian Ford—and the road that led through Brandt's Crossing to Selby Hall?

Speculation along these lines, as Yancey knew, was useless. Thanks to the welter of rumor, he could not even strike a reasonable balance between the die-hards (who were sure that Hood would destroy Sherman once he took the field again) and the crepehangers who had already surrendered in their hearts. He could only pray that the Selby luck (which had brooded above the mansards of the Big House, like a dark angel, all through the war) would survive the next hammer blow of Mars. . . . Cracking his whip more sharply, he forced his mind to dwell on matters within his control, such as the maternity call from the tenant farm that had used up his afternoon.

LORENA

By all the rules of logic, maternity calls from Selby tenants should be rare these days. Nearly all the husbands were in uniform: the wives were busy with their men's work, in fields and gin. Nan Purdy's man had served the Confederacy from the beginning—but Nan had given birth each year, as predictably as the deep-uddered cows in the Selby barns. The Purdys, Dr. Yancey reflected, deserved a place of honor in the farmer's almanac. A single leave (in each ten lunar months) was all that Sergeant Ben Purdy needed to insure his immortality. There would always be Purdy men to till his forty acres, to drive his cotton wagons to Selby for the annual division of the profits.

Regardless of the outcome of this coming winter of lost causes, the Purdy clan would find ways to endure. So far, Yancey could not say as much for his own people—though the white mass of Selby Hall, and the green demesne that enclosed it, seemed eternal as time when his gig swung into the drive.

Sentinels were on duty at the gate. In the cedar grove a few late cook fires gave evidence that Captain Bradfield Selby's cavalry troop had not yet received orders to rejoin his brigade. Other than these, nothing indicated that the breath of war had touched this corner of the South. In the clean bath of starlight the lawns that flanked the drive were cropped velvet-smooth (they could hardly be otherwise, with the cotton in and hands to spare for such chores). Along the drive itself the famous double file of oaks was rigorously pruned: tonight, more than any single feature, those immaculate lines of trees drove home the continuing miracle of Selby Hall. Here, thought Yancey, was a true enclave of repose. What outsider would guess the repose was only surface-deep?

The great manor house itself—rising like an Athenian temple on its man-made hill, set off by its rose gardens and its boxwoods—was the focal point of this strange aloofness. The ordered blocks of work buildings, the looming shapes of gin and packhouse, were a world apart. So were the five thousand acres of still-green furrows that were Selby Hall's reason for being: the glow of light at its tall glass doors could not dispel the illusion that it was some splendid, half-forgotten tomb. . . . Appropriately, the barns were divided from the formal gardens by a windbreak of cedars. It was broken at a single point, where a utility road branched off from the noble curve of the drive. In the stable yard, Yancey surrendered his reins to a groom, who had emerged from a stall at the sound of wheels.

The plantation doctor had intended to report at once to the Big House. Lowering his tired legs from the gig, he saw that his boots were red from the wet clay in the Purdys' yard—and swung instead toward the lighted rectangle of the overseer's office. Mud-caked boots did not belong in Selby Hall. Besides, he was eager to learn if Luke Jackson had returned from his mission to Decatur.

There was no sign of Luke in the office, though a hanging lamp burned above his desk. Saladin, the young Negro who had recently been promoted to the job of plantation bookkeeper, was hard at work on a ledger. His handsome ebony profile stood out boldly against the whitewashed bricks of the office wall. Again Yancey changed his mind and moved toward his own domain, without entering Luke Jackson's. Sal was a friend of long standing, but he was in no mood to converse with him now.

In the memory of man no slave had moved so far at Selby—or so fast. Yancey could still recall the storm of disapproval that had swept Cray County last spring when Lorena Selby had put the Negro in the overseer's office—without even consulting her absent husband. . . . A few years before, the county had chuckled indulgently when old Judge Selby (who was known to have queer notions) had made Saladin a protégé: the county had nodded its approval when the Judge had given Sal to his new daughter-in-law as a wedding present. At the time, there had been no shortage of white bookkeepers in Georgia. It had been inconceivable that a coal-black bondsman would one day be poring over the Selby ledgers—simply because the overseer was too overworked, and too unlettered, to handle such a task.

Abandoning the unsolved status of Saladin, Dr. Yancey entered his surgery. This was a small clapboard building standing between Luke Jackson's office and the quarters. Since the health of three hundred field hands was his direct concern, the plantation doctor had found it simpler to maintain a dressing room and study in a lean-to. Here he could sleep when there were emergencies in the cabins—or when epidemics threatened. Here he kept the brandy that had been his after-dark solace for more years than he cared to count. Here, too, were the books and pamphlets that would have seemed heretical, had he displayed them openly in his formal suite at Selby Hall. . . .

After he had changed his clothing from the skin out, the mirror assured him he could pass muster at Lorena's soiree. He had supped after a fashion in the Purdy kitchen, so the fact he was late for dinner was hardly disturbing. Food had never been an important item on Yancey's schedule. Not when brandy and good Havanas were still available.

He finished his first brandy while he adjusted his cravat. The cigar he lighted for his evening walk through the quarters—and blessed Quenten Rowley as he struck the lucifer. Only Lorena's brother could bring cigars to Selby now: like the gown of *peau de soie* she planned to wear tonight, they had come through the blockade on one of the runners Quent still chartered out of Wilmington. Such luxuries were considered bad form, now the enemy was on Georgia soil: a Spartan disdain for the amenities that made life bearable was mandatory among the die-hards—even when those same Spartans had bombproofs among their menfolks, or had been prudent enough to send their hard money abroad.

Lorena, Yancey reflected, was above such hypocrisies. She had given all she could to the Confederate cause, from the day of the first secession. Tonight—it was her husband's last at home—she deserved a dinner party. By the same token, she could afford to ignore gossip—even to the point of installing a slave as her overseer's helper. Thanks to her management during Brad Selby's absence in the field, three hundred slaves and their progeny still slept in quarters tonight—as tranquilly as though the Judge still ruled here. What other landowner in Cray County could say as much?

The slave cabins lay in triple crescents, in the hollow behind the barns—each resplendent in new whitewash, the roofs fresh-shingled against the autumn rains. Doors and windows were closed and barred—a sensible precaution on moonless nights, when haunts were stirring. Yancey's practiced ear caught no echo of nightmare behind the portals. Save for the snoring of tired sleepers, there was no sound but the whimper of a newborn child in Big Jody's cabin —and the crooning of Jody's woman had already begun to still that feeble wail.

LORENA

A careful shepherd (even when his flock was safe in its enclosure), Yancey retraced his steps on the hard-packed earth before he ended his tour. All of them slept now—even Big Jody's woman and his newest get. At the door of the head driver's cabin Ajax's snores seemed to set his roof dancing. Ajax (the one headman at Selby privileged to wear a bull whip coiled round his neck while he paced the cotton rows) had earned his repose tonight. So had the twin carpenters, Castor and Pollux—again the Judge's whimsy was apparent in the naming—who had produced miracles of ingenuity to keep Selby in repair during these trying years. So had Prome (short for Prometheus), the Mozambique giant who was the best picker in quarters—and next to Ajax himself, the best baler at the gin.

Lorena, thought Yancey, had done her utmost to make these three hundred lives secure—and she had promised them what she could for tomorrow. . . . He faced north again on his climb back to the lawns. Looking across that mass of dark rooftops, he could make out the turnpike where it followed the riverbank to the pasture land that marked the beginning of Greentree Plantation. The November stars were timeless beacons above the pulse of the stream. It was beyond belief that occupied Atlanta lay a scant thirty miles beyond that pasture. Or that the invaders who now manned the city's hard-won defenses awaited only their commander's word to wipe out all that Selby stood for.

When he had mounted the southern portico of Selby Hall, Yancey found it even harder to admit the threat was real.

On this side, the house faced its formal gardens across a velvet-green apron of lawn. There was a distant view of the belvedere beside the swan lake. Beyond, a stand of virgin lightwoods masked the turnpike where it curved toward Macon. Those noble trees, Yancey knew, had been left deliberately, as a landmark in a country rich with memories. They had formed part of the Selbys' original quarter section. The first Selby had cut logs there to raise his cabin when this part of Georgia was still a wilderness.

In those days, too, this earth had been a battleground. Indian wars had raged round the first generation to take root. Some of the older work buildings (standing as relics today) bore the marks of bullet holes—though most of the red man's raids had passed the fledgling plantation by. From the start the Selbys had been canny traders, buying land from each warring faction but giving allegiance to none.

Lorena had absorbed the Selby genius for husbandry, with the Judge as her tutor. Her first loyalty was to the land the Judge had left her husband. Was it possible she would ride out this storm as well?

Reluctant, even now, to join the soiree, the plantation doctor lighted a second cigar and settled on the top step of the portico. With his back to a pillar, he frowned at the scene within, as brilliantly lighted (and as artificial) as a play without words. Not that the scene needed dialogue, thought Yancey as he studied the seven figures grouped round the oval table in the dining room. He was glad, in fact, that the panes of the tall french doors muffled the voices. Having sat at Lorena's right through a hundred such dinners, he could have spoken most of the words from memory.

Old Colonel Hamilton was in the doctor's usual chair this evening—a portly caricature of the retired officer in civilian dress. The empty coat sleeve was part of that hero façade—a proud advertisement of the arm Hamilton had lost at Shiloh. Beside him was one of Brad's lieutenants: another faced him across the board. Both young men glittered in immaculate dress uniforms. Both were medallion soldiers who had gone to war with valets in attendance —and had cursed Richmond roundly when Mr. Davis had forbidden such practices in the field. The Cray County Crusaders were an elite troop, outfitted at Selby's expense. Today they wore homespun into action. But there were dress tunics in reserve for galas such as this.

Bradfield Selby lounged in the host's place with his fixed, unchanging smile. His own coat, Yancey knew, had been cut in London: the fine dove-gray cloth and the golden hieroglyphs on the high collar set off his Byronic good looks perfectly. Once again the spectator on the portico reflected that Brad was too handsome to be flesh and blood: those classic features, like a Roman coin, seemed minted to outlast eternity. From this distance the hints of sparrow pouches beneath the eyes went unnoticed—telltale half-moons that spelled out dissipations only a plantation nabob could crowd into thirty years of living. Nor would an outside observer have guessed that the master of Selby—who was master in name only—was roaring-drunk. Brad carried his habits well, along with his liquor.

Quenten Rowley sat at his sister's left. His dead-black evening coat was relieved by a frilled shirt front of Irish linen and ruby studs. Quent seemed slender in contrast with these martial males. When he glanced their way, his lips curled into a lazy smile. He seemed utterly at ease—and quite absorbed in a mock flirtation with the colonel's lady. Though she looked all her fifty years, Clara Hamilton was responding as coyly as a girl.

Yancey's inventory had saved the hostess for the last. A glance at Lorena told him that her guests were still in control, that Quent and Brad had yet to lock horns. Tonight the mistress of Selby (who ruled here in more than name) had never seemed lovelier, never more certain of her destiny. *It's her Charleston manners,* thought the plantation doctor. *They've seen her through five years of marriage. They'll see her through tonight.*

The dinner was almost over. While Yancey watched, Lorena and Clara Hamilton billowed up from their chairs in waves of silk and crinoline: when they left the table they seemed to float rather than walk. Quent Rowley, flapping his napkin, moved to open the foyer door for their departure. But Brad was also on his feet, his glass lifted. Shouted in his ringing baritone, his toast set the pendants in the candelabra tinkling: the echo reached the portico.

"My friends, I give you the Confederacy. And its gallant women, of whom my wife is a proud example."

Hamilton's glass was lifted too. Like the aides, he was already at dress-parade attention. "To the Confederacy—and its ladies!"

Quent had made no move to touch his glass. It was Lorena herself who swept into the breach. Returning to her place, she took up her wine and raised it head-high. This, too, was a defiance of custom: in Cray County ladies received most compliments with lowered eyes.

"To our brave soldiers—and to the sons who will preserve the future they die for now."

Yancey let a chuckle rumble in his throat while the glasses were drained. Brad, he saw, had been startled by Lorena's words. It was well known that Selby Hall was still without an heir. Had his wife's toast been a challenge—or a portent? Moving slowly down the portico, the plantation doctor shrugged off the teasing question.

He paused at the row of french doors for a final survey. The ladies had crossed the great circular foyer—moving like silken argosies from the shadow of the famous spiral stairway to the double parlor that lay beyond, its shadowed vastness starred by a few standing lamps. In the dining room the four soldiers had settled to begin on the port and brandy. Viewed from this angle, the scene resembled a museum diorama—a celebration of a time that would not come again. Or was it a curtain scene in a melodrama—one of those tableaux so dear to the sentimental dramatist? A final curtain, guaranteed to send an audience home in tears?

Quent Rowley supplied the answer to the watcher on the portico. Refusing Brad's offer of a drink, he strolled to the piano in the alcove and let practiced fingers run down the keys. The music that filled the Big House was both sinister and sweet. Recognizing the theme, Yancey knew that Lorena's cynic brother had chosen it deliberately. It was the third movement of Chopin's Sonata in B Flat Minor—the funeral march of the dead.

Perhaps it was the mockery of Chopin—or merely the autumn dampness that had begun to seep into his bones—but Yancey decided on another brandy before he faced Lorena's guests. Back in his lean-to, with his daybook open on the desk, he felt some of his detachment return with his entry for the date:

Nov. 14, 1864

Returned from Purdy farm, 9 PM, after delivery of Nan Purdy's fifth son—a fine ten-pounder. Mother and offspring flourishing.

Heavy fog on road, lifting on return to Selby.

Quarters quiet.

Again the plantation doctor downed his glass. Liquor was a necessary medicine these days when he studied Lorena Selby with candid eyes and measured the debacle she was facing here. Already the brandy had begun to replace despair with acceptance. While the protection lasted, he could endure the fact he was on the wrong side of sixty—with nothing to offer Lorena but advice. The sort of old man's wisdom she would discard in advance.

No sign of Luke Jackson (who was sent to scout the roads around Decatur). It hardly matters. I can spell out his report, sight unseen.

Judging by the behavior of our dinner guests, the enemy might still be in Washington. Does this show courage—stupidity—or both?

2

Her party had been successful, Reen decided, regardless of the portents. ("Reen" was the best her house slaves could make of her name, and Lorena had grown used to the contraction.) Even Brad had behaved well, considering the wine he had taken.

She had been briefly unsettled by the appearance of Uncle Doc —as she had called Yancey since childhood, though he was not a relative. Knowing his moods by heart, she had refused to be troubled by his abrupt withdrawal after the toasts that had ended dinner. Still, she was glad that no one else had noticed his presence. Obviously Uncle Doc was tired of pretending—and too fond of her to burden her with his weariness. He would come in later, when he had drunk enough brandy to sustain him.

She was also aware of her brother's malicious joke at the piano —Chopin's *marche funèbre* was meant for her ears alone. True, the colonel's lady was pretending to hum the melody between her bursts of small talk—but Clara Hamilton had no ear. Reen dismissed the implication with a toss of her head. Quent, busy with a difficult passage, pretended not to notice: it was enough, for him, that the comment had registered.

Reen kept her resentment in control while she continued to talk with Clara Hamilton. It was the sort of lady chatter appropriate to a drawing room in the nadir hour between dinner and the return of the gentlemen, flushed from too much drink and bombast. On other occasions she had managed her part well enough: tonight the effort was almost beyond her. Weary or no, she could wish that Uncle Doc had come in ahead of the others—even though he would probably have begun by scolding her.

After all, he had good reason: she should have taken his advice long ago. Now that the crop was in at Selby Hall, its chatelaine had earned the right to go south (to Macon, at least) to sit out the present military crisis. So far, she had refused to budge. The Hamiltons, the Randolphs, and the Buells had clung stubbornly to their homes—and their hopes. The Selbys could do no less.

The plantation had escaped harm during more than three years of war: thanks to Quent's blockade runners, its books had even continued to show a profit. Quite apart from the cult of *noblesse oblige*, the need to prove her courage under fire, she could not resist the urge to play the Selby luck to the end. Now that she was entertaining a warrior husband on leave, she might justify that long and dangerous gamble. The challenge she had just flung in Brad Selby's teeth had been deliberate: her toast had been a demand that he give her the son they had never had. She did not regret the dare.

When the Yankee threat was revealed, she would face it squarely. While Brad slept under the Selby rooftree, she would never admit their marriage was tottering on the brink. Or that Selby Hall itself (which had become the center of her existence) might be a ruin tomorrow.

In the dining room the men's voices boomed on. Quent had begun to play a Viennese waltz against that pompous counterpoint. Clara Hamilton, rising on her toes, was dancing with an imaginary partner. Reen knew that her guest's solemn pirouette was a prelude to her retirement upstairs, where she would spend the next half hour re-doing a chignon that was already arranged perfectly, to the last lovelock. Admitting that she should follow Clara, Reen put down the impulse. For once, manners could yield to memories.

Her marriage had begun on a high note of romance. Where had she taken the first wrong turning?

Oddly enough, they had been playing that same waltz when she and Bradfield Selby had met. The time was her debutante year in Charleston, the place one of the great houses on the Battery. Brad had been wearing the uniform of the 1st Georgia Dragoons when he asked her to dance (though the country was at peace, he explained, volunteer regiments had been organized to give the Southern answer to a fast-brewing impasse). War had seemed a remote threat that night when she moved into his arms, to the sighing of the fiddles. It had been a long time since she had had a handsomer partner—or a gayer one. Charleston had already labeled him the catch of the season: a debutante could do no less.

It had been a love match from the start—and, though some of her friends called it a union of opposites, they agreed that she had made a brilliant choice. Not that the Rowleys gave the Georgia Selbys an inch on breeding. Reen's ancestors were among the oldest settlers in the Carolinas. Like so many Scotsmen, they had crossed in the late sixteen hundreds to take part in the founding of Stuart's Town. When Indian raids forced them back to Charleston, they had proved adept in trade. Lorena Rowley had descended from generations of successful merchants. Her bailiwick was part and parcel of the South—no less than Brad's red clay acres.

Regardless of background, the alchemy of Eros had done its work in that debutante spring—by established custom, the season of mating. She had felt she would die if Brad Selby failed to propose. And yet when the offer of marriage came (logically, at the last cotillion of the season), she found herself accepting it almost calmly. After all, she was a Rowley: it was no more than her due.

Even then she knew Brad was attracted by her strangeness. There had been prettier girls in Charleston that year—but few who equaled her animation, and none to surpass her in education or in brains. Had some inner weakness (unadmitted even to himself) drawn Brad to her strength, her quiet assurance that she could more than match him in wits? She remembered his astonishment when he found she was a graduate from the seminary for young ladies at Raleigh, an honor that meant even more for women than his own sheepskin from the University of Virginia. Like many Southern gentlemen, Brad Selby had assumed that women (including wives) were a compound of queen and servant. As such, they deserved to be cherished—and used as needed. It had been a novel experience to discover that his bride possessed a mind.

Lorena was sure he had loved her at first, after his fashion. Perhaps, for all his mocking ways, he loved her still. To her their wedding journey (to London and the Continent) had been strangely numbing. She had not dared to wonder why.

When she first came to Selby Hall she had accepted the great chain that held the housekeeper's keys: it was part of the ritual installing her as the chatelaine. The Judge was still in residence—and firmly in charge, though his health was failing. From the first day, he had made his daughter-in-law welcome, even as he trained her rigorously in her new duties. Thanks to that kindly discipline, Lorena found she could adapt well enough. But the numbness had persisted until Uncle Doc's arrival from Charleston. The Judge had proved a friend: he was not a confidant. She could open her heart only to a man from her own country.

During the courtship she had told Uncle Doc of her love for Brad. She had insisted he was a true knight, a Lochinvar out of the West (in Charleston, Brad's part of Georgia was considered a frontier of sorts). Even then she had sensed the misgivings her mentor was too cautious to put into words: when he was presented to her dashing fiancé, she had watched his eyes probe deep. Now she realized that Yancey had looked beyond the uniform, to discover a swaggering boy who had yet to attain maturity—who might never understand the give-and-take that true marriage demanded.

After her return from the honeymoon Uncle Doc had given up a Carolina practice for her sake and become the plantation doctor at Selby. She had been eager to explore her unspoken doubts. The day of his arrival she had burst into the surgery before he could unpack his bag—making no attempt to hide her tears as she buried her face against the familiar, threadbare shoulder. But she had insisted on taking him for a tour of her new domain before speaking her mind. Even then the first questions had come haltingly.

"Wouldn't you say I'd done well here?"

"Better than that, Lorena," he told her with the raised eyebrow that reminded her of home—and the grin his lazy man's beard only half concealed. "I trust those were tears of joy when you greeted me."

"You know better."

"Want to tell me about it, girl?"

She fought off the craven urge to hold back. "I've grown up at last, it seems. I can't bore you with my troubles forever."

"Don't grow up too fast. Not until you decide just what you want from these Selbys."

"What *do* I want, Uncle Doc? And why do I want it? Tell me that, and you'll cure your first patient here."

"Skittish brides can't be cured in a day," he said. "First things first. I take it you're partial to Georgia."

"I love it. Selby's been like home from the start. The Judge couldn't be kinder——"

If he noted the omission of her husband's name, Yancey gave no sign. "You prefer this outsize mansion to your aunt's place in Charleston?"

"Yes, Uncle Doc. Truly. It's the first time I've managed to forget I'm an orphan. To feel I'm close to growing things. Even the land seems to live and breathe."

"It's a rich country, when it's cared for," he said. "You can trust Judge Selby there, I'm told. Will you love it as much when winter comes—and the frost kills everything that's green?"

"Selby will stay alive under the frost—making ready for spring."

"So it will. Like a woman carrying a baby."

"Will I have a baby soon?"

"Reckon you'd better answer that one. I didn't go on your honeymoon."

Reen knew she was blushing, but she made herself answer steadily. "I'm praying I have a son. It's all I need to belong here."

"Every bride wants a son," said Uncle Doc. "Leastways, if she deserves her wedding ring. 'Course, the *reason* she wants one has plenty to do with whether or not she gets him."

"And what is that supposed to mean?"

"Only that it takes all kinds of women to make a world—to carry on the race. The lucky ones really love their husbands. Enough to give more than themselves when they go to bed. Such wives have no problems but the happy ones—a houseful of children. Incidentally, most of 'em are poor as Job's turkey."

"Poor but fulfilled. Is that what you're implying?"

"Fulfillment takes its price. In my experience most of those mothers die young—from overwork. Or should I say from too much giving?"

"And the others?"

"The others are a different breed. They want children for themselves alone. To take the place of a husband they've stopped loving. Or even started hating."

The words stabbed at her vitals—but the pain was oddly comforting. For the first time, she could see her problem plainly.

"I hope I understand you, Uncle Doc."

"Don't try to move too fast, young miss," he said—using an upcountry drawl to hide the sting in his words. "You're still a bride."

"But it gets worse—" She blushed, hotly at what she had revealed, and knew she was struggling between tears and laughter. This time, the laughter won. "You *are* an old devil. Tripping me with such talk—and shocking my modesty."

"Go on speaking your mind," he said. "This time, don't hold back."

"Does being married ever change? Will it get so it isn't *all* pain —and disgust?"

"Only you can work that out," he said.

"But I feel I'm being used," she cried. "Never that I'm giving."

"Many wives do," he told her. "Others learn better. Or hadn't you heard that love is what the woman makes of it—not the man?"

Remembering Brad in the big master bedroom upstairs, the sudden, savage assaults that left her helpless with unuttered terror, Reen closed her eyes. "Say what you mean. I can listen now."

"Put it this way, Lorena. You've been in houses where people didn't make you welcome. Doesn't that describe a lot of marriages —after the couple's gone upstairs?"

"Perhaps." Her eyes dropped before his level gaze.

"There are other homes where you know you're expected—and wanted—even before you knock. You can feel the happiness come through the walls. Knowing these folks inside are happy—you're happy too."

"You're saying it's my fault then?"

"I'm saying a marriage takes a deal of planning—on a woman's part. And a deal of earning. You'll have to earn yours at Selby. Right now you're young and scared: things have just mounted up.

They'll turn out easier later on. Didn't you drop a stitch or two when you first learned to knit?"

"More than a few."

"When you went on that wedding trip you were the smartest needlewoman in Charleston. Marrying's like knitting—it takes practice. 'Course, it's different too. Knitting follows the same set of rules, no matter what yarn you use. No one has invented a fool-proof pattern for what comes after the wedding."

"Doesn't practice make perfect?"

"Yes and no. But if I were you I'd do no knitting until my mind was on my work. Now you've settled in, I don't think you'll make that mistake much longer."

"Thanks for your faith," she said. "I can use a little right now."

"You'll have faith to spare, girl, when you really need it. Something inside that head of yours sets you apart from most women: believe me, I've known all kinds. For want of a nicer word, I'd call it grit."

She laughed then—amazed that she could take refuge in mirth. "Is that bad?"

"Not if it's used in moderation," he told her. "And kept a secret from your husband. Shall we walk up to the Big House and see what's in the cupboard?"

"You mean the cellar, don't you?"

"Naturally, girl. Why else would I follow you here? We've married the best liquor bin in Georgia."

After her confessional with Uncle Doc, Reen had felt some of her confidence return. Her spirits had risen still higher when she began to realize that Judge Andrew Selby—who had begun by accepting her as a daughter-in-law—now seemed to regard her as the custodian of his land and its future.

Brad, as befitted a son and heir, had made ritual visits to both gin and fields. Bored and more than a little disdainful, he had gone to the cotton auctions, when buyers from Mobile had bargained for crops that were scarcely in the ground. In the fall he had glanced over the bookkeeper's shoulder when the year's figures were tidied up and the fantastic profits deposited to the Selby accounts. It had taken his bride but little time to find that Brad had no head for business—or the dull but vital chaffering that had pinned those profits down.

Reen herself had always had a knack with figures—and a genuine interest in plantation economy, in the complex of forces that had built Selby Hall, and kept its magnificence inviolate. Judge Selby, she perceived, had created that magic formula—but the Judge was dying, though he would refuse to admit as much until his funeral. There was no visible successor.

In the beginning she had not dreamed he was training her for the part. During her first year on the plantation she had assumed that her father-in-law's kindly but detailed instructions were given from the goodness of his heart, so she might enter more fully into the life there. When he began inviting her to his bartering sessions with the brokers, when he opened the plantation books for her perusal (down to the repair bill for the guest wing, and the list of new Negroes he had purchased in the New Orleans market), Reen saw his intentions were serious. Judge Selby had discovered she had the brain of a born manager, and the will to use it. It was already an open secret between them that the Judge's son was a wastrel.

Brad would inherit Selby Hall in the near future: that much had been evident soon after Reen came there as a bride. The line would endure, if Brad's young wife could give him an heir. Meanwhile it was essential that plantation business proceed as usual. In a crisis-haunted era the rule of King Cotton had remained secure: Selby's proven ability to deliver prime bales must be maintained at all hazards. Two years before the first shells fell on Sumter, Lorena Selby had taken over most of the duties that would normally have fallen on her husband. When an undeclared war was made official, she was in complete command.

With the Judge beside her to explain its mysteries, she had explored the workings of the mill—from the great stone dam beside the river to the massive overshot wheel, which ground corn enough to feed each field hand at Selby, as well as the Negroes at Greentree and Hamilton Hundred. She had studied the machinery of the gin at harvest time until she grasped each stage of the separation of seeds and cotton. As she grew familiar with the routines of carpenter shop and forge, of bake oven and smokehouse, she had realized that this vast demesne was self-sustaining—save for importing such necessities as iron ingots and the drugs for Uncle Doc's shelves. Or such luxuries as the Judge's calfbound London editions, and the Paris fineries that made life here gracious as well as bountiful.

In the fields (wearing boots beneath her skirt to protect her from the ground-rattlers in the furrows) Reen had followed the chanting drivers from dawn to dark. She had memorized each item in the complex timetable of cotton raising: plowing, planting, chopping to thin the line of green growth and remove grass and weeds. She had observed the laying by, the appearance of the brilliant blooms with their odd shape, the growth of the bolls (and their bursting to reveal their snow-white contents), the picking, ginning, and baling.

More than once, at picking time, she had scandalized the Judge by working side by side with his field hands—until she could pluck the cascading white abundance as expertly as they, and cram her trailing crokersack with its precious freight. She had known no other way to measure that backbreaking task accurately—to decide, with her own muscles, what an honest day's work should be.

She had visited the cabins in the quarters until she knew each mammy (and her offspring) by name. In the surgery she had helped Uncle Doc with the birthings. She had read the prayers for the dead and dying—and learned the thousand ministrations that came between, insuring a rule-of-thumb happiness for Selby slaves, as well as the creature comforts of abundant food and shelter. . . . The Judge was a stern taskmaster. Demanding obedience without question, he had always respected his land, and the men who worked it, whether black or white. The respect had become a first principle in her own book of rules.

As for Brad, he had paid but little heed to such abstract subjects as profit or loss. Or the need to plan for a stable future, when the South had broken free—in fact as well as intent—from Northern tyranny, to become a separate nation. Intent on his own pursuits (which included training hunters and supervising the racing stable that had made the Selby name famous), he seemed unaware of his father's labors in his behalf—or the fact that his wife had joined in wholeheartedly. Brad was seldom home in those last, hectic months before the war. As master of the hunt, his services were in constant demand. When the racing season opened, he traveled with the Selby stable, to keep an expert eye on trainers and jockeys.

If these activities had given him but little time for a recent bride, so much the worse. As a husband he could insist that his conscience was clean. He had all but insisted she accompany him to those racing meets, and had sulked properly and briefly each time she refused. When Georgia joined South Carolina in the first secession from the Union, he had been toasting a winner in the victor's circle at New Orleans. When his father died (a week after the first brilliant repulse of the Yankees in Virginia), he was already in the field.

Reen had managed Selby thereafter, in name as well as fact.

Brad had made only a token protest when she had urged him to sign an agreement with Quent's syndicate of shipowners. This fleet of blockade runners had captains in every port from Mobile to Cape Fear: the agreement had specified that it would transport Selby cotton to Nassau and the English Midlands, in return for an equal division of profit. . . . It had been Brad's only business gesture since the war began. He had yet to ask how Reen managed to hold his slaves on the land (without a single desertion to freedom road), or how she had kept Selby itself in such amazing repair.

Actually, she was pleased that he had taken her ability for granted, along with his continuing prosperity. It was her special pride that his plantation—like her own spirit—could still flourish, now that the Union noose had tightened in earnest. Her work had absorbed her utterly, saving her from brooding on the future. Only one element was lacking. Selby Hall remained without an heir— and her marriage was entering its sixth year. . . .

Tonight (pretending to take her ease on a love seat covered with the rose-point damask Quent had brought from Paris) Reen watched her brother's fingers fly down the keyboard. As children she and Quent had never been close. It had taken a shared rebellion to remind them of their kinship—and its advantages.

True, they quarreled on occasion. Like Uncle Doc, Quent had stormed at her because she refused to take refuge in South Georgia or Florida. He had scolded her even more harshly for her stubborn loyalty to the plantation—and to Brad. It was Quent's opinion that she should leave Brad Selby to his fate, with the war so clearly lost. Her brother did not understand that the fortune she had poured into now worthless bonds had been given gladly—along with the second fortune in beef and flour she had sent to Confederate quartermasters. Nor could she speak of her need to produce the son Brad demanded. Quent was both a sophist and a bachelor. He would never see that this need for a child was the strongest chain that bound her to her husband, the one drive that kept the marriage alive.

Breaking loose from the skein of old frustration, Reen approached the piano. "I'm going to the overseer's office," she said. "Tell Brad, if he asks."

Shaping a difficult chord, Quent did not look up from the keyboard.

"When will you learn to separate work and play?"

"Not tonight—if you insist on driving down to Macon. I want you to have our final accounting."

Her brother broke off his playing. "Sure you don't plan to corner Luke Jackson ahead of Brad? Just in case he *has* brought back the truth about Atlanta?"

"Meaning, of course, that Brad can't face the truth?"

"Brad and I were at the university together. Even then he never permitted cold facts to interfere with his fun. He won't today."

"I'd resent that, if I had time."

Quent smiled, and let his hands glide into a long, mournful arpeggio. "You're excused, Lorena—regardless of your motives. Just don't desert your guests too long."

"I'll return in five minutes," she said. "Word of honor."

On the portico November was chill on her bare shoulders, but she did not return for the stole she had left on the love seat. The fresh night air revived her instantly, along with the scents from the rain-soaked garden. Knowing it was a pagan gesture (and making sure that no eyes observed her), she dropped to one knee on the path and let her fingers touch the soil of a flower bed.

Bizarre as it was, the gesture soothed her instantly. It was a confession that she and this Georgia soil were one: she would go on serving it to the end. Even though she still remained barren, this red clay had yielded another rich harvest. . . . Was there a grain of truth in the classic legend that the earth mother, Demeter, could restore all those who stood in need?

Brad would be riding out tomorrow: he had said as much at dinner. On his last night at Selby they might still atone for her five childless years.

The lamp burned brightly above the ledgers in Luke Jackson's sanctum. Reen climbed the porch knowing she could not face Quent without some proof that her walk through the night was justified. At first glance the office seemed empty. When a figure stirred beyond the pool of light, she drew back a trifle—startled, for the moment, out of her hard-won calm. Then, realizing it was Saladin, she stepped over the threshold.

"I'm sorry you must work late, Sal."

"Marse Luke tell me to finish, ma'am. He say you want dese 'counts fo' Marse Quent leave." The young Negro's voice was firm: only the elisions in his speech betrayed his origin. Otherwise it was hard to believe this had been a mere field hand when the war began. Wondering if she had been wise to bring Saladin forward so rapidly, Reen knew she had had no choice. . . . Regardless of the color of their owners, brains were now beyond price at Selby. The Army had drained Cray County in its search for men. Sal was worth three Luke Jacksons when it came to keeping the accounts: he was a tireless pace setter in field and gin. By contrast, the overseer was a patient bull, a bellwether who kept the hands in line without inspiring personal devotion. There was a point beyond which Luke could not go. So far, the mistress of Selby had found no limits to Sal's horizon.

She felt a vague stir of resentment at the admission, and heard the sound of ancestors whirling in their graves. Obviously, the white man was born to rule in a plantation economy. He was destined to give the orders, dispense largesse, and—in the end—to play God in his own fashion. She had challenged that ancient concept when she had admitted Sal to her countinghouse, even as a wartime measure. Would he be willing to pick up his mattock again at the war's end? And would the county forgive him for rubbing elbows, however briefly, with her overseer—on terms that implied equality?

Reen put the question from her mind and bent over the ledgers, with her slave at her elbow. It still faintly troubled her to admit she felt no trace of strain in his presence.

"We'll want all these books in the Big House tonight," she said coolly. "Mr. Rowley will be returning soon to Wilmington. He should check our bills of lading against his own." Wilmington, in North Carolina, was one of the few Confederate ports not closed by the blockade. Quent's shipping syndicate had established its offices there, and continued to do a thriving business. But Saladin knew (as well as she) that Wilmington was no longer an outlet for Georgia-baled cotton. Sherman had cut the rail lines that linked Cray County with the East via Atlanta.

"How do we ship, Miss Reen?"

"We don't," she said. "I'm only preparing, in case the situation improves. Meanwhile Mr. Rowley should know just what we have in the packhouse."

"C'n he sell it to de contrabanders, ma'am?"

The word fell awkwardly between them. It was common knowledge that Northern brokers (moving on the skirts of the Union armies) were prepared to padlock cotton barns in the battle zones, with the connivance of the provost marshals. Once it was so labeled, the cotton could be sold for whatever price the Army decreed—and resold later at its true value. . . . Reen hesitated over her reply. Saladin, it seemed, had picked up the white man's stratagems easily.

"Even if such contracts weren't forbidden by Georgia law," she said, "Captain Selby would never permit it. The Yankees will always be our enemies. We can never make deals with them—or make peace. Not after what they've done to the South."

The former field hand's eyes were lowered humbly—but his voice contrasted oddly with his manner. "Miss Reen, we sold cotton up No'th *befo'!* Cain't we sell agin, now de fightin's 'bout ended?"

"Dealing with contrabanders is quite another matter, Sal."

"'Scuse me, ma'am. Reckon Ah jes' didn't think."

Reen turned away, baffled by the logic of the question. In the quarters, she knew, the Negroes talked of little but the day when their freedom would be fact as well as promise. Saladin intended to marry one of her own house slaves (a handsome wench named Florrie) the moment such unions were legal. Reen had already half given her consent. Without Sal, and the vast influence he wielded over her workers, she could never have brought in the last crop. It was hard to oppose him now with the same timeworn arguments.

"The enemy hasn't whipped us yet," she said mechanically. "My husband is sure we'll drive them out of Georgia."

"Mebbe so, Miss Reen. But Yankees doan' drive easy."

When she left the overseer's office, her departure was too poised to resemble a flight. It was only when she crossed the lawn that she admitted she had left Sal without a single straight answer— since any answer she could have offered would not have deceived a child. *If your slaves have the last word*, she told herself, *your cause is really lost*. Mounting the portico steps, hearing Clara Hamilton's laughter ring out in the parlor, she hesitated a moment more before leaving the world of reality for make-believe.

Her husband's lieutenants had emerged from the dining room and now hung above the love seat, flirting dutifully with the colonel's lady. Quent was playing Mozart—a gay travesty of an army patrol, filled with the beat of idiot drums. It was another of his mockeries, offered for her ear alone. Humming a snatch of the melody, drawing her Charleston manners about her like a cloak, Reen swept into the house to rejoin her guests.

3

Brad Selby breathed deep above his brandy inhaler before he tossed off the last of the fragrant contents. At the table's head old Hamilton was describing the tactics he had used to surprise (and all but destroy) Grant at Pittsburg Landing—as though the strategy of that catch-as-catch-can battle had sprung full-bodied from his own brain. Brad could have repeated the harangue verbatim. Feigning to listen, he let his lids droop a trifle. Not that he was tired. He was, in fact, buoyantly awake, at the precise mid-point of drunkenness when the next move (undecided as yet) could seem an enticing adventure.

Orders had not yet reached him from brigade, but he was sure

the troop would ride out tomorrow. Since this was his last evening
at home, it must end with a fight or a frolic—and the choice was
his alone. Whatever his decision, Reen had no right to complain.
Having changed places with the colonel, he now faced the portico
windows. He had seen her leave the house, en route to the overseer's office. Sometimes he was convinced that Reen's interest in
her ledgers transcended a natural loyalty to himself. Or that his
wife (immersed, as she so clearly was, in her own self-importance)
had forgotten he had offered his life, on a score of battlefields, to
preserve her privileges.

During those enforced absences he had given her far too much
say in the running of Selby—on the sound theory that it was unwise to tether her on a short rope. He was prepared to admit she
had done reasonably well, for a woman. But he'd be damned if
he would thank her for what was, after all, only a take-over of his
father's methods. And he'd be double damned if he would condone her assumption (as serene as it was infuriating) that the take-
over was permanent.

So far, the *status quo* had produced results, and Brad had made
no protest. He had shrugged off the whispers when news reached
the regiment that his wife had installed a black bookkeeper, that
she was paying actual wages to his field hands . . . Luke Jackson
had assured him the boy knew his place; he could hardly blame
Reen for using the readiest means to hold his slaves on the land.
But there would be drastic changes when Sherman was expelled
from Georgia—and this insane talk of freedom was scotched
forever.

Meanwhile it would do no harm to remind his wife who was
master here.

When had she decided she could manage a plantation as well
as he? Or that her business judgments were even better? Brad had
paid Selby but little mind while his father lived. Engrossed in more
stimulating pursuits, he had assumed the place would run itself,
that it could easily finance the sowing of a bumper crop of wild
oats. Reen's take-over, of course, had been an inevitable by-product
of the war. When the war was victoriously ended, he would tell
her he understood—and, if she was truly penitent, forgive her. To-

night he would merely teach her an interim lesson, in terms that would hurt the most.

Pray God those tardy orders were on the way; he was eager for more campaigning. His heartbeat quickened at the thought. War and Brad Selby had been boon companions from the start—and he had thoroughly enjoyed each tour of duty, despite the obstinacy of an enemy who refused to admit defeat, after years of continual drubbing. Since tomorrow meant yet another good-by, Reen would surely expect him to come to her when the soiree ended. At such a time a warrior husband's ardor was unwritten law—but Brad obeyed no laws that clashed with his prevailing mood. Tonight (despite that rocket burst of rhetoric at the close of dinner) he felt no urge to repossess his wife. At the moment, his ruling emotion was closer to hate than love.

He had loved Reen once, he supposed—especially during that whirlwind Charleston courtship. She had been a bewitching little thing in her aloof fashion, spare as a thoroughbred filly and every bit as fiery, once her dander was up. Lorena Rowley had been better than a tonic during his Carolina holiday. She had also been a welcome relief from the opulent belles who had swooned in his arms (and, on occasion, invaded his bedroom), convinced that he would choose one of them as the chatelaine of Selby.

Naturally, even a thoroughbred filly must respond to the thorn bit of marriage. During the wedding trip he had taken his bride when he saw fit—casually or brutally, as the spirit moved him. That, too, was part of his code: how else could he prove he was the man, the owner—and she the weaker vessel? When she had failed to match his own desire, he had shrugged off her weakness. Compliance was all a man really expected from a well-brought-up wife— and, eventually, a son to carry on his name. While he waited for Reen to adjust to these reasonable demands, he was willing to take his fun elsewhere.

Once they had settled down at the plantation, he had lost no time in renewing his liaison with a mistress in New Orleans. He kept a second fancy woman in Mobile; he had always taken the pick of the girls at Madame Julie's when he visited Atlanta. Just as naturally (when fox hunting or bad weather kept him at Selby) he had fathered his share of brats in the quarters, following the traditional *droit du seigneur,* honored by custom since antiquity. Surely there was no need to discontinue so pleasant a routine— simply because he had drawn a chilly bride in the matrimonial sweepstakes.

To give Reen her due, he could see that she was deeply shamed at her failure to provide Selby with an heir. During his present leave he had done his part to remedy the omission. It was not his fault that his wife (intent though she was on conceiving) had all but proved herself barren.

Thank God he had found other ways to keep his self-respect in prime repair, to forget the galling fact that he and Reen were childless. There were few officers of his rank who could match his citations for valor. He had won battle honors with the Army of Northern Virginia, at both Antietam and Gettysburg. During the Peninsular Campaign he had stormed across the Chickahominy, with a hundred gray devils behind him, to threaten the enemy headquarters: official record stated that the raid had convinced McClellan his whole position was untenable, that it had forced the enemy's general retreat. . . . Brad Selby's esteem for Brad Selby (which his father had once described as monumental) had refused to admit defeat in love or war. Why should his pride stoop now—to pick up the challenge Reen had flung down at dinner? There were better ways to end an evening.

Colonel Hamilton's booming voice had trailed into a frank, full-bodied snore. The hero of Shiloh had fallen asleep in his chair, his beard lifting gently, like the quills of a lazy porcupine. The colonel's host leaned forward to rescue a freshly opened bottle, as Hamilton's hand flailed suddenly, in response to some ancient dream of glory. Rising quietly from the table, Brad Selby tucked the bottle under his arm and slipped from the room.

On the portico he was careful to stay clear of the file of french doors that opened to the first half of the long double parlor.

Reen's party was going full blast: the rattle of voices told him that. After he peered cautiously in—and discovered that Yancey had finally joined the others—Brad had no desire to mingle with his guests. Quent Rowley was bad enough. Quent and Uncle Doc together were a pair of antagonists he could no longer bear to face—

not without a brace of dueling pistols, and carte blanche to dispatch them in order.

The night air had gone to his head a bit: he was swaying when he paused in the shadows, and supported himself by leaning against the nearest pillar. Yancey, he saw, was talking nineteen to the dozen with Cal Lambert, stabbing the lieutenant with a finger to drive his points home. (The plantation doctor was never windier than after too many brandies in the surgery.) At the moment, he was proving, with his own crackpot logic, that England would never recognize the C.S.A., that the promised intervention of the Emperor Maximilian from Mexico was also a myth—in short, that this war of liberation was lost beyond recall. . . . Actually, of course, it was common gossip at headquarters that Sherman had hopelessly overextended his supply lines to take Atlanta. The invaders could be cut to ribbons, once that line was severed. Matched against Butcher Grant's incompetence in Virginia, such a defeat would be more than enough to swing the balance abroad.

For an instant Brad played with the impulse to shout the near-traitor into silence. The fellow was at least kissing kin of Reen's— and he had been tolerated at Selby for that reason. Loyalty to a wife's past had limits, however: when he came home for keeps he'd send the old idiot packing. . . . Tonight, he told himself dourly, Yancey could win this duel of words with Lambert.

Following an unsteady course down the portico, Brad paused at the last of the french doors. Save for a single lamp, the second half of the double parlor was in darkness. The sliding doors that separated it from its twin were closed. Another example of Reen's management, he thought: it was considered unpatriotic to waste candles in wartime, even though the wicks in those lamp chimneys had been dipped in Selby tallow. . . . In the Judge's day the Big House had blazed like the morning sun on party nights. Had the Judge's son given the orders, each room would have shone as brightly now.

In the far wall a door stood open to the Judge's study: a second lamp, in a bracket above the flat-topped desk, outlined the towering bookcases. Since Brad's departure Reen had made this room her personal retreat: it was here she kept her own plantation records. It would serve her right, thought Brad, if he took back his

father's sanctum until morning and settled there with what was left
in the bottle. Generations of Selbys had slept downstairs in their
boots when the spiral staircase in the foyer proved too hazardous.
Tonight the present master would follow custom.

About to cross the darkened parlor, Brad paused in surprise as
another study lamp was lighted. Florida, one of the house slaves,
hovered just inside the door with a taper: with the light behind
her the girl's lush figure stood out in pleasant relief. He had noticed Florrie before, going about her tasks demurely, with a flirting
motion of her hips that was no less interesting because it was innocent. He watched her a moment more, without advertising his
presence. It was not the first time he had stripped her in his mind,
as casually as an Indian husking corn.

Sixteen, Brad thought—seventeen at most. Yielding to a familiar,
secret stirring, he moved to the door to investigate this unlooked-
for bounty—and paused with a scowl when he found that Florrie
was not alone. Evidently, she had gone into the study to light the
way for her companion, who was placing the first of an armful of
account books on the desk.

Even in the half-light Brad realized the man was Saladin, the
field hand Reen had assigned to the overseer's office. Now, incredible as it was, he had dared to enter the Big House itself. Watching
the pair narrowly, Brad observed that Florrie, at least, was taut with
anxiety: the girl knew Saladin was a trespasser, that only a house
slave could come and go in the Judge's study.

The transgression took on added meaning when he recalled another bit of news: only yesterday Luke Jackson had told him that
Sal now spoke openly of his plan to marry Florrie, once the Union
armies had enforced Lincoln's promise of emancipation. Marriage
between bondsmen was unheard of at Selby—save for the few who
had been given their freedom. Even had Reen wished to make an
exception, she would have needed his consent, as Florrie's present
owner. Florrie, Brad told himself, was still his property, to deal
with as he chose.

The two slaves were still unaware of his presence. When he
spoke, his voice was a whip.

"What's this mean, boy?"

Florrie whirled so rapidly she just escaped falling. So did Luke

Jackson's helper. Side by side, with the glow of the study lamps upon them, they made a striking contrast. The girl was a light octoroon, her skin a smooth *café au lait*. Saladin had the mark of Africa on every feature—but he was graceful as a panther, the flower of his race. Brad made the observation freely, with a shrug of acceptance. Perhaps he would breed them later, if only for the blood lines.

"Answer me, damn you!" he shouted. "What's a field hand doing in my house?"

The black man spoke at last—and his chin was still high, his voice firm. "Ain't no field hand now, Marse Brad——"

"Are you calling me a liar?"

"No, suh! I ain't——"

"Surely I know my own stock," Brad drawled. "Step into the parlor, boy. Let's have a look at you."

Sal obeyed the order promptly: Brad was pleased to observe that his arms had frozen about the rest of the account books. Florrie, her eyes rolling, stood flattened against the parlor wall. Enjoying the fear he had created—and quite willing to prolong it—the master of Selby lifted the taper from her hand and lighted the mantel candles before he picked up the cane that lay beneath his father's crossed shotguns. When he spoke again, he touched Saladin's cheekbone lightly with the lead-shod point.

"What's your name?"

The question, of course, was needless, and Brad smiled as he spoke. He saw that the Negro had guessed his purpose, that he was forcing himself to make the expected response.

"Ah's Miss Reen's Sal, Cap'n. Marse Jedge give me to her fo' a weddin' present."

The cane lashed at Sal's cheek. It was a practiced stroke, hard enough to raise a welt without drawing blood. "Don't tell me what I know. I've already asked what you're doing here."

Sal had taken the lash without flinching. Brad watched carefully, ready to strike harder if he found a ghost of resentment in the black man's eyes.

"Miss Reen want her books, Cap'n. I brung 'em hyah befo'. She doan' mind——"

The cane moved again, to raise a welt on the other cheek. "I mind, Sal. Will you remember next time?"

"Ah'll remembuh, Cap'n."

"See you do. *Now get out!*"

The order was thundered. When Sal accepted it with bowed head, Brad tossed the cane aside. "Take the books, Florrie," he said. "Put them on the study desk. I'll look at them later."

The octoroon snatched the remaining ledgers from Sal's arms: as she did so, she gave him a pleading glance that mingled love and fear. Brad continued to observe him narrowly. Obviously, Sal hoped he and Florrie would be permitted to leave the room together; when the Negro made no move to go, Brad let his fingers play with the pistol holder at his belt. He regretted he had left the weapon itself upstairs. He had shot slaves before to enforce discipline, taking care to wound rather than kill. It was a fact of life here, which Sal knew as well as he.

"I said get out, boy. Are you hard of hearing?"

"No, suh. I's goin'." The slurring voice was almost a parody— but Sal had moved at last, into the open french door. Here he paused to meet Brad's stare before he walked into the night. For a moment Brad thought of calling him back for the punishment he so clearly deserved: considering his offense, Sal had gotten off lightly. Then a second thought crossed his mind—and he sank into an armchair that faced the open study door.

Sal would be sure to linger in the darkness outside. There was a better way to punish him for the belief he possessed a brain. Or that the brain could harbor an impulse, however vagrant, which might threaten his master.

In the study Florrie was stacking the last of the account books on the desk. She was making much of that small chore in order to hide her nervousness. Brad felt his face muscles slacken at the sight: now that he had decided on his next move, he felt ten years younger.

"Bring me a cigar, Florrie," he ordered. "There's a box in the cabinet."

He had made his voice gentle: now that his mouth had ceased its twitching, the smile that wreathed the handsome lips was benign. The girl emerged from the study, with a Havana in one trembling hand and a lucifer on the outstretched palm. He took the cigar with a nod of thanks, savoring its aroma before setting it between his teeth.

"Hasn't Mrs. Selby taught you to strike a light?"

"Marse Brad, Ah'm skeered of matches."

"They can't hurt you," he said pleasantly.

"*Please, Marse Brad——!*"

He studied her blank eyes, and read the fear behind them. Neither of them spoke while she fumbled with the match, produced a flame at last, and held it to the cigar end. Brad steadied the flame with a hand on her wrist, puffed deeply—and held her with his eyes, like a hunter about to dispatch a stricken doe.

"When are you off duty?" he asked.

"Now, suh. Ah was jes' leavin'."

"Do you sleep in the quarters?"

"No, suh. Ah lives inside now."

"The room behind the kitchen?"

Florrie nodded, her eyes rolling in terror.

"Go there and wait. I'll join you later."

"This yo' las' night at Selby, Marse Brad. Woan' Miss Reen——?"

"You saw what happened to the field hand," he said mildly. "Do you want the same lesson?"

She left him then, dragging her steps just a little—the simile of the stricken doe, Brad thought, suited Florrie at the moment. Pouring himself another brandy, he carried glass and bottle to the study —knowing that Sal had observed the exchange from the dark garden, and happy in the knowledge.

The Judge's den was too bright for his taste, and he blew out the desk lamp before settling on the long horsehair couch. It was always a comfort for a soldier to be sure of a resting place between battles. After he had finished with Florrie he would end the night here. Sleeping in his boots, he would be ready to ride out at a moment's notice when his orders came.

4

Sal had watched in helpless, hot-eyed stupor from the shadow of a boxwood. He was still there when Florrie emerged from the Big House and began to circle the west wing. He had not heard the words when she faced Captain Selby in the armchair—but there had been no mistaking their import, or Florrie's frightened acquiescence. Only when she was safely outside the radius of light from the portico did he step forward.

"Wait, Florrie——!"

She was in his arms, letting her terror pour out in tears.

"Ah wants to *die*, Sal. Ah wants to die in little pieces!"

"He knowed Ah'd be watchin', didn't he?"

"Bettah yo' hadn't been, Sal."

"Lissen to me," he said. "When he knocks, jes' turn yo' lock—an' *keep* it turned."

"Ain't no locks on a black gal's room, Sal."

"So help me Jesus—someday Ah'll *kill* him!" Once the words were out, he was not sure he had really spoken them. Yet the utterance gave him a curious relief: he could even manage to smile at Florrie's gasp.

"Hush 'at talk, Sal! Marse Brad'll whup yo' daid——"

"Marse Brad's whupping days are endin'," he told her. "An' he got no right t'harm yo' now."

"He got every right dey is. Doan' he own me?"

"Ownin's past an' gone——"

"Not at Selby it ain't. Not while dey's still fightin' Yankees——"

He left her then for a moment, striding down the length of the shadowed boxwoods, clenching his fists in impotent fury. "Go tell Miss Reen," he said. "*She'll* stop him."

"Yo' ain't makin' sense, Sal. Miss Reen b'long to him too. White skin, brown skin—whut dey mattah?"

Sal did not speak at once. What she had said was true, but he had a truth to match it.

"So he owns her—now," he said quietly. "Reckon he owns Selby too. But he ain't earned Selby. *Miss Reen* made dis plantation. An' if she ain't hyah t'keep it green, it'll die tomorrah."

"Forget 'bout tomorrah," said Florrie doggedly. "Now's whut counts. T'night I do whut Marse Brad say—an' so does Miss Reen. She's no diffrunt."

"Florrie is right," observed a new voice. "She has the wisdom of the earth. Don't argue with it."

Sal turned—and gasped his relief when he saw the white shape in the dark was the plantation doctor.

"How much yo' heah, Doc Yancey?" he asked hoarsely.

"Enough. Better hustle back to quarters, Sal. And stay there until Captain Selby leaves."

Sal threw a look at Florrie, who nodded her endorsement. With something like pride, he saw she had regained much of her composure.

"It ain't right, Doctah. You know it ain't."

"Who's talking about right? This is law."

"Ah aim t'be mahself. Not somethin' a white man own. How long does Ah wait?"

"Not too long, Sal—the way things look. Right now there's just one thing to remember. Peace is always harder to win than war." Yancey turned from one Negro to the other, leveling a finger at each in turn. Sal had heard him give such lectures in the surgery, at calomel and weaning time. He had soothed Big Jody thus— while he set Jody's arm, broken after an encounter with Brad Selby.

"Cain't we fight back?"

"Not while the law says no. Look at Florrie. *She* understands."

"Does she have t'*wait* fo' him—jes' lak he say?"

"Yes, Sal. It's probably the last time he'll be able to give such an order."

Florrie had already started toward the kitchen wing. Yancey's fingers closed on Sal's arm as he moved to detain her. The gentle pressure brought him to his senses.

"Reckon yo' right, Doctah," he said resignedly. "They's nothin' we c'n do—now."

He would have gone on that, unwilling to face the splendor of the Big House a moment more, since it was a visible reminder of his shame. But Yancey was not quite at the end of his lecture.

"Look at it this way, Sal. You're a power here—a real force for good. That sort of power means responsibility."

"If you say so, Doctah." It was true that the Negroes had obeyed him when he preached patience. After Miss Reen had made him her paymaster, they had stayed on in their cabins instead of deserting. Sal knew it was not only the wages she paid them, in defiance of custom. He, too, had been part of the persuasion—a living proof that there were white people in the South who looked on Negroes as something beside animals.

"They'll listen harder tomorrow," said Yancey. "After you're free. Mrs. Selby will really need help then, to keep her labor force in line. Think of what she's done for you so far. Shouldn't you pay her back?"

Sal could only bow his head beneath such heavy wisdom. Miss Reen had changed him, quite literally, from slave to man: it was not her fault that he could not yet cast off his yoke. It was true that she would want help desperately in the coming peace. Workmen aplenty would be required to till the land for the first postwar crop—and Luke Jackson could never recruit such a force, though he could handle it in the field. Nor could the overseer keep the books in his office, or find ways to show a profit. Sal broke off his musings, aware that he had left no place for Brad Selby in the picture. The problem of the captain, he told himself, must be solved on its own terms, when this promise of freedom was a living thing.

"Ah'll make no trouble, Doc Yancey," he promised.

"Then I'll sleep with a clear mind," said the plantation doctor. "Go to your cabin—and don't stir until the morning bell." He fumbled in a pocket and came up with one of his round pillboxes—as much a symbol of authority in the quarters as Ajax's never used bull whip. Or the conjure beads, tucked in the chink above the cabin door, where visiting Bible-backs would never think to look. . . . Sal blinked back the tears that had clouded his vision. Why should he think of whips and conjure beads when he stood on the threshold of another, finer world?

"Swallow this," said Yancey. "You'll be sure to sleep."

"Ah'll sleep 'thout pills, Doctah."

But he found the promise was easier made than kept, once he had closed his cabin door. A dozen times he started up at the sound of footsteps outside—only to realize he had dreamed of Florrie's return, through his restless dozing. Once, in the shadow of true oblivion, he imagined his fingers had closed on Captain Selby's throat. He smiled then, and shook the captain's limp body thoroughly, to make sure he was dead.

After the vision had run its course, he lapsed into true slumber —proud that he had refused the doctor's medicine. Tonight he could avenge Florrie only in dreams. The revenge would be real (he told himself fiercely) before Brad Selby's life had run its course.

5

When Dr. Yancey made his belated appearance at the Big House, the gaiety had been at its peak: only a trained ear would have questioned the men's swagger or the timbre of the ladies' laughter. The fact that Colonel Hamilton continued to snore over his brandy had gone unmentioned: so had Brad's absence . . . Now (stumping out his last cigar and watching Sal's departure with a shrug of dismissal) the plantation doctor sensed that Reen's soiree was finally dissolving.

It was a matter of intonation, of pauses in the repartee: even from the portico he could judge it perfectly. Reen's guests were responding, as they must, to a conviction that night's candles were guttering, that the stock of merriment and compliments was exhausted. Telling himself that he had already made his contribution, Uncle Doc was careful to skirt the lighted portion of the house as he made his way toward the empty half of the double parlor. He knew just where to look for the master of Selby at this hour. Not that he relished the meeting, but Brad deserved a few verbal blows.

The collision of master and slave he had just witnessed had been an easy triumph for the owner. Brad had held all the weapons; he had used them with insolent ease. There would be other, more violent collisions later. No man would dare predict the result. No one could say how Lorena, trapped between the warring factions, might be spared the hideous aftermath.

Observing her long duel with Brad, Yancey had tried to be an impartial judge. Tonight he could tell himself that Lorena deserved the victory, though the contest had gone against her from the start and the prospects were dark indeed. Lorena had proved herself the earth woman, the giver of abundance. Brad was the atavism, the destroyer of all he touched. Representing only an infinitesimal part of the South and its culture, he and his kind were the rotten apples that had ruined the barrel.

There was even a certain justice in the fact that the marriage had been without issue. Sterility, after all, was the stock in trade of men like Brad—despite the brats he fathered so regularly in quarters. . . . The basic fact remained: Lorena would never justify her union, save in the creation of Selby's heir. When Brad rode off tomorrow, it seemed all too likely he would leave her barren. It was even more probable that Selby Hall would be a smoking ruin when the year ended. How could its chatelaine survive—without the work that sustained her, with no child to replace a husband's love?

Brad lay spread-eagled on the couch when Yancey opened the study door. From all outward signs, he had slipped into a brandied nirvana—yet he sat up abruptly at the sound. With the opening of his eyes he appeared almost sober. Here, it seemed, was a Southern gentleman to the manner born—a two-fisted drinker who could ride into the dawn with a song on his lips, ready for his stint of fox hunting or Yankee-killing.

"Next time," said Brad, "you might have the courtesy to knock."

Yancey tilted himself comfortably in the swivel chair behind the desk. "Did you find the account books heavy reading?"

The master of Selby knuckled the drowsiness from his lids. "Don't be so sharp, Yancey. You'll cut yourself."

"Read the figures again," said the plantation doctor. "You'll see the black ink is in the proper column. In your place, I'd be thankful for that miracle."

"I still don't see how we've shown a profit."

"Praise your wife for that—and your brother-in-law's runners. Isn't it time you admitted Lorena is quite a manager?"

"I'll admit it freely," said Brad. He rose from the couch and adjusted the skirts of his beautifully cut gray tunic. "I can't pretend it sets well on me."

"Lorena isn't the first wife to handle her husband's business while he's in uniform—and handle it well."

"Two years before Sumter she ran the plantation."

"Blame that on your father's whim—after all, you were usually away."

"Are you singing that old tune again?"

"Perhaps I am, in another key," said Yancey: his mild tone was in sharp contrast to his words. "Certainly I don't blame you for spending your patrimony as you saw fit. Not while there were foxes to ride down and duels to fight—and Creole ladies waiting in New Orleans. You're a master at such things. Lorena has been willing to finance you, now the Judge is gone. Worse bargains have been made in marriage."

"Don't tell me to meet Reen halfway," said Brad. "That's another tune I've heard too often."

"This is your last night here," said Uncle Doc. "Couldn't you stay sober?"

"I *am* sober, damn it!"

"Sober enough to realize your wife will be heartbroken—if you don't join her by midnight?"

"You old lecher, what are you driving at?"

"Do I have to spell it out?"

"Go to hell, Yancey. Is it my fault Reen's harder to stock than a skittish mare?"

They faced each other for a bristling moment: once again Uncle Doc admitted he had lost the argument in advance. "You've led a charmed life in this war," he said. "What if your luck doesn't hold? Wouldn't you be happier with an heir?"

"Of course I would. I've wanted a son more than anything in this world. Is it my fault Reen hasn't foaled?"

"Maybe. You've neglected her shamefully on this leave—and every other."

"Are you calling me a bastard to my face?" Brad shouted.

Uncle Doc kept his temper. "No, Brad. At Selby the bastards are always high browns—or high yellows. You, unfortunately, are legitimate."

"What's that meant to imply?"

"Nothing. I was trying to be witty—and failing for lack of an audience. As for Reen, she's had good training at widowhood. She'll survive your death nicely, if we're fortunate enough to lose you."

"That's enough, Yancey——"

"More than enough," Uncle Doc agreed. He looked up as a figure appeared in the double doors that divided the two parlors. "Here comes your overseer. Try cursing *him* for a change."

They fell silent while Luke Jackson pulled the panels shut and came limping toward the study. The plantation overseer was tall and sallow, with an almost equine face. His expression (which should have been humorous, in the traditional rustic fashion) remained merely dour. The limp, the result of a near-fatal encounter with a rutting bull, seemed part of his awkwardness. Having paid his respects to the company on his way through the house, Luke could afford to shed his formal manners. Before he spoke, Yancey guessed the news he bore was bad.

Brad strode into the parlor, scowling in lieu of greeting. "Where have you been hiding, Jackson? I've had a dozen things to ask you."

"Sorry, Cap'n. I've been runnin' errands for Doc Yancey." The man's speech placed him. Despite his linen coat and broad-brimmed planter's hat, it was evident that Luke Jackson was a red-neck from the backlands—in this case a mountain white from Tennessee, who needed time to shape his prejudices, but clung to them grimly.

"Since when d'you work for Dr. Yancey?"

"Mrs. Selby said I should go."

"I give orders when I'm home—not Mrs. Selby. Is that clear?"

"Sure is, Cap'n," said Luke. "It's only that the doc needed quinine from Decatur. Since I'd gone that far, I figured I'd have a look around."

Brad's face was a thunderstorm in the making, but Uncle Doc saw his temper was in control. He suppressed a bitter smile. A field hand who dared to set foot on the master's carpet could be whipped without mercy: the flogging of a Negro was a natural outlet for passions. But no Southern gentleman would think of losing his temper with his overseer. White inferiors could be neither thrashed nor challenged.

"Don't you know the Decatur road is closed to civilians?"

"Maybe so, Cap'n—but I didn't see hide nor hair of our military today. Only a powerful lot of dust around Atlanta—and bluecoats everywhere."

"The enemy has sent no patrols out of Atlanta. They haven't dared."

"They did today, Cap'n," said Luke with the same oxlike calm.

"I won't suggest you're lying, Jackson. Only that you're mistaken."

"Since when has one of our own patrols reported here?" asked Yancey.

"That, I'm afraid, is a military secret," said Brad.

"Not that it matters. We all know it's only a question of time before Sherman makes his move. If he's sent his outriders to Decatur he's ready now."

"Since when did you turn strategist, Yancey?"

"Even a civilian can see we're whipped, Brad. Why not admit it too?"

"If you weren't Reen's kin, I'd call you out for that."

"Have it your way," said Uncle Doc. "I believe in facing facts. Real news is welcome, after a week of your bombast."

Brad's fingers had curled into a fist: Yancey braced for the blow. Instead, Brad slapped his thigh with a contemptuous glare. The gesture was meant for Quenten Rowley, who had just strolled in from the other room. As always, Quent seemed a trifle withdrawn —and secretly amused, as though he were smiling inwardly at a joke he would not share.

"Do me a favor, Quent," said Brad. "Tell your Uncle Doc he's turned coward."

Lorena's brother took the best armchair the parlor boasted. When he spoke he seemed to be thinking aloud—and only half aware of Brad's restless pacing.

"A little old-fashioned fear makes sense at times," he said. "For my part, I expect to be in Macon by morning. I hope I can persuade my sister to join me."

"Don't tell me *you* believe this old-woman gossip?"

"It isn't gossip, Brad. You'd know better yourself—if you hadn't lost touch with your own army."

"I've had constant reports."

"When did the last one come?"

"I can't answer that. It's taken General Hood time to regroup——"

"Don't worry. You'll get orders by morning—and I'll guarantee you won't like them."

Brad had fallen back a pace at this cool statement. He was aware of Quent's connections on both sides of the battle lines—and knew his reports were accurate. "So you think Sherman will risk a fight?"

"I'm sure of it. And there'll be damned little risk involved—after the beating we took around Atlanta."

"What's the enemy objective?"

"Savannah."

"Savannah's on the coast, man!"

"Don't give me lessons in geography," said Quent drily. "My guess is they'll reach it without a major engagement."

"No army under heaven can cross Georgia and live."

"This one can and will. The day Hood gave up Atlanta, the South lost the war."

"Georgia will rise up and destroy them."

"You've got that backwards, Brad," said Quent. "*They'll* destroy Georgia. This time, you're facing a new kind of war. One that has nothing to do with chivalry—and still less with cavalry charges. It will end resistance in the Deep South by the New Year. And I'll give you odds Virginia surrenders by spring."

"Think what you like," said Brad in a thick voice. "It isn't my business to correct the bombproofs. But don't use the word surrender in my presence."

Quent's cold eyes did not flicker. "Go waken Colonel Hamilton with that battle cry. He'll endorse it."

"Old Hamilton's a fool. I don't need his opinion."

"That's your first reasonable remark," said Quent. "When I left the others, he was still snoring in his after-dinner armchair. You can hardly blame him: it must be the first decent meal he's had since his slaves deserted him." Quent sighed and poured a brandy. "The colonel is luckier than most of us tonight. He's a complete exile from the present. Right now I'll wager he's dreaming he has the arm he lost at Shiloh—and the two sons he gave to Lee for cannon fodder——"

"No man can criticize General Lee to my face, sir. Not even my wife's brother."

"I'm criticizing no one—not even our generals. And I'll let you die defending Selby without turning a hair. But I don't want Lorena to be hurt—just because *you're* doomed and damned."

"Reen's my wife. If I'm damned—we'll be damned together."

"A noble sentiment," said Quent. "Let's hope she ignores it, and comes south with me."

"Lorena won't leave," said Yancey. "I've done my best to persuade her."

Belatedly Brad recalled Luke's presence, and jerked a thumb toward the door.

"You'd best leave us, Jackson. This seems to be a family quarrel."

"Why should Luke go?" asked Quent. "Since you turned cavalryman, he's worked hard for Selby. He's entitled to hear what we say."

"Thanks, Mr. Rowley," said the overseer—but he had already edged toward the door, obviously eager to escape this quarrel among his betters. He paused only when Quent addressed him directly.

"How much cotton do you have in storage?"

"Nearly a thousand bales."

"Prime?"

"It's all we raise here, sir."

"I've good cause to know that," said Quent. He was speaking straight at Brad now. "So do my factors in England. As you're aware, we can no longer ship direct—except from Wilmington. I might still make a deal, if I move fast."

Brad's eyes, Yancey observed, had taken on a sudden gleam. The cavalry captain had been woefully short of hard money lately—and Quenten Rowley's accounts were always settled in gold.

"What's your game?" he snapped.

"I've a friend in Atlanta——"

"You've friends everywhere."

"I won't deny it," said Quent in the easiest of drawls. "This friend is also a cotton broker. He isn't quite on Sherman's staff—but he's close enough to call him Uncle Billy. With carte blanche, he can sell those thousand bales before the bummers steal them."

"Damnation, sir! I won't deal with Yankees."

"Some of my best friends are Yankees," said Quent. "Selby cotton has already reached New England mills, by way of Nassau. Why object to one deal more?"

"I refuse to listen."

"Not even for Lorena's sake? Each year of this useless war, she's sunk your profits in Confederate bonds——"

"Selby Hall could do no less——"

"*This* would be a hard-money deal. Cash in London. You'd have enough to start your next crop."

"When Richmond redeems our bonds, we'll have a fortune."

Quent drank his brandy. "Finish things your way then. I don't doubt you'll survive. Your sort of pot rot always does—no matter what language you speak."

The argument broke and died as Reen came in from the twin parlor. With a quick glance behind her she pulled the door panels shut and faced the four men with the special smile she used for such meetings. Brad (who had been sulking in an armchair) was on his feet instantly.

"I *will* end things my way, Quent," he said. "And I'll tell you more. My wife will back me."

Reen crossed the carpet slowly: the silken whisper of her hoops was loud in the silence.

"Forgive me, gentlemen. Do I intrude on an argument?"

"On the contrary, Lorena," said her brother. "This concerns you directly. I was scheming out a way to dispose of your cotton——"

"If it's a contraband sale, the answer is no."

"Think twice before you close your mind," said Quent. "It's entirely legal, if the purchase is handled at staff level. A provost guard at your gate could save Selby from looters——"

Reen threw her husband a flashing smile. "My gate is guarded now—by our cavalry. I ask no better protection."

"You're my sister," said Quent. "You *can't* play the fool forever."

"I'm a lady turned farmer, with work to do," said Reen. "The war is Brad's department—and he doesn't seem too concerned." She smiled at the overseer. "Did you bring good news, Luke?"

Luke Jackson swallowed hard as he felt Brad's eye. "Dr. Yancey will tell you, ma'am. I just gave him my report. If you'll excuse me, I'm plumb weary: it's a long ride from Decatur." He went out, his sad horse face seeming to brood over wrongs too great to be borne.

Reen watched him leave, with her composure unshaken. *You*

already know what news Luke brought, thought Uncle Doc. *If you're play-acting now, it's only for your dunderhead husband's sake.* Aloud he said cautiously, "It seems the enemy's on the move outside Atlanta. Brad tells us the situation's in control."

The cavalry captain spoke instantly—and his voice rang with sincerity. "Cray County is in no danger, my dear. If a single patrol dares to cross Indian River Ford, we'll shoot them down."

"That's all I need to know, Brad." An outside observer would have sworn that Reen's confidence in her warrior was absolute. "Selby will sleep without nightmares tonight then. Clara and the colonel are leaving. Your lieutenants are riding them to the Forks. Would you care to say good night?"

"An excellent thought," said Brad. "I can check on my pickets." He nodded to each man in turn with sullen politeness. It was apparent he welcomed an excuse to escape the reality of Luke's chilling news. "I hope you've conceded the argument, Quent," he said. "What husband could ask for greater trust—or greater loyalty?" He left them—with his panache and his insolence unshaken.

"That was quite an exit, Lorena," said Quent. "Mr. Booth himself could hardly have done better on the stage."

"There's no need to reproach Brad," Reen said. "Selby is a feudal preserve. As lord in residence he has certain illusions to maintain." She turned to Yancey. "Now tell me what Luke said. Tonight that's more important."

She listened in silence while the plantation doctor repeated the overseer's report. When he had finished, she lay back in her armchair for an instant and closed her eyes. He could see now how tired she was.

"You sound ominous, Uncle Doc. Are you trying to frighten me?"

"No, my dear—only to give you the facts. The Union vanguard could be here by morning. Take my word, it will be a blue avalanche."

"Will there be fighting?"

"I doubt it. Once Brad has made contact—if he lingers that long —he'll have no choice but to skedaddle."

"So the enemy is visiting us at last. I suppose it's my just reward for pretending they didn't exist."

"Call it what you like," said Quent. "It's time to get out."

"For you, perhaps."

"You can't play Brad's game forever."

"You've said that a dozen times this year—and the clock at Selby ticks on."

"A bullet could stop it tomorrow."

"I'm not afraid of bullets. You just said there'd be no fighting."

"What *does* it take to frighten you?"

"I can't believe General Sherman will harm civilians," said Reen. "Nor do I think he's the two-headed dragon people claim. Besides, the main road goes through Brandt's Crossing. That's five miles north of here. They could miss us entirely."

"My bags are packed now," said Quent. "I'm taking the morning train from Macon. Open your eyes and come with me."

"Where are you bound this time?"

"London, I think. Most of my cash is there."

"Brad took me to England on our wedding trip. It did nothing but rain."

"Winter in France then. Get a Paris lawyer to draw up your divorce. I'll foot the bill—and help you find a real husband later."

"I'm married now," said Reen.

"To Selby?"

"To Selby, Quent. So is Brad—though he won't admit it."

"You can't go on living in a battlefield."

"This house was a battlefield before the war began. I'll find ways to take cover."

Listening to the argument, knowing the girl would not budge from her resolve, Yancey shot a questioning look at Quent. Judging by the latter's shrug, he was about to concede defeat.

"You've a point there," he put in quickly. "But your brother's right. You can leave the field with honor."

Reen moved toward the portico, to fling one of the glass doors wide. For a moment she stood against the night, as though its repose could somehow give the lie to Quent's prediction.

"Uncle Doc, did you ever see a plant bed burned off?"

"I've burned 'em myself. Why?"

"Tell Quent what happens. Being city-bred, he's probably forgotten."

"You pile on wood until the whole bed's covered," said the

plantation doctor. "Then you set fires at each corner. The earth is cooked to kill the weeds. Later it's hoed and molded. The new plants come up fresh and green."

"That's what will happen in Georgia." Reen turned and faced her brother. "We'll plant again—when this fire's burned out."

"It's a useful metaphor," said Quent. "I'm not sure it applies to the South. War leaves its special crop of weeds. They thrive in scorched earth."

"I still say we'll make crops at Selby."

"With no hands to drive the plows?"

"Our slaves will work as freedmen."

"Can you picture old Hamilton paying wages to a free Negro? Or the Randolphs? Or the Buells?"

"Even they must follow, if someone leads. When they see it's the only way to survive——"

"How can Selby set the example, with Brad the owner?"

"I'll worry about Brad when the time comes," said Reen. "The fact remains: this plantation is my job. It's work I can't delegate. Nor can I avoid it by running away."

"And what more can you accomplish here?"

"A hundred things. Just keeping in repair is a full-time task. There's still cotton to be ginned——"

"With the packhouse bursting?"

"We'll find room somehow. When the last bale is stored, we must plan next year's crop. Brad will expect it in the ground when he's mustered out."

"Damn Brad—and what he expects! This place should be yours, Lorena. Perhaps that's the only solution of your problem." Quent was on his feet now: Yancey could see that he was prolonging the argument only for his peace of mind. "Let me raise the cash to buy him out. It shouldn't take much—with an army of occupation in the county."

"Brad would sooner die than sell his land."

"Who gives a continental damn for his feelings? He could be forced to sell. How does he propose to pay taxes when he takes off his uniform?"

"Perhaps he won't," said Reen. "If this campaign goes against us, he's talking of joining forces with Mexico."

Yancey rumbled into speech at last. "You can leave us with a clear conscience, Quent. *I* can't persuade her to go where it's safe. Why should you?"

"Promise you'll stay, Uncle Doc?"

"I'll leave when Lorena does," said Yancey. "Not before."

"Keep her safe, or you'll hear from me."

"Uncle Doc and I will protect each other, Quent," said Reen. She put up a cheek to be kissed, then led her brother toward the door that gave to the west portico and the stables. The visitor, Yancey observed, was being dismissed firmly, but with perfect manners:

"Take the yellow gig," she said. "It's the fastest in the stables. Ajax will drive you to Macon."

"I'll drive myself," said her brother. "And I've already commandeered the gig. My bags were put in before dinner."

"See, my dear? You *had* decided to leave me to my fate."

"Have it your way, Lorena. I wish you luck."

"I'm luckier than you'll ever be, Quent," she said with a smile. "I've a place to fill and work to do. All you're good for is coining money."

"At least I don't squander it on knights without armor," he said. "That's my last sneer until we meet again. I'll return the day Mr. Davis admits the war is over."

"You'll find me here," said Reen. "That's another thing you can count on."

Uncle Doc did not speak until the side door had closed. Quent's departure, he thought, had been quite in character: the Quenten Rowleys in the South would always move a bit faster than history —sidestepping its debacles neatly, since they could guess the outcome of the next chapter before it was written. The Lorenas (who were no less wise) were born to face the music. He would have respected Reen far less tonight had she consented to flee with her brother.

"What's the next move?" he asked, settling in his favorite chair by the fireplace—and wishing his old man's heartbeat could match the booming assurance of his voice. The false exuberance, of course, had not deceived Lorena. He did not look up when she moved behind his chair, leaned both arms on the back, and stared down at the flames.

"Are you good at prayers, Uncle Doc?"

"Fair to middling. I seldom expect them to be answered. On occasion I'm pleasantly surprised to rediscover there's a God."

"Try this one. Pray the Union Army misses Selby."

"And burns out the Hamiltons instead?"

"Not at all. I meant what I said about firing the plant bed. But if we *are* spared—isn't it the turn of the game?"

"This time, I'm afraid the odds are against you. Quent says the enemy has Cray County mapped, down to the last hen roost. For more than three years this plantation has supplied the Confederate armies. Obviously it's on their black list."

"Then I'm a fool to stay on?"

"Put it another way, girl. You can't give up the game, even when it's played out. You're trapped by your success here."

Reen put a soothing hand on his shoulder. "Don't most women cling to their homes, to the last gasp?"

"Is Selby Hall a home—or a symbol?"

"Symbols are important too. Few of us have the home or the husband we've dreamed of. Will you admit this is a fair substitute?"

"Where does that leave your cavalry captain?"

"I'm still Brad's wife. And I mean to give him a son. That's why I was created."

"I won't deny it was an important reason."

Silence fell between them, broken only by the hiss of a collapsing pine knot on the hearth. "I hoped I'd conceive, before his leave was over," said Reen. "Is that immodest enough to suit you?"

"Nothing could be more natural," said Yancey. "In fact, it's a good hope to sleep on. If you can sleep, with an enemy army moving this way. Shout up the stairs, if you need me. I don't expect to close my eyes."

He did not stir while Reen put out the candles in the parlor. Nor did he move to help her when she took a light from its bracket, pushed back the sliding doors, and climbed the noble rosewood stairway. Ulysses, the ancient butler, was snuffing the candles in the second parlor. He honored the mistress of Selby with a bow as she swept from view.

The guests are gone, thought the plantation doctor, *the revels ended.* He took up a candle of his own just before darkness invaded the great downstairs rooms. It was the start of his ritual midnight prowl—the self-indulgence of a man past middle years who needed sleep badly yet was reluctant to seek his couch.

Tonight he prowled with extra care, testing the bolts on each window, and the chains on the heavy mahogany door that opened to the southern portico. Ulysses had long since banked the fires—but he roamed from hearth to hearth to check the flues—ending his tour in the wide, copper-gleaming kitchen. Here the open fire-places were stacked with plate warmers, ready for the breakfast Penelope (the senior cook) would serve an hour after sunrise. The tall Terry clock—a present from a grateful mill owner in Massachu-setts—was loud in the stillness. Comparing it with his watch, and finding it exact to the minute, Uncle Doc smiled faintly. He had recalled Reen's challenge to her brother. War had come and gone across the ravaged South, but the clock at Selby ticked on.

It was odd that this clock should be a Yankee's gift.

6

Reen dismissed Mammy Jo when her undressing was only half over. The old slave's clucking had soothed her at first. Now an obscure impulse caused her to finish her preparations alone.

Her gown was on its hanger, its hoops in the special wardrobe. She was free of her camisole and the high, whaleboned corset—though the marks of each stay were still livid on her flesh, thanks to merciless lacing. With only her shift to cover her, she stepped out of beautifully stitched linen drawers and rolled down her stock-ings. Hesitating but a moment, she stood before the cheval glass in the dressing alcove and let the chemise fall to her feet. Once again she told herself she need envy no woman her looks.

It was true she was too slender for the bombastic gowns now à la mode, the flounces that turned a woman into a kind of floating argosy. Her breasts were not large, but they were proudly firm. Her milk-white skin was smooth, her figure constricted sweetly at the waist, then tapering to hips and legs a sculptor would have called perfect. It was the beauty of a greyhound, without the full-blown

enticements of an odalisque. . . . Were such bodies meant for love?
How could she know when she had done no more than yield to a
husband's lust?

Reen selected a vial of perfume from her dressing table. It was a
present from the *Albemarle* (the flagship of Quent's fleet of blockade runners) a French scent heavy with musk. Half closing her eyes
in distaste, she touched the stopper to her ear lobes.

Without risking another glance at the mirror, she felt she was
blushing furiously. At such moments she could believe hostile eyes
were upon her, though the drapes were drawn on the balcony that
opened to the upper story of the portico and only a single night
light glowed beside the bed. Her eyes flinched from that imposing
monument to Eros. Should she bring another lamp to the night
table? She preferred darkness for the marriage ritual: Brad insisted
on a night light. It was almost as though he enjoyed the spectacle
of his dominance.

Uncle Doc had told her that some women conceived because of
their wanton nature—that fertility was a by-product of the pleasure
they offered their husbands. Try as she might, she could take no
joy in this rite of Venus: her only wish was to give Selby Hall its
heir . . . As always, she thought of these bountiful acres as a person
rather than a place. In the heat of anger Brad had once accused
her of marrying Selby outright: it was the land she loved (he had
raged) and not its owner. Tonight she could admit the truth of
his accusation. It was Selby she meant to renew with Brad, not
Brad himself.

Her husband—she could admit it frankly now—was beyond re-
newal. She had tried to make a marriage. It was not her fault she
had failed—and he could still father her child. Selby's heir would
not be the first conceived without love.

Reen's house slaves knew many odd things, folk memories out
of their primitive past. Only tonight Mammy Jo had whispered that
this was her best time to "make a baby." Now, repeating the crude
phrase aloud, Reen took relish in its crudity. While the thought
lasted, she was close to wanting Brad. Even then she knew her desire sprang from no yearning of the flesh. Brad was merely the blind
male force that could bring her fulfillment.

Bemused as she was, lulled by the warmth of the room, she had been unconscious of her nudity. When she glimpsed herself again in the mirror she moved with flaming cheeks to the bed and picked up her nightgown. The robe (chastely concealed in an embroidered case) was of sheer silk, brought from Japan in one of her father's ships. Letting its folds rustle over her shoulders, Reen saw that it lay taut across her bosom and molded her hips like a second skin.

On another night she would have chosen a more modest garb. There was something indecent about this wisp of honeymoon finery. Surely it was what kept women wore (though her classmates at Raleigh had whispered that such women wore nothing at all). *He'll climb those stairs tonight,* she told herself fiercely. *He must.*

On her dresser the clock pointed to an hour after midnight. If only to distract her thoughts, Reen moved to the portmanteau that stood open beside the bed and began packing the clothes Brad would take into the field. It was a task soon ended. Cavalry kits were on the Spartan side these days—when saddle space must be saved for extra bandoleers.

Reen had no clear image of her husband at war. Nor could she feel the dread most wives endured when their men rode back to join their commands. There was something in Brad that rejected death, an iron will to endure that had taken him through every blood bath. Whatever his faults, he had courage: the medals that spanned the tunic of his dress uniform were proof of that.

Quent had talked often with Brad's brother officers: most of them agreed (if only in whispers) that Captain Selby courted peril for peril's sake. Three horses had been shot under him at Chickamauga. In a raid after the retreat from Gettysburg he had led a company of volunteers across Meade's vanguard—and returned, with three other survivors, to report the mission accomplished. Reen could understand such stories perfectly. Brad was a born soldier. From his first battle he had found his true calling.

When the portmanteau was closed, she took the field uniform from the armoire for a final inspection, though she knew it was cleaned and brushed. The buttons were wooden pegs today instead of gilt—but the double bars at the shoulders had been burnished until they shone. She folded the uniform neatly, and placed it on the portmanteau, where Brad would be sure to find it by daylight. Making the gesture, she felt hot tears fall upon her hands. It was monstrous that she could send him on his way so coldly—but he would perform his last function in her life when he gave her a son.

Such reflections, she told herself, were as dangerous as they were unseemly. Above all, she must not fret at his tardiness—nor could she risk reproaching him when he joined her at last. A carafe of brandy stood on the table, with a single glass beside it (no matter how much he had taken below, Brad always liked a final drink at bedtime). Reen herself had seldom tasted anything stronger than a sip of wine at table. Tonight she poured out a full glass of the tawny cognac and drank it at a toss, as she had seen Yancey do so often.

The effect, after a moment of burning torment, bordered on the miraculous. She found that she could mount the two carpeted steps leading to her nuptial couch and lie there (abandoned as some Oriental sultana in the vast nest of pillows) while she poured a second glass. Again the stimulus seemed to reach her instantly. This time, however, the reaction was more profound.

In another moment she found herself drowsing: her lids had drooped shut as predictably as the eyes of a china doll. She started up just once, at the sound of a creaking floor board, contracting in the cold on the balcony outside her window. For a moment she was sure that the enemy had already invaded Selby. Then, shut off from reality at last in a warm cocoon of alcohol, she slept—without caring that she slept alone.

She wakened to the pelt of rain outside, her limbs aching in the icy cold of morning. The fire had died on the grate: clad only in a sheath of silk, she trembled violently as she fumbled her way to the chaise longue and put on the quilted robe Mammy Jo had left there.

The light burned on the table beside the bed, and the hands of the clock hung on four. When she pushed her window drapes aside, night still pressed down on the earth, though there was an eerie, reddish gleam behind the clouds that might presage the dawn.

Muddled as Reen's senses were, she was not too certain of her next moves—though she recalled groping in Brad's armoire until she found one of his riding crops. The board creaked again on her balcony: this time, it was the pressure of her foot when she moved toward the stair that led down to the portico. . . . Sleepy as she was, she had taken this route by instinct. She knew she must corner him: if they met in the foyer, he might brazen out his absence.

Long before she opened the study door she could hear his snoring. As she had expected, he was sleeping in his clothes on the horsehair couch, with an empty bottle beside it. The light above his head gave him a brutish look, enhanced by the unbuttoned tunic, the shirt-tail he had neglected to tuck in. It was not the first time she had found him thus. In the past she had summoned Ulysses to help him to bed—then slept, as best she could, in the dressing alcove. Tonight such kindness was beyond her: until she died she knew she would shrink from Brad Selby's touch.

Her fist knotted on the whip. Taking a step nearer the couch, she lifted it to strike—just as Uncle Doc's hand closed on her arm.

"I told you I was a light sleeper, girl."

Reen shook her head like a woman emerging from a bad dream —and stared at the hand that held the riding crop. Yancey took it from her gently and laid it aside.

"Right now," he said, "it'll take more than that to rouse him. Shall I fetch a shotgun?"

Shaking with an ague that had no relation to the cold, Reen let her face rest against his shoulder. "How did I get here? I feel as though I've been sleep-walking."

"Reckon you were close to it, Lorena."

"What was I trying to do?"

"Give back a beating," he said. "God knows he's flogged your spirit enough down the years. Still and all, it's better to let him lie. He's out of the world till morning, to judge by that empty decanter. He'd never know who thrashed him—or why."

Uncertain whom she hated more—the figure on the couch or herself—Reen was really weeping. "I've never been shamed like this before," she sobbed.

"I'll agree," said Yancey. "Didn't I just say he deserved a bull whip?"

"While I waited upstairs, I had two glasses of brandy. But I can't blame it on that."

Neither of them spoke while he led her from the study. The strange red glow had deepened on the windowpanes. Wide awake at last, Reen exchanged a baffled glance with Yancey as she heard a continuous low wailing—a sound that could come only from the quarters. It was not the first time her field hands, terrified by a phenomenon beyond their ken, had raised their voices in supplication to half-forgotten gods.

"What is it—a forest fire?"

"The enemy is burning Atlanta," said the plantation doctor.

"*Atlanta?*"

"Local fires were set two days ago," he said. "Tonight the whole town's ablaze. We had the news an hour ago."

Reen broke free and rushed to the north portico. Standing on the wet lawn, she saw that the sky was pulsing with a monstrous, man-made aurora borealis, with its center in the northwestern quadrant. Far off though the fire was, there was no mistaking its origin—or its portent.

The wailing continued from the cabins, muffled by closed doors. Only a few of the younger Negroes had ventured out to watch; most of her slaves, obeying the urge to hide from what they could not understand, had locked themselves in. She knew they would cower in those cabins until the rising bell. . . . Asking herself if they would obey that brazen summons tomorrow, Reen had the answer: even now they would obey a routine to which that flaming portent had written finis. Here in letters any man could read, was the spelling out of freedom—but the field hands of Selby still relied on the chatelaine to guide their footsteps. The knowledge was a bitter tonic as she turned to Yancey.

"The Union Army's on the move then?"

"It can mean nothing else. Atlanta has been their bivouac since September—and they've destroyed it."

Reen turned to the driveway, and the wink of sentinel fires that marked the cavalry camp. "Surely Brad's troop can't stay until morning?"

"So far, they've had no order of movement. I've just talked to Lieutenant Lambert."

She found she was shaking with laughter. It was fitting that Brad Selby could snore through the destruction of Georgia's capital.

"Perhaps we should get what rest we can," she said. "We must be prepared for refugees tomorrow."

"I've given orders for a canteen," he told her. "Ulysses and Penelope will set it up at the gate. My guess is most of the county will move out ahead of the Yankees. It's senseless, of course, but people take fright easily——"

"I'm glad you thought of that, Uncle Doc. The moment it's light, I'll join you there."

Reen pushed back the hair from her forehead with a tired hand. Now that she had struck rock bottom in her relations with her husband, now that the enemy threat was as tangible as that flame on the horizon, she felt strangely calm—and almost too drowsy to stand. "I'm going to sleep while I'm able," she said—aware, even as she spoke, of the anti-climax. "Even if we could waken Brad, he can hardly save Atlanta now."

In her room again, she staggered into bed and twisted a fold of blanket about her. Tired as she was, she had not even closed the door that opened to the landing. The last sound she heard was Brad's contented snoring. Its vibrations seemed to shake the whole house, once she had identified the source of that volcanic rumble. . . .

For a while she wept quietly in the dark. Then, just before dawn, she felt her dilemma unwind as though a strangling noose had been loosened. An escape had come to her unasked, rising from the mind's underworld, where knowledge is older than speech. It was as though a pagan voice had whispered in her ear—assuring her that no dilemma was insoluble in times like these, when an enemy army was on the move and old values must go by the board.

She opened her eyes just once, to realize the rain was a downpour. For a moment she was staring wide awake—shocked to the soul by the stratagem that other, primitive Lorena had offered so brazenly. And then, remembering a family legend (which proved that one of her ancestors had been a pirate), she found she was smiling before she slept again.

Uncle Doc would smile in turn, if she dared to confide that reckless, half-formed resolve. The fact it had come to her at all—even in a dream—was proof that her cause was desperate.

7

The rain ceased at sunrise; the clouds, lifting in a freshening breeze, were gone with the first glimmer of light. Major Daniel Carroll, of the 2nd Pennsylvania Cavalry, reined in with his staff on the slope above Indian River Ford, reflected that it promised to be good fighting weather after all—assuming (as he must) that the Johnnies would contest this strategic crossing. While his aide spread a field map on the saddle, he lifted a spyglass to sweep the country to the south. Despite his preoccupation he was conscious of the green, smoky beauty of the Georgia earth. *Land like this,* he thought, *is too rich to spoil in battle.*

"Shall we send out scouts, Major?"

"Not yet. Hold the battalion in cover until it's really light."

In the end, it was Carroll himself who got down from his horse to move through the stand of yellow pine for a closer view of the stream and the road on the far bank. A tall, broad-shouldered man in his late twenties, he was handsome in a craggy, sunburned fashion—his good looks marred only by too-intent eyes, the by-product of a trade where alertness could spell out the difference between survival and extinction. He stretched his long legs gratefully at the first contact with the springy turf. Then, like a cautious cat, he made himself one with his cover. After three years of fighting he had learned the arts of invisibility, and of silence.

Today's tour of duty was routine—a scouting expedition well beyond the right flank of the Union vanguard. Its objective was a testing of enemy resistance on the roads around Brandt's Crossing, the only settlement of consequence that Cray County boasted, besides the county seat. Intelligence reports had stated that most Confederate units had retreated with the main body of Hood's army —but Carroll had learned to check such reports on his own. Established firmly on the northern bank of the river, he had refused to expose pickets to needless risk.

With four companies of seasoned fighters behind him he was confident that he could meet the faltering enemy resistance on better than even terms. It would be a simple matter to command the ford—and to sweep the nexus of roads beyond it. He had also learned to take even a foregone victory seriously.

Creeping through the bracken (and recalling, for no clear reason, a game of Indian-hunting he had played as a boy in the Alleghenies), Carroll moved to the very edge of the forest screen. Here the piney woods gave way to a meadow that rolled in gentle contours to the turbid red river below. At this distance it was possible to confirm first impressions. An advance by the enemy, even in strength, could be stopped dead from his present position. Indian Ford had been aptly named. In dry weather horsemen could sweep from bank to bank with ease. This morning, thanks to heavy rains, the river was lapping its banks. The ford was passable—but it would be necessary to swim the horses at its deepest part.

In such circumstances a crossing under fire would be suicidal. Carroll decided to remain in the shelter of the woods until he was positive his arrival had gone unheralded.

"Do we sit tight, Major?"

He turned to grin at his aide. For a boy just turned twenty, Jack Keller was developing into a first-rate tactician.

"How would you manage things, Lieutenant?"

"I'd pass out rations, sir—and wait awhile. It's too early for a swim."

"Much too early," Carroll agreed. "If there's cavalry between here and Macon, it's bound to be looking for us. We'll play hide-and-seek while we can."

The order to breakfast in the saddle was obeyed quietly. The 2nd Pennsylvania Cavalry was a veteran group, and Carroll's troop was among the crack battalions: even its recruits, seasoned in the field since Chickamauga, had become part of that compact ax of war. Munching a cold bacon bun while he continued to study the map, the major found he was remarkably alert, considering the long ride from Atlanta. It was a relief to be on the move again, to sense the gauge was down.

Finishing his Spartan meal with a tot of rum, Carroll felt his nostrils distend to a familiar aroma: it was the odor of frying fish, drifting up from the riverbank. He had noted the cabin that stood there, and decided against checking on its occupant: a Confederate observer would hardly advertise his presence so openly. He was sure

of that estimate when a Negro emerged with a hound at his heel
and moved toward the fish weirs that stood in the river current
upstream.

This, obviously, was the abode of a field slave whose task was to
seine the river and supply his master's kitchen. It was typical of
Georgia's plantation economy that a black man could continue to
perform such a task. To the north the roads around Atlanta were
already clogged with refugees. Here, in the idyllic peace of morning, it was unthinkable that death (in the shape of five hundred
Union carbines) was waiting in a ready-made ambush.

Carroll breathed deep of the nostalgic cooking smell, letting his
mind drift back to the Pennsylvania hillside he called home. There
had been meadows and fish weirs in those uplands—and fine farming land in the valley, until his father's oil derricks had raised their
grotesque heads among the furrows. The Carroll acres, of course,
had yet to feel the tramp of marching men. . . . Yet he could not
believe that this final Georgia campaign was an evil thing—though
resistance might have been ended by other, less drastic means. If
it could shorten a now senseless war by a day, it would serve its
purpose well.

The Union major sighed at his oracular musings: perhaps it was
inevitable that a farm boy turned Philadelphia lawyer should think
in abstractions. At least he could tell himself he had donned this
uniform in the spirit of an honest crusader. So far, he had not let
his insignia tarnish.

It was good to remember that today's orders called for no in-
discriminate barn burning. He planned to occupy Brandt's Crossing by noon, after he had fought the expected action at the ford.
Thereafter he was to take over an estate called Greentree, of which
this meadow was a part, and Hamilton Hundred, a second estate
on the Macon turnpike. If he kept to schedule, he would reach a
third plantation (called Selby Hall) well before sunset: it would
serve as his bivouac.

Hamilton Hundred and Selby Hall. He spoke the names aloud
to test their exotic ring. Each was a world removed from the labels
of home. Would their owners be as strange—and as hostile?

Part of his force would guard Brandt's Crossing; other units
would take over along the turnpike. Selby Hall would serve as

his personal headquarters. With four cavalry companies fanned through the area, the danger of enemy reprisal would be slight. If Hood chose to fight again (and this was highly unlikely), the action would take place far to the north.

During his occupation of Cray County, his instructions were explicit. His first task was to police the roads until the Union host had rumbled safely on its way: the enemy, as such, now included civilians as well as men in rebel uniform. The former were to be treated with military courtesy—but the slightest resistance would be dealt with instantly, including the razing of whole establishments as examples. Such measures were at the discretion of all senior officers. In no event was mercy to be shown to acts of violence. (How else could the lesson be driven home—that surrender this time must be total?)

Inevitably, some Georgians would resist this type of coercion with their lives, rejecting the hard lesson to the end. Others would pretend to yield—and strike back when the Army moved on. Still others would flee to Mexico, to the mirage of gray hosts re-forming beyond the Rio Grande. . . . The lesson was still worth learning, thought Major Daniel Carroll. If a nation was to emerge from this holocaust, North and South must learn to obey one law, to speak one language.

"It will take time," he said. "Time and patience."

Lieutenant Keller, still busy with his map work, looked up in mild amazement. "Beg pardon, Major?"

"Don't mind me," said Dan Carroll. "I was thinking aloud."

8

Four miles to the south Brad Selby wakened to a bugle call in the brand-new morning. Aware of his aide's hand on his shoulder, he rose from a well of slumber. His headache would have shamed Nero—but last night was still a happy memory, despite the price he was paying now.

"Orders, Captain. They just came in."

Brad grinned into the worried face of Lieutenant Cal Lambert. Cal was in field uniform, he noted. It meant they were riding out at last.

"I hope you read 'em before waking me," he said.

"I did, sir. We're to proceed to Indian Ford. Take care of the Yankees when they try to cross——"

"Yankees at *Indian Ford?* Don't be a fool."

Brad was wide awake now, and his throbbing head was clear enough. He listened with rising anger while his aide retailed his dire news. Atlanta, it seemed, had been evacuated between midnight and dawn. The whole Union force was now moving southeast, with strong screens of cavalry on its flanks. So far, there was no evidence that the main column would cross the Indian River: strategy dictated that it follow the main road, on the northern bank. Brad's own regiment—taking no chances—had long since retreated in a prudent arc, to join forces with Hood to the north of Atlanta. During this maneuver it was vital that the enemy be denied access to the ford. Brad was to make this denial stick.

"Shall I question the order?"

"We don't question orders, Cal. Not while I command this company."

"But we don't even know their strength, Captain. Or their intentions——"

"Their strength doesn't worry me," said Brad, pouring his first drink of the day. "We'll outride 'em—and outthink 'em too. Haven't we always?"

"Still and all," said Cal Lambert, "I'd like to confirm that order. I'm holding the courier."

"Are you telling me you're itching to cut and run?"

The aide flushed darkly. "What if we've no real way to stop them?"

"We'll stop them, Cal. Leave that to me." Brad closed his eyes, letting a wave of vertigo dissolve in the brandy. "Are we saddled up?"

"Give me ten minutes more, sir."

"Make it five. I've had my rest. Now I'm ready for action."

When the aide had left the room, he did not regret the bluster. Cal Lambert was a graduate of the Virginia Military Institute, and an excellent officer. Why should he question today's command to attack another enemy unit, no matter what its strength? . . .

At Chickamauga the troop had deflected a whole regiment from a key crossroad simply by keening into its midst as darkness fell, in a cyclone of flailing steel. Afterwards Hood's Texans had stormed up to finish the job: it had been one of the turning points of the battle. Today, unfortunately, there would be no infantry to end the action.

A second brandy took care of the worst of his headache. It could not quite erase the shameful fact that—despite his predictions—Yankees had somehow forced their way into his home county. Everyday chivalry dictated that the lady of the manor remove to a place of safety until the action ended. . . . Quent could take Reen to Macon, he decided (if Quent was still in the house). In any event, he would detail a squad to escort her and arrange for transport.

Leaving the study, Brad needed a real effort to mount the stairs. Puzzling over his reluctance, he knew he was ashamed, for the first time in years. . . . Not for last night's romp with Florrie (a wife must take such matters for granted). Not for his failure to join Reen afterwards. But he could curse himself heartily for his neglect in providing for her escape: a gentleman did not treat his lady thus when the danger was real. Later (when this ridiculous invasion was driven back) it might even cause talk in the county.

He had expected his wife to be dozing at this early hour. It was a shock to find the bedroom empty. Even so, he was glad to observe that Reen had thought of his welfare: his portmanteau was packed, his fatigues ready. Donning that sun-faded uniform (and careful to put his dress grays on a hanger, to await his next home-coming), he felt suddenly carefree. It was a familiar phenomenon at these moments of departure.

Selby would come through its ordeal, he told himself (it was impossible to picture an existence which failed to include the Big House and its cornucopia of abundance). Meanwhile his duty lay elsewhere. Once he had sent Reen outside the battle zone, he could say, with perfect truth, that he had done his part. It was unfortunate, of course, that he had been warned of her danger so tardily: he could allow her but a few minutes to prepare for departure. . . . Even that, in a way, was a blessing: he was in no mood for tearful good-bys. Not while there were Yankees to kill at Indian Ford: no sport on earth could quite equal Yankee-killing.

His whipcord riding trousers, despite their patches, fitted perfectly: the tunic clung to his taut body like pliant armor, giving it a new dimension and meaning. Once again he was about to convince a rascally invader that the Confederacy would never be defeated on its own soil. His headache had vanished: while the moment of dedication lasted, he felt completely alive.

He was humming wordlessly while he stamped into the brand-new boots he had taken from a Union colonel he had cut down at Resaca. Bit by bit the words of the tune took form—until he was singing them aloud. It was a sentimental ballad, one of the great favorites of the war. It brought back a hundred bivouacs—the good fellowship that went with firelight and a bottle, the certainty that all one's enemies were born to fight and run away:

> *We loved each other then, Lorena*
> *More than we ever dared to tell.*
> *Ah, what we might have been, Lorena—*
> *Had but our loving prospered well!*

Lorena. The hearts-and-roses tune had brought tears to his men's eyes, while they sang its endless verses in winter quarters between their victories. It was odd that his wife had been given the same name at her christening: he could hardly imagine a woman more remote from this figment of a soldier's dreams. . . . Yet, oddly enough, it was Reen's song too.

The words died on his lips as the hall door opened. She stood on the threshold—fully dressed, in the homespuns she wore on her trips to the fields. A man's hat of roughly woven straw all but concealed her dark hair. She seemed unaware of his presence in the room until she crossed it to take a cloak from the armoire.

"I thought you'd gone," she said—and wrapped the cloak about her.

"Why are you abroad, at this hour—dressed like a pickaninny's mammy?"

"You've seen me in these clothes before," she said in the same cool tone—almost as though she were addressing a stranger. Brad felt his jaw clamp down in anger. He had met these moods before and broken them.

"Couldn't you wait until I'd left to play the field hand?" In his resentment he had half forgotten his reason for lingering. Hoping to temper the harshness of his news, he forced himself to address her gently. "Not that it matters today. In fact, you may be wise to dress as a poor white—after the report I've just had from Atlanta."

"I've had the same report, Brad. A bit sooner than you, it seems."

"How could you?"

"Look out that window if you want an answer," she said. "The whole county's on the move. We've set up a field kitchen at the gates. Ever since dawn we've been feeding all comers."

"Was that necessary?"

She moved toward the door with another of those stranger-looks. This, he realized, was more than a temper tantrum over last night's neglect. "I could hardly do less," she said. "I must go back now."

Brad moved to bar her path: already this unexpected contretemps had driven him to exasperation. It was quite like Reen to play Lady Bountiful at such a time. His aide had spoken of a heavy influx of farm wagons on the road—but he had hardly listened. Civilians had a way of infecting one another with panic at the first rattle of gunfire; the mere rumor of troop movements could scare them out of a year's growth. Most of these skittish rednecks, he felt sure, would return to their homes tomorrow—after he had righted matters at the ford. Still, prudence dictated that Reen leave Selby for a while.

"Listen to me, if you please," he said sternly. "This business has gone far enough."

"We've scarcely begun. Already the roads are jammed. There'll be still more, now it's really light."

"Put that human cattle from your mind, my dear. We'll get you out ahead of the stampede. If need be, I'll send Cal Lambert himself to escort you."

Reen had made no protest when he stopped her. Now she was halfway through the door before his parade-ground bellow held her frozen on the sill.

"*Wait, Reen! That's an order!*"

"Give your orders in the field," she said. "You're wasting breath here."

"You've five minutes to pack a bag. Then you're leaving Selby."

"How can I—now?"

"The county's invaded. You can't help yourself."

"Last night you said you'd wipe the enemy out if he crossed the county line."

"So we will, my dear," he said patiently. "Unfortunately, such things take time. I don't want you here while lead is flying. Quent can keep you company to Macon——"

"Quent left at midnight," she said. "I refused to go then. Why should I change my mind this morning?"

"Because I'm your husband. Because I fear for your safety if you stay."

"Clara Hamilton isn't leaving," said Reen. "Mary Buell is alone with her slaves at Greentree. Think how they'd gossip if I ran away."

"Who cares for old hens' cackling? I won't leave my wife unprotected."

"No one will censure you, Brad. Our friends know I belong at Selby, just as you belong with your troop."

They were eye to eye in the doorway now. The tensions of crossed wills crackled in the stillness like visible lightning. When he turned away he knew she had won her point, that she was not to be budged.

"I can't wait much longer," he shouted.

"There's no need to wait, Brad. I'm staying here, and I'm keeping Selby whole. I'll be quite safe, I promise you. When the fighting's over, you'll still have us both."

"What good is a barren wife? Or land without an heir?"

"Perhaps I'm not so barren as you think."

He had stormed about the room while he railed at her—cramming cigars into the portmanteau, charging to the gallery to toss his gear into the arms of his orderly. Her last words spun him toward her again.

"Are you pregnant, Reen?"

"I'll answer no more questions. If you'll excuse me, I'm needed at the gate."

[68]

"Let's hope I understand you," he said. "When I return I'll repeat the question."

He moved forward to kiss her, but she shrank back. There was no fear in the withdrawal—only a repulsion she could not have expressed more plainly in words. Brad shrugged and drew his dignity about him.

"I'll go at once since you're speaking in enigmas," he said coldly. "And I'll leave you here, if you insist. Wish me well in the campaign?"

"Tell me just one thing before you leave," she said. "What if we do have a son? Could we make a new life together?"

"If I knew the Selby line was assured, I wouldn't mind stopping a bullet," he said. "But you aren't yet a widow. If I must go on without issue, I'll be a long time dying."

"The Selby line will go on," she said. "Leave that part to me."

"Suppose the Yankees cross the river? This won't be the first place they've gutted."

"Uncle Doc and I will camp in the ruins—and rebuild when we can."

"You've staying power, Reen," he said grudgingly. "I'll grant you that. You may even have courage. Or is it only pride?"

"Does it matter, if I keep what's yours—and give you what you want? Get about your war, Brad. Leave me to my job."

They faced each other for the last time, like spent fighters with no strength for another blow. Then, as the bugle shrilled, he picked up his hat and went out. Reen had been too much the lady to blurt out the fact she was with child, he told himself. Once the boy was born, she would have discharged her debt to Selby—and he could find ways to endure those Charleston manners. There would be time enough to repay her for her coldness—after he had killed his last Yankee.

Twenty minutes later he rode down his driveway at the head of his column. Cal Lambert was at his right. A pair of sergeants rode just behind, each with a company guidon whipping bravely in the morning breeze. The troop was in parade formation, but their laughing voices belied that precision. As always, they were singing lustily: the words seemed to issue from a single fervent throat.

Brad had ridden to war with music since he had served with Stuart: the thumping obbligato of two banjos was part of it. The players were Negroes who had once performed at the Atlanta Hotel. He had purchased them to entertain plantation guests, and had given them the status of orderlies when he organized the Cray County Crusaders. . . . Today he was glad to find that he could join in the singing as gaily as any subaltern. Ducey and Crown, in his opinion, had never played better.

9

Major Dan Carroll, sweeping the river with his glass, could not believe his ears when he heard the song drift through the pines that masked the southern bank.

For the past hour he had clung to his cover, hoping the enemy would show his face before the day was too far advanced. Now (incredible as it seemed) he had seen fit to advertise his arrival with music. Dan edged his mount forward in the thicket: Jack Keller followed at his nod. Beyond the muddy sheen of the river a covey of quail whirred into flight, startled at the approach of the invisible horsemen. Save for the rhythmic chorus, and the whacking accompaniment of two banjos, there was no other sign of life.

"What d'you make of it, Jack? Are these soldiers? Or field hands turning out for work?"

"Not a chance, sir," said Keller. "*That's* Captain Selby, and the Cray County Crusaders. The company's famous. They always fight to music."

"They're strangers to me."

"I've tangled with 'em twice," said Keller. "Once in a crossroads town near Gettysburg, the day after Lee's retreat. The battle was lost—but *they* hadn't heard the news. We met again at Chickamauga. Selby's hellions hacked their way through a whole infantry corps. Judging by the way they yelled, they meant to reach Nashville."

"They sound like fighting fools."

"So they are, Major—the sort of fools who are damned hard to kill. If it's really they, I'd suggest we alert our reserve line. They'll be just as hard to stop today."

"Surely they've no intention of crossing the ford. Any sensible commander would dig in on the south bank. They could make things hot for us there."

"Not Captain Selby. His idea of fun is a charge in the open."

"In that case," said Dan Carroll, "we'll do our best to oblige him."

Both men fell silent as a red pocket handkerchief of flag showed among the pines. It was followed by another—both of them streaming gaily in the morning as the two riders galloped forward. The guidon-bearers were close behind, flanking three officers who rode in formation, as classically correct as though this were the prelude to some grand review. Carroll choked down a gasp as the entire company burst into the open—riding at a hard gallop now, and still keening its song.

"It's Selby's troop, all right," said his aide. "Those are his guidons."

"Is that the captain on the roan?"

"Must be, sir. At Chickamauga, I couldn't see him for dust."

Carroll studied the cavalry leader minutely, while the man bore down upon the ford. Brad Selby (leaping into focus as he bent low above his horse's mane) was a handsome warrior indeed. His saber was unsheathed. Riding just behind his color-bearers, he was slashing the air to left and right with expertly vicious strokes, as though he had already engaged the enemy. There was something larger than life about this caricature of the fire-eater—but he was still a threat, for all his dandified air.

Dan had crossed swords with other Selbys in this war. He had found them lion-brave—and even more dangerous in retreat than attack. *Here*, he thought, *is another living legend.* This was an enemy who would fight by the book—as debonairly as an earlier ancestor would have charged in full armor to a jousting.

"By all that's holy—he means to cross the ford."

"Looks that way, sir," said Jack Keller in an awed whisper.

While they spoke, the roan went spatter-dashing into the shallows. The standard-bearers were already swimming their mounts through the deeper reaches of the river. The company, without slowing its pace by a single drawn bridle, followed their captain. Intent on the difficult crossing, they had ceased their singing. But the banjos still thumped out their measure, dampened not one whit by the wallowing of three hundred mounted men.

In another moment the tune reached Dan's ears. With no surprise, he found himself humming the words. The situation was already grotesque enough.

A hundred months have passed, Lorena,
Since last I held that hand in mine. . . .

Who had said that the rebels' *Lorena*, like the North's own *Battle Hymn*, had made this brothers' war worth fighting? Dan himself had first heard the tune from on a disputed field in the Shenandoah. For two days a freak snowstorm had made fighting impossible. During the truce the opposing forces had traded the usual insults and tobacco, while chaplains and burial parties had gone out from the lines. When night fell, that song had made even winter picket duty bearable. The syrupy words, like the tune itself, had spoken of wisteria and moonlight and the trills of mockingbirds. Bringing the past alive, it had promised a still more fragrant future—when the old, longed-for abundance had returned to a ravaged homeland.

At the time, Dan Carroll had been only a recruit: the action in the Valley had been his first campaign. Listening to those heroes' voices (as brave as Homer, for all their lugubrious sentiment), he had prayed the snow would fall forever. . . .

"Do we hit 'em now, Major?"

Dan returned to the present with a guilty start. The enemy was floating in midstream, swimming his horses with practiced ease. The roan charger had found its footing: Captain Selby, half out of his saddle to ease the animal's progress, sat firm again and leveled his sword at the meadow. On either side the flags sprang upright, their crossed stars gleaming against a blood-red background. As though on signal, a rebel yell rang from stream to shore. Even now, that hated keening ran down Carroll's spine like water.

"Hold your fire, Jack," he said. "And try not to laugh out loud. So far, this is pure comic opera."

"It won't be funny for long, sir."

The Confederate strategy (if it deserved the term) was glaringly evident. Ignoring the usual precautions, the Cray County Crusaders had poured into the ford without even slowing their headlong pace, relying on superb horsemanship to gain the northern bank. Without so much as a skirmish line to guard against surprise, they now intended to stake out a position beyond the ford—which they would defend to the death, in the best tradition of the underdog. It was a schoolboy's version of combat, based on daring rather than tactics. Carroll could applaud the daring, while the Confederate flag-bearers moved into rifle range. Had he commanded the troop, he could not have arranged an approach more suited to his purpose.

Had he wished, he could have stormed down on Selby's company while it still wallowed in midstream. Such a move, however, would have brought his own far superior force into the open. No matter what the casualties, some of the enemy would have escaped —and he wished today's defeat to be total. Once they had gained the northern bank, with the Union cavalry deployed (in deep cover) on either side, they would be boxed in a classic trap.

"*Now*, sir?"

"Stop acting like a bounty boy, Jack. We're playing this close to our chest."

Still bunched in parade formation, two thirds of the Confederate horses had reached dry land. When the last units emerged, the battle flags moved to higher ground, with the captain's sword signaling orders in flashing arcs. The two ebony-dark musicians still plucked out their sad-sweet melody. They ceased their playing only when the captain signaled for silence.

"Halt all units!"

"*Halt all units!*" The sergeants' voices, barking the command down the line, seemed oddly small in that vast meadow. The echo, bounding from the wall of pines, mocked the flourish of the drawn sabers.

"Stand by for orders!"

Selby and his officers (a pair of lieutenants whose black-browed scowls made up, in some measure, for their youth) rode slowly toward the pine grove. Behind them the troop lolled its saddles at parade rest—an unbroken line, facing the Union guns. Three hundred sitting ducks, thought Carroll, could not have made finer targets. A familiar wave of compassion engulfed him. Before it ebbed, he considered a shouted warning—an offer to hold his fire if the enemy would ground his weapons. Such an offer, of course, would be futile. He had been ambushed no less ruthlessly at Seven Pines, and again at Fredericksburg—today he would return the compliment.

"Now, sir?"

"Now, Jack."

Dan's gloved hand lifted—and waited—until he was positive he had caught his sergeants' eyes. When the gauntlet swept downward, the first volley roared out from five hundred carbines.

At that easy distance the blast found better than one target in four. The second volley was no less deadly, since it all but overlapped the first. The enemy reeled under the impact, but did not break ranks. Instead, his flanks wheeled instantly, changing a motionless target to a flying wedge of horse flesh. The officers, turning their own mounts with the same amazing sang-froid, formed its apex in a twinkling.

"Charge!"

Carroll was not sure if it was he or Selby who had first given the order. He knew only that blue and gray horse had obeyed a common impulse—that they needed but a moment to come into deadly contact, with a merged battle shout that all but drowned the thunder of flying hoofs. Schooled in this brand of combat, the hostile forces exchanged a running fire as they joined—but the contest was already a hopeless one, thanks to those two punishing volleys. This, quite literally, was an action ended before it had begun.

Two hundred Confederate riders had been shot from their saddles before the first clash of steel. It was ninety men against five hundred now—a wolf Iliad that made up for crushing odds with the frenzy of its counterblow.

Jack Keller led the massive envelopment while Dan watched from the command post. He saw that the Confederate leader, still unhurt, had flung himself into the melee, cutting down the first Union soldiers who engaged him. Already it was evident that Selby had earned a reputation for a charmed life: such invulnerability sprang from a deeper cause than luck. This (thought Carroll) was the bellwether who led others to death. Each Union carbine—blasting enemy riders into oblivion—had saved that splendid target for the last. . . .

There was little time to ponder such a fantasy. Rising in his stirrups, shouting his own challenge, Dan Carroll rocketed from ambush to meadow to finish what his staff had begun.

The enemy, ringed in a circle of steel that contracted with each exchange of blows, was now close to extinction. Carroll saw as much before he could join Keller—anchored on the perimeter of the action and bellowing the precise orders that made the debacle complete. He was in time to watch the flying wedge of gray (smaller now, but no less irresistible) as it smashed into that lethal circle. It was an all-or-nothing charge, careless of broken knees in the cannoning of horse flesh.

Carroll's pistol, aimed at Selby's head, missed fire. In another instant he was exchanging saber cuts with one of the Confederate lieutenants—a youth with a mad brown monkey face, who fought like a dervish until Dan's stern swordsmanship disarmed him.

The brief duel was the finale of the action. Jack Keller (who had just dispatched the second of Selby's aides) tackled Dan's antagonist from behind, spilling him to the meadow in a tangle of thrashing boots and bad language. The blue horse had already reformed—responding to a series of bellowed orders to take the field.

The Cray County Crusaders, Dan observed, had been demolished—almost, though not quite, to the last man. Those who had survived the volleys from ambush had fought back like terriers—refusing to surrender even at gun point. At first glance it seemed that Keller had unhorsed the only live prisoner. . . . To the north, where meadow and piney woods merged, a blue squad was galloping in futile pursuit of the only enemy horsemen to break free.

Extended in a thin line, they were hardly twenty strong. Dan saw that Captain Selby was leading the escape—firing as he rode, and still howling his rebel yell.

Inured as they were to grisly aftermaths, the 2nd Pennsylvania Cavalry hastened to begin the count of noses. In their thunderbolt attack they had lost just nine men—all of whom had fallen in hand-to-hand combat. Over a score were wounded. Of these the less serious cases were sent back to the crossroad, to await the hospital wagons that always rode with the infantry. The two battalion surgeons did what they could to save the others.

The Confederate dead lay in tumbled rows—over two hundred and seventy, by careful count. As Carroll had feared, there were almost no wounded. The enemy had sold their lives dearly. Whenever they could, they had refused to sell their honor.

Lieutenant Cal Lambert (the only prisoner who had been subdued without a scratch) wept tears of rage and begged to be shot out of hand. When his shame had subsided, Carroll found him ready enough to answer questions. The troop, he said, had been ordered to cover the withdrawal of the last sizable infantry unit in Cray County. Despite its appalling losses, he refused to blame Captain Selby—or Selby's almost childish disregard of tactics. In the captain's place, Carroll reflected, Lambert would also have stormed across the ford.

"Do you always prefer such odds, Lieutenant?" he asked. "Is it a matter of pride? Or do you really believe that one Johnnie is worth ten of us?"

The boy managed a grin. Now that he had accepted the fact he survived, that his share in this war was paid in full, he seemed a model prisoner. "Didn't Captain Selby prove it today?"

"At least he avoided capture," said Dan.

"He always will. And he'll never surrender."

"I wonder why, Lieutenant? Is he one of those deathless leftovers we read about?"

"Come again, sir?"

"They've existed in every culture since Rome. The soldier who doesn't die—but only fades away."

Lambert's china-blue eyes were hard as marbles. "There isn't a finer cavalry officer living. Most of your generals will vouch for that."

"Now I've seen him in action," said Carroll gently, "I couldn't agree more."

"Then I'll thank you, sir—if you'll refrain from tagging him with fancy labels. What are you, a preacher in a uniform?"

"No, my friend. Just a Philadelphia lawyer, with a passion for the verities. Why did your captain go on fighting when he knew he was surrounded? Where can he hide, now he's broken free?"

"If you ask me, Major," said Lambert, "he'll be reporting to

Hood's staff by nightfall. Even if it means riding that roan stallion to death."

Dan nodded. Captain Selby (though he was now forced to head north, through the Union vanguard) would live to fight again. His version of this suicidal blunder would then be part of the official record—rather than the sober truth that he had behaved like a fool. Carroll considered imparting this judgment to his prisoner, and stifled the impulse. Young Lambert had been punished enough today.

"I've a plantation on my field map named Selby Hall," he said. "Is it the captain's home, by any chance?"

A film dropped over Lambert's hard blue gaze. "I've told you my name, Major," he said. "*And* my regiment. Not even a Philadelphia lawyer should ask for more."

Dan put a hand on the boy's arm. "Don't think I'm complaining because the captain got away," he said. "I won't burn his birthplace out of spite, if that's what is troubling you."

"Then you only burn on orders? Is that the size of it, Major?"

Carroll stiffened and signaled to his prisoner's guard. He was beginning to regret that final question. "We needn't discuss my orders," he said. "But I'll tell you this, Lambert. You're damned lucky to end your military career this morning."

"Not if it means a Northern prison."

"That's another thing I'll promise—you won't be a prisoner for long."

He saluted crisply as the erect young figure stalked away between the guards. The 2nd Pennsylvania Cavalry was ready to cross the ford—leaving its own dead side by side with the enemy's to await the burial details. The way to Brandt's Crossing was clear: there was no logical reason for his uneasiness. Selby Hall had been marked down on his chart as tonight's bivouac long before the action at the ford. Only a born romantic would yield to a conviction of fates converging.

Dan had seen a dozen plantation houses on this campaign. Busy with more urgent matters, he had ridden past their entrances with no more than a curious glance. Why did he look forward so keenly (and so fearfully) to his first glimpse of Captain Selby's domain?

Or ask himself how that visit could explain a hell-roaring hero who bought his laurels so dearly?

10

All the long day, Reen worked with Yancey at the improvised canteen outside her gate. From dawn to midafternoon refugees had poured by from the northern reaches of the county. Most of the forced *émigrés* huddled in farm wagons. Others (who had sold their last mule to the Confederacy) trudged wearily in the dust. The marchers had been glad to accept the food Selby offered. Almost without exception, they preferred to eat while they moved on.

So far, none of these frightened plodders had seen a Union soldier in the flesh. Last night's spout of flames in Atlanta had been warning enough that Sherman was on the prowl again—that a prudent Georgian should move even faster. All that morning, rumors had flown down the dusty column. An army of a hundred thousand men had been sighted at Brandt's Crossing. Families had died in their beds, in a dozen back-country farmhouses. In Gant County (which lay to the north of Indian River) not a corn crib had been left standing. . . .

Busy as she was, Reen had heard these tales with but half an ear. At last, as the day wore into evening, the column had dwindled to a trickle, then ceased. Only the haze of its passing remained, like a red halo above the land. Now that even the dust had settled, she saw that the turnpike to the north was empty too. Somehow the road had been less sinister when it was choked with humanity. The very emptiness suggested the all-devouring monster was close behind.

"Better go back to the house while you've the strength to walk," said Uncle Doc.

Reen took off her planter's hat and fanned herself slowly. It was a profound relief to pause thus—and find that no haunted eyes were facing her across the trestle she had used as a serving table.

"I'm not tired, really," she said. "It's just that I've been working too fast to think. Now that road is empty, I'm not sure I *want* to think. What does it mean?"

"Only that a farming county can empty fast when it takes up its bed and runs."

"They're saying that Greentree is burned out. That a thousand men were shot at the ford. That Hamilton Hundred's crawling with bluecoats. But no one saw the smoke—or a single enemy uniform."

"It's possible they took North Road rather than the turnpike. Even a hundred thousand men can't cut that wide a swath."

"You know they'll be here before dark, Uncle Doc—and so do I. Why else would we tell Sal to bury the silver—and the brandy?"

"Sal didn't bury all the liquor, girl. This is the time of day I take my first glass. Why not join me—and await our visitors in comfort?"

It was easy to yield to the pressure of his hand at her elbow, to turn from the empty serving table (and that strangely silent road) to seek the shade of her driveway. The field cart was waiting inside the gate, with Sal at the reins: he made a small ceremony of bowing her in. All that day, Sal had labored with a picked squad of field hands—men who could be trusted to hold their tongues. They had buried the last of the silver service in the ditch between the truck garden and the greenhouse—and planted ferns above the hiding place so cunningly that no bummer could smell it out.

Sal had worked harder than the others—yet he was bandbox-neat in his white linen, now the task was done. It was part of the young Negro's system of authority that his clothes must set him apart from other slaves, even the house servants.

"I'm afraid that was a long ditch, Sal."

"Nevah mind, Miss Reen. It's done—an' we got it all listed."

"Every piece in a chamois bag—and burlap," said Yancey.

"Cain't tarnish much, ma'am," Sal added. "Not 'less we have a real rain."

"What about our cash money?"

"Safe 'twixt the walls of Marse Luke's office. Castor done a right smooth job."

The cart bowled smoothly up the drive in a silence oddly free from strain. Reen was still marveling at her acceptance of the inevitable when they swung into the gravel circle before the house and Sal leaped out to hand her down.

Thanks to the vagaries of a Georgia fall, the afternoon was warm and sunny. In the sunken flower garden that was Selby's pride, there were still banks of chrysanthemums, dahlias in formal rows, and a bed of gladiolas to keep summer memories alive. Moving through her garden, Reen could not bring herself to believe such beauty might be destroyed: already she found herself wondering if she could spare a field hand to pack the caladium bulbs in peat moss before winter really came. . . . A cardinal's wing flashed scarlet against the bright green of a holly tree. Her eye followed the bird's flight, and the familiar balm of day's ending settled on her spirit.

This was the walk that always ended her working hours, no matter what the season. If weather permitted, she took tea on the portico afterwards, while Uncle Doc inhaled the aroma of his first bourbon—and exhaled the musings that belonged specially to this hour. Today (she told herself hopefully) would be like the others: if there were enemy troops in Cray County, they would forage elsewhere.

Ulysses was presiding over the tea table: he had placed her chair in a spot where the sun warmed the flagstones. All around her was the muted stir of the plantation—audible proof that nothing had changed here, that the refugee-choked road beyond her gates belonged to another planet. Scythes were busy in the west hundred, cutting the last of the hay. In the carpenter shop the whirr of a lathe told her that Castor and Pollux were shaping a rooftree for the new cabin in the quarters. Even the voice of Penelope, chanting supper music to her pullets at the kitchen stoop, was in key with the bucolic symphony.

Reen climbed the worn bricks of the path with an armful of dahlias. Arranging them in the bowl that stood waiting on the table, pretending that the tea she poured was the best oolong and not sassafras, she smiled at Uncle Doc, who seemed to doze in his chair.

"Was I right, trusting Sal to hide the gold? I felt he should have the responsibility."

Yancey nodded with his eyes on his glass. "As you say, he's the sort of helper who responds to trust."

"It seemed a needless thing to do. I simply won't believe an army is rolling down on us."

"Not after your stint at the gate?"

"Uncle Doc, we've sat here for ages and planned a better world. Why shouldn't we go on sitting and spin the same daydream?"

"*That's* one reason," said Yancey—and jerked a thumb toward the northern pasture, a rolling sweep of green that dropped, in easy stages, to the river road. Reen's eye followed the gesture incuriously. Brad had ridden down that road in the early morning. Remembering the brassy farewell of his bugles, she was not too startled to hear another call to the colors, beyond a green crescent of willows. The sound was faint and far away. Yancey, whose hearing was acute, had caught the echo before her own ears.

"Maybe it's Brad returning," she ventured.

"Listen carefully. That bugle talks another language."

"Yankee language?"

"There was action at the ford this morning, Lorena. One of the Buells' slaves saw it from the fish weirs."

"Why didn't you tell me?"

"You had enough on your mind."

"*Was* Brad——?"

"Never fear—he got away without a scratch. But the troop was almost wiped out. In a moment I think you'll see why."

The bugle repeated—nearer this time. At the same moment, Reen heard the rattle of the cart's wheels on the drive. Sal, his eyes wild with excitement, burst into view.

"Union cavalry, Miss Reen! Crossin' de wes' meadow!"

"You're sure?"

"Jody brought de news, ma'am. He was cuttin' wood—he seed 'em, plain as day." In Sal's breathless state his tongue and his grammar were a trifle thickened. "Dey's movin' slow. Makin' sho' dey's no one t'fight hyah——"

The bugle spoke again, and received a ringing answer from the west. This time, there was no mistaking the plantation's response. As the brazen notes died out, stillness fastened on Selby like a vise. When it broke, Reen heard (in no real sequence) the patter of running feet, the squeal of a snatched-up infant—and, finally, a banshee wailing that spelled terror in any tongue. At this hour, she knew, the women were preparing the evening meal in the cabins: the hands, save for a few odd-jobbers, would be resting in their doorways. . . . On the drive the pony lunged at the traces as Sal cracked his whip; his quick mind had caught her wish.

"Sal will keep the slaves from bolting," she said quietly. Now that the enemy was all but visible, she found she had regained her poise. She had expected this moment to be ushered in with gun-fire, with an outright charge across her lawns. Anything but those clashing bugles—and the sudden, take-charge action of a slave in a field cart.

Luke Jackson, limping from the barnyard, supplied the note of anger she had missed. He was winded from running.

"Damn Yankees, Miss Selby——! Crashin' our fences 'thout a by-your-leave——!"

"Better go inside, Lorena," said Uncle Doc.

"This is my home," she told him firmly. "I receive callers on my portico."

She saw her first bluecoat then—a dust-caked lieutenant, who rode as though his horse were an extension of his own lean body. The man approached at a canter. He was followed by a squad in open order. It took them but a moment to cover the driveway, and each corner of the house. A second squad, led by a sergeant's guidon, deployed between house and quarters. Still other horsemen, Reen saw, had moved in from the meadow to guard each barn door and the porches of the gin.

No heads showed in the cabins while the investment was com-pleted: Sal (she gathered) had done his work quickly. . . . Below the portico the lieutenant reined in and sprang from his saddle. He was little more than a boy, despite his martial air. When he ad-dressed Yancey, his smile was almost friendly.

"Any Johnnies about, sir?"

"We're alone here, Lieutenant," said Uncle Doc. Breathless as she was, Reen could admire his aplomb.

"Mind if we make sure?"

An instinct she could not define, lifting her clean out of her trance, made Reen step forward and face the man in blue. A mo-ment before, she would have barred her door against these invaders —with her own body, if need be. Now that this young man had asked permission to enter—with perfect manners—it seemed only right to grant it.

"Go in, Lieutenant," she said firmly. "We've nothing to hide."
Nothing but silver that goes back to Queen Anne, she added silently. *Nothing but a little hard money to keep my hands from starving—and a thousand cotton bales that will never find a buyer now.* She thought of the account books in her desk, listing her contributions to the Confederacy: if she could believe the rumors, those lists alone could consign Selby to the torch. . . . Yet this boy in uniform did not resemble a barn burner. Nor did the two alert sergeants who followed him into the foyer, joshing one another in a flat, drawling speech she only half understood.

"What do they want of us?" she whispered.

"Nothing we can't supply, I hope," said Uncle Doc—but he did not meet her eye.

On the portico step Luke Jackson gave a taurine bellow as a corporal searched him for hidden weapons. The lawns were alive with horsemen now, all of them moving in precise patterns. Here and there a flower bed was trampled. Reen closed her eyes briefly when she heard a tinkling crash that could only mean the ruin of a greenhouse. . . . In the house itself there was only the sound of hurrying footsteps.

The search, it seemed, was soon ended. The lieutenant appeared on an upstairs balcony in short order, followed by his sergeants.

"All clear, Major. Can we set up shop?"

As though in answer to the shout, a rider detached himself from the blue mass and rode into the gravel circle of the drive. Reen did not need the marks of rank at his shoulders to guess this was the enemy leader: even at that distance he seemed tall enough to blot out the sky.

The illusion, she knew, was part of the aura that wrapped these strangers. Telling herself that she must hate the major on sight, she felt no hatred whatever. Watching him dismount, she could not even feign aloofness. Instead, she felt an overmastering urge to meet him halfway. To put out a hand and touch him, if only to make sure he was real.

"Major Daniel Carroll, Mrs. Selby," the invader said quietly. "Second Pennsylvania Cavalry. With your permission, I must take over your home."

[83]

Reen stared at him blankly—glad that his attention was distracted by an aide who had hurried up with a map case. It was shocking enough that he spoke her language (with just enough harshness to prove himself an alien). It was worse that he knew her name, that Selby was evidently marked down on the map he was studying. . . . What shook her, to the roots of her being, was the insane urge to move into his orbit, to let her fingers close on his arm.

She spoke quickly, while the desire was in control.

"Selby Hall has yet to refuse visitors a night's lodging," she said. "I won't pretend you're welcome, Major Carroll. But I'll ask you to be our guest."

The Yankee's eyes lifted from the map. For the first time, Reen saw that he was handsome in a gaunt, sun-bitten fashion—that his air of ease was not a mockery, but an attempt to establish some rapport between them.

"I appreciate your courtesy, Mrs. Selby," he said. "Let's hope my men and I deserve it."

"Just what do you wish of us?"

"My orders are to use this plantation as a temporary command post," he said with that same disarming air. "We expect no further action. Nothing's to be harmed while I'm in command, providing no one interferes in the discharge of our duties. As you can see, we'll need a largish field to bivouac. We have tents, and our own rations. All we ask of you is fodder."

"Dr. Yancey will show you the way," she said. "Mr. Jackson, my overseer, will see to the horses." The sense of fantasy deepened while she made the presentations—as solemnly as though the major were an expected guest. Carroll acknowledged the courtesy as Uncle Doc offered the semblance of a bow. Luke Jackson contented himself with a lynx-eyed stare—but Luke had yet to disobey her orders. Shambling forward, he pointed mutely to the nearest hay barn.

"Thank you again, Mrs. Selby," said the Major. He indicated the aide on the balcony. "This is Lieutenant Keller. We'll billet here, if we may."

"Rooms will be ready in a half hour," she said. "What of your other officers?"

"They stay with their men."

"We dine at seven," she said. "Does the hour suit you?"

If the invitation surprised him, Carroll gave no sign of it. "Seven will give us ample time, Mrs. Selby," he said. He was gone—before she could quite recover from her own astonishment at the words that had just issued from her lips.

A quartet of captains, dismounting in unison, hastened to trail their commander as he disappeared into the hay barn, flanked by Yancey and the overseer. The battalion (shepherded expertly by its sergeants) wheeled by platoons and followed its officers. Reen was still frozen to the portico when the last cavalryman vanished among the work buildings.

"May we use your parlor for our map room, Mrs. Selby?"

Lieutenant Keller had descended from the balcony, and stood at her elbow; on the bottom step of the portico the orderly with the map case awaited his orders. Nodding her permission, Reen moved aside. The orderly strode into the house with the air of a man who had staked out a score of headquarters in similar settings; the young lieutenant offered a punctilious bow and followed him.

It took an extra effort, but Reen found she could stand in the foyer to watch them at work. Some measure of calm returned to her when she saw that this enemy headquarters would be established with a minimum of disturbance. The lieutenant had just carried a Sèvres vase from table to bookcase as carefully as though it were a sacred relic. Clearly, the major's promise of hands off had been genuine. . . . Was it possible that the man was a gentleman, instead of the blue-coated ogre she had visioned?

He knew my name, she thought. *He knew this was Selby Hall. Was he sent here by the devil—or by God?*

11

Yancey paused with a foot on the stile. The step-over crossed a hogproof fence, dividing the barnyard from pasture land that had been marked to lie fallow until spring. Within the hour, those sixty acres had blossomed with a new crop—a geometric pattern of canvas tents, grouped about a common cooking area. Already, as the shadows lengthened, fires had begun to turn a score of field stoves cherry red. The scent of frying ham that drifted across the tent poles was proof enough that the 2nd Pennsylvania Cavalry had established its tenancy.

In the far corner of the pasture a split-rail pen enclosed the horses and their grooms—the latter still busy transferring hay from the high-sided cotton wagons that waited at the gate. Officers were everywhere, checking the open bedrolls beneath the canvas. While Yancey watched, one of them turned to question Luke Jackson. The plantation doctor sighed his relief as the overseer answered, civilly enough. . . .

There had been no incidents during the take-over. It was unlikely that Luke would fight back—now he realized he was not to be shot down, that the invaders had no immediate plans for razing Selby.

Measuring each act with a cautious eye, Yancey had concluded this was a routine occupation, with no sinister overtones. If the enemy seemed almost happily at ease tonight, he could grasp the reason. The action at the ford had been decisive: Cray County was now a conquered province. . . . Carroll himself had said as much. Selby had been chosen as his headquarters because of an accident of geography. It seemed unlikely that the major himself intended its destruction. Nevertheless, it was true that he held their fate in his palm, for all his flourishes of good will.

On their tour of the plantation he had seemed deeply impressed by the miracles Lorena had wrought. He had praised the model quarters warmly, and the provisions for the field hands' welfare. Perhaps his interest could be turned to Selby's advantage later. Sherman's foragers would surely stay clear while the battalion remained. Could the protection be made permanent when it rode on?

Observing that the major was about to join him on the stile, Yancey resumed his mask.

"Lieutenant Keller was along just now to collect your gear," he said. "Mrs. Selby has given you the south suite in the guest wing."

Soldier and civilian moved down a path that wound through five acres of truck garden. They did not speak at once, but there was an odd lack of tension in the silence.

"Mrs. Selby has been more than generous," said Carroll. "I must say it puzzles me a little."

"She's a Southern lady—and you happen to be her guest."

"Why did she ask me to dine?"

"That's part of it."

"Are you telling me the invitation was offered freely?"

"Come, Major," said Yancey, "surely you aren't that unintelligent?"

Carroll smiled. "It's a New England trick, answering one question with another. I hardly expected it in Georgia."

Yancey accepted the challenge. "Are you asking if she's eager to appease you? The answer is yes."

They had paused at the bottom of the rose garden—lifting their eyes (as though by common consent) to the soaring majesty of the south portico. Selby Hall seemed to take on an added dimension, now the day was dying and Ulysses had begun to move through the downstairs rooms to light the candelabra. Tonight every sconce was ablaze. Yancey nodded a silent approval: in Lorena's place he would have made the bravest show.

Carroll spoke quietly, with his eyes on the Big House. "If you'll pardon an unoriginal observation, Doctor, that's a beautiful sight. Like a temple left over from Rome."

"A temple that's outlasted its time?"

"*You* said that, not I. When I told Mrs. Selby we'd harm nothing beyond her flower beds, I spoke by the book. Didn't she believe me?"

"Does that mean we're to be spared?"

"It does—so long as I'm in command here."

"I suppose that's natural, since you're using us as a bivouac," said Yancey drily. "What about afterwards?"

"Afterwards is a slippery word in war, Doctor."

"May I take the plunge and ask the only question that matters?"

"Try me," said Carroll quietly. "You'll get a straight answer."

"I've been told that your provost marshals can protect property at will. All that's required is a poster for one's gatepost——"

"True. Such posters do exist."

"Could a man in your position leave one at Selby? And a guard to see it was obeyed?"

The major's eyes did not waver. "You've given me more importance than I deserve, Doctor."

"May I ask why?"

"Our provost guards are assigned at corps level."

"Surely you're free to make such a recommendation."

"That's part of my function. It's also my duty to condemn property when it deserves destruction."

Yancey felt his spirits plummet. He was realist enough to recognize that Sherman's march had several aims. His bummers were the hungry crows found in every army. At a higher rank his officers had orders to wipe out installations that served the Confederacy—guerrilla nests, the depots of Army contractors, plantations that might be a source of enemy supply later. Obviously, Selby Hall could go on such a list—unless this enigmatic Yankee's report suggested otherwise. . . . At least, it was evident that he had bivouacked here with more than one purpose. Selby's fate would be decided elsewhere—but he could still influence the verdict.

"You'll forgive my plain speaking, Doctor?"

Yancey collected himself quickly. "I'm honored by your frankness," he said. "And I'll ask no more impossible questions tonight. Will you join me in a drink before we dine?"

"I'll be delighted, once I've made myself presentable." Again Carroll seemed oddly detached, after that burst of candor. "Perhaps you'll allow me to supply the whiskey. I've Pennyslvania rye in my saddlebags."

"Guests are permitted to drink no liquor but ours. That's an iron rule at Selby."

Carroll smiled. "Surely you've buried your *good* whiskey long ago."

"Only the brandy, Major. Not the bourbon."

"Bourbon has its points, I'll grant you. But I'll match our rye against it when it's aged in wood."

"Perhaps we can make the comparison when the war is over."

"Stranger things have happened," said Carroll. He led the way toward the Big House—as naturally as though he had lived there always.

The guest wing opened from the long gallery—which connected

it with the parlor adjoining the master's study. When he had shown Carroll to his suite, Yancey hastened to seek out Lorena.

The dining room, he found, was empty. He smiled over the floral display on the centerpiece, the placing of Selby's second-best china and wineglasses. The pewter dinner set, he saw, had been arranged as precisely as though it were the Judge's matched silver. His brows lifted again at the two bottles of Johannisberger, already decanted on the sideboard. A magnum of Pommery stood ready in the cooler, still beaded from its immersion in ice-cold spring water. He knew it was the last champagne in the bin. . . . Lorena was evidently prepared to entertain the enemy in style.

Following the aroma from the kitchen, Yancey found a brace of pheasants in the oven, stuffed with the wild-rice dressing that was Penelope's secret recipe. There were creamed onions and candied yams beside them: the clock of Selby ticked on, it seemed, even in a stage of siege. Ulysses was sharpening cutlery in the pantry, and Florrie knelt before the oven to baste the fowl in their own rich juice. The plantation doctor studied Lorena's house slaves carefully before announcing that Major Carroll would be ready to dine at the appointed hour. He detected no glimmer of resentment. It was apparent they had taken the enemy arrival in stride, that their loyalty was unshaken.

"Where's Mrs. Selby?"

"Down at de gin, Doc Yancey," said Ulysses. "She say doan' yo' fret. She be back right soon."

Uncle Doc smiled despite his heavy musings. Now that she had adjusted to the presence of Union forces on her land, it was quite like Lorena to visit her packhouse. She could hardly dress for dinner until she had made sure her precious cotton was untouched.

He found her on a bale in the shadow of the loading platform. Reen's head was bent in thought, and her fingers twisted a wisp of cotton that had escaped the burlap casing.

"Don't brood too long," he said. "You've just a half hour before we receive your guest."

The chatelaine of Selby flushed, and did not raise her eyes. "You showed him everything?"

"We toured your domain from end to end."

"Tell me what he said. And don't skip."

"The major has convinced me he's both a gentleman and a philosopher," said Yancey. "Granted, he isn't one of us—but he understands us well enough. On balance, I'd say we could have drawn far worse conquerors."

"Will he leave us in peace?"

"That depends on two factors. The orders he receives from his corps commander—and you."

"What can I——?"

"Let's take his orders first. He's completing an inventory of Selby's resources. If he feels we're still useful to the Confederacy, it's his duty to burn us out. Or, rather, to recommend such a procedure to corps."

"Then we haven't a prayer."

"Perhaps we do, after all. That, my dear, will depend on the second factor I just mentioned."

"Are you hinting I appeal to his better nature? As a Union officer he can use but one standard."

Yancey sat down on the cotton bale: he spoke carefully, with his eyes on the girl's averted profile. "That's a rather hasty judgment, Lorena. Don't forget the man is from back-country Pennsylvania: I'm told there's no finer farming land. Certainly he admires what you've done here. Your care of the fields. The fact you've treated your slaves as men, not as chattels——"

"Our records stand. He's sure to find just what we've given General Hood——"

"Our usefulness to General Hood is ended—and the general's cause is lost. Doesn't that exempt us?"

"It won't be that simple, Uncle Doc. How can Major Carroll neglect his principles—or his orders?"

"Let's forget his orders and explore those principles a bit. I've already called him a philosopher. Would you like to know his background?"

"If you insist," said Reen. "I must say I thought *you'd* take a gloomier view."

"So I would, if Carroll were a case-hardened regular who worked by the book. This major is a great deal more. He attended the College of New Jersey at Princeton—and read for the Philadelphia bar. When the war began, he was already a successful lawyer. To my mind, his choice of professions is significant. If he'd wished, he need never have worked at all. His family's a wealthy one——"

"Did he give you his pedigree too?"

"He didn't mention it. But even I have heard of the Pennsylvania Carrolls. They began with oil in '59; they were already in iron. Today they own a fleet of river steamers. Coal mines and Pittsburgh mills——"

"What's that to do with us? We're enemies."

"Perhaps not, if you plead your cause adroitly."

"What does *adroit* mean in a cynic's dictionary?"

"Translate it yourself," said Yancey. He was still careful not to meet her eye. "Carroll is a man of the world, not a hell-roaring abolitionist. He can see both sides. My advice is to throw yourself on his mercy. Swear your husband forced you to supply Hood's quartermasters, if he asks for your books——"

"I'll tell no lies. Not even to save Selby."

"Very well—if you must be noble. Point out that three hundred Negro laborers, and their families, will starve without your help. Insist they'll make better freedmen if he spares their means of livelihood. My guess is he'll agree."

"Suppose he doesn't? What then?"

Yancey paused. "How well do you remember your ancient history? The Punic Wars, for example?"

"Well enough."

"Are you familiar with the career of Hannibal—the general from Carthage?"

"The one who conquered Rome?"

"He didn't *quite* conquer it. That's my point. Hannibal rode up to the gates with the finest army the world had ever seen—ready to sack the city. The next day, he marched on. History has never given us a valid reason. The poets insist a woman changed his mind."

"Do you believe I can charm Major Carroll into sparing us?"

"You could try," said Yancey steadily.

"He'll be moving on. Others will follow. What's to keep *them* from destroying everything?"

"Something I'd heard existed but couldn't be sure—until Carroll himself confirmed it. If he leaves a provost marshal's bulletin on your gatepost, forbidding all Union troops to molest us, we could get off scot-free." Watching Lorena narrowly, Yancey saw her shoulders straighten at the thought—and knew his point had sunk home.

"You're sure he can do that?"

"The actual orders come from above. But I'd gamble Carroll's superiors listen to his recommendations. He's that kind of man."

Lorena nodded slowly. "You'll help?"

"Of course, girl."

When she got to her feet the light in her eyes told him all he wished to know. "It's time we were dressing for dinner," she said. "Selby doesn't keep its guests waiting."

12

Surveying his clean-shaven face in the bathroom mirror, Dan Carroll concluded he would pass muster. Granted, his tunic had seen hard service—but it had been cut by the best tailor in Philadelphia. Tonight he could wish it were a less violent blue. He could still take comfort in the expert fit, in the boots that shone like fresh-rubbed chestnuts.

Moving into the bedroom, he dismissed his orderly and opened the shutters wide. Alone at last in this fabulous house, with a day's work behind him and a conscience at rest, he breathed deep of the fresh November air and leaned out to survey the vast sweep of gardens. Once again (it was a feeling he could no longer question) he had the sense of destiny closing, of the timelessness of time. . . .

A figure was drifting across the shadowed velvet of the lawn—a white moth in the dusk, with a darker shadow in attendance. He saw it was his hostess and the plantation doctor, deep in talk. Dan sighed and closed the shutter hastily. Guessing the subject of that earnest conversation, he could wish for a confidant of his own.

Jack Keller would have served, but his aide had ridden away with the day's dispatches. Carroll had just informed the major-domo that he would be the only guest. Knowing it would take Dr. Yancey a moment more to change, he stretched himself on the chaise longue that stood between the bedroom casements, and surrendered to his fancies. Few tours of duty ended as neatly as they began. This one, so far, was a shining exception. The victory at the river had been climaxed by his reception here. Not even in his wildest dreams had he pictured such a manor house as Selby Hall, or such a chatelaine.

Carroll's knowledge of the South was adequate—but it was based on his reading, on judgments not too far removed from prejudice. True, there had been firsthand glimpses in his campaigning—but these were too fugitive to make a coherent picture. He had also met his share of Southerners, who had sung the discordant symphony of defeat from Virginia to New Orleans. Standing at his commanding general's side, at a reception given in Nashville to sweeten the gall of conquest, he had met a dozen ladies who insisted their devotion to the Union had never wavered. . . . Clearly, the mistress of Selby was forged from sterner metal.

So far, her poise had seemed perfect. Was there a way to break that shell and reach the woman beneath? If they could meet and talk as equals, would he understand her land more fully?

Smiling at his own eagerness, Dan began to roam his opulent quarters, examining the Persian carpets, the portieres of maroon velvet at each window, the painting above the fruited marble mantel, which he recognized (with a low whistle) as a Romney. The bath he had just quitted was almost Pompeian in its splendor. In the dressing room a marble table contained enough bottles and unguents to serve a dozen Brummels. The regal bed had four fluted columns, surmounted by classic love knots and a tester starred with the golden bees of France. Yet there was nothing ornate about this deep-piled comfort. It belonged to Selby Hall, like those formal boxwoods outside, and the quarter mile of driveway arched by live oaks that had been centuries in growing.

Nor did it detract from its mellowed beauty to admit that this empire had been built on black sweat. Lorena Selby might be the flower of a culture he had vowed to destroy root and branch. Her allure was no less potent.

Dan shook his head over the enigma—and moved from guest suite to gallery, to study the row of painted ancestors. The portraits were in order, beginning with the first Selby to set foot in the New World—an ornately wigged Georgian whose plethoric glare named him a three-bottle man as clearly as though a doctor's report had been added to the canvas. Later Selbys were leaner, but the arrogant stare was constant. These, after all, were the conquerors of a wilderness, with a king's patent to back them. Naturally, they had taken their mastery of the land for granted—and the human chattels that tilled it.

The next to last portrait was a man in judge's robes. There was an open tome on his knee, and his hand rested lightly on a globe. The brow beneath the snow-white mane was a noble one; the eyes were warm, for all the aloofness of the nose. Here, thought Carroll, was a man who took all knowledge for his province. Judge Andrew Selby was rather out of place among these fox-hunting nabobs— yet he dominated them by majesty alone. Was it because his was the one face where intelligence ruled rather than pride?

The final portrait, a tall, superbly endowed man in a Confederate uniform, restored the dominant strain of the Selby line. Carroll recognized his antagonist of the morning instantly. Bradfield Selby's gauntleted hands were folded on a saber hilt; the artist had painted him in profile, with a stormy sky as a backdrop. Perhaps it was the setting that made him seem more façade than man. It was a painting that spelled out end of the road in letters even the casual visitor could read. Especially if the visitor had faced other Brad Selbys on the battlefield.

There was no woman's face in all the long gallery. Dan gathered that only the male line was deemed worthy of portraiture at Selby Hall. He shrugged off the implication and moved on to the twin parlor.

The plantation doctor rose from his place beside the fire. "This is the time for my second drink of the day," he said. "Sometimes my third, if the news from the front is bad. I think you'll find our bourbon to your taste, Major."

Choosing a facing armchair, with the crackle of lightwood knots between them, Dan accepted the glass. It was superb whiskey— and he felt his tensions unwind with the first sip. Had he been seated at his father's fieldstone hearth (sampling a toddy after a day's hunting on the mountain), he could not have felt more serene. It was as though an unseen door had opened, admitting him to Selby Hall—if not to Selby's secrets.

So far, he had been accepted as a visitor from another cosmos

—an invader who would continue to receive this formal welcome until he proved himself an enemy. Basic questions remained. He would press on for answers when he faced his hostess at dinner.

Thinking of Lorena Selby, he was conscious of her arrival before he glimpsed her. First came the rustle of her gown on the stairs, then the sound of her voice while she conferred with her butler. Her muted greeting, spoken from the foyer, brought both men to their feet. When she paused for an instant in the archway between the parlors, Dan could only stare blankly. It was as though another portrait had come suddenly alive, completing the picture of Selby in a last, bold stroke.

Tonight she wore a gown of watermelon-green silk, cut low and fastened at the bosom by a sunburst of diamonds. There were other jewels at her wrists and hair—gathered into a high chignon that did the most for milk-white neck and shoulders. When they had met on her portico, he had thought Lorena Selby a strikingly handsome woman. Here, in the setting of her home, with the candlelight warm on that dark hair, her beauty took his breath away.

He saw that she was aware of his homage. For a moment more, the snapping black eyes swept him from head to foot. Then she moved forward and held out her hand. The gesture put a formal seal on his presence. As her fingers touched his, he half bent to kiss them—but they had slipped from his grasp before he could make his homage complete.

"We can go in when you like, gentlemen," she said. "Ulysses has announced dinner."

An hour later, warmed by perfect food and wine, Carroll had fenced with the chatelaine of Selby on every level, with her plantation doctor as a quiet umpire. So far, he had yet to win a match (though he could tell himself that he had held his own). He bore her no ill will for her prowess—since this was her special domain. Until he challenged her authority there, she had every right to rule.

He had debated the same topics with other Southern ladies, as the Union advance had rolled from state to state. Tonight he had been told once again that the North, not the South, had begun hostilities. Desiring to live at peace with its "peculiar institution," the South had merely resisted invasion. Naturally, the army with the most guns must gain the final victory. His hostess was prepared to admit that the conquest was all but complete, despite the genius of Lee in Virginia. . . . She still insisted that the war was needless, that there should have been a meeting of minds across the invisible border that divided two hostile nations.

As for the slaves, they remained the South's problem. Regardless of proclamations from Washington, the South must solve that problem in its own way, on its own timetable. Here at Selby (she could prove it from her ledgers) her field hands lived better than many New England factory workers. In time, as their status grew, education would have been feasible—with manumission the final goal. Enlightened Southerners had always believed in eventual freedom. With patience, it could have been achieved without bloodshed, the sowing of dragons' teeth that would fester in Southern soil for a century. . . .

"Tell me just one thing, Mrs. Selby. Were it in your power, when would you have freed your Negroes?"

"The moment they could *use* their freedom."

"Tomorrow? Fifty years from now? Or never?"

"I'll reveal two secrets," said Reen. "Even in Judge Selby's day slaves who could profit from it were taught to read, write, and cipher. Since I've managed things, they've been paid wages. It was my way of keeping them safely on the land until I saw the future plain."

"You're in charge here then?"

"Completely, since my husband joined his command."

"Would *he* have freed them in time?"

"Perhaps. I hope so."

"Forgive me, but I can't believe that."

"How can you judge Captain Selby, when you haven't met?"

"We met today, at Indian Ford—as you must have heard. I'd already known him by reputation. I don't mean to slander the absent, but it's men like Captain Selby who made this war inevitable."

Reen's lips tightened, but her voice was still calm. "I won't contradict that estimate, Major."

"Slavery and states' rights, in the fire-eaters' view, are synonyms. When there's peace again in Georgia, they'll do their best to keep the Negro in bondage."

"It's their privilege."

Dan smiled down at the wineglass Ulysses had just refilled with champagne. This was a duel he intended to win, no matter what the risk. "Tell me one thing more, Mrs. Selby. Why was this Civil War fought? What is our real bone of contention?"

"The right of a region to live by its own rules," said Reen. "And we don't use the term *Civil* War in Georgia. To us, it's the War between the States."

"Precisely. Mr. Lincoln said long ago that he would not have interfered with slavery if he could have preserved the Union. Once the shooting began, however, we couldn't end things honorably without freeing our Negroes——"

"*Our* Negroes, Major. They're not yours."

"Our joint responsibility then," he said quietly. "Let's ignore slavery for the moment. What really counts is the survival of these United States. When we lay down our arms, they'll be *really* united for the first time. This war will prove to the world that we're a nation—that a whole is stronger than its parts." He broke off as Yancey applauded from the table's end. "I didn't intend to make a Fourth of July oration," he said. "Still, I'm glad the doctor agrees."

"So does our hostess," said Yancey. "Not that she'll admit it in your presence."

"We can all agree the war was senseless," said Dan. "Can't we proclaim a separate peace among ourselves?"

"Hardly," said Lorena, "if you mean to burn us out."

It was a statement of fact, not a query. In the silence its implications seemed to expand, like circular ripples when a stone falls into a pool. For the first time, Dan had caught a note of near pleading in Lorena Selby's voice. Though her eyes did not waver, they seemed to implore an answer to her doubting. Wishing with all his heart that he could supply that answer, he forced himself to voice his thoughts.

"I'll tell you this much now," he said. "My aide is en route to our corps commander with a complete report on what I've seen here. I've said we encountered no resistance and expected none. I've added that, in my opinion, such stores as you now possess will never reach the enemy. But I've already told Dr. Yancey that the final decision is not mine. Our corps commander may well disagree with my estimate." He forced a smile to cover the heavy portent in his words. "There the matter stands, at the moment. I wish I could be more sanguine, but I won't delude you with false hopes. And I'm afraid I must add some news you're sure to hear tomorrow. Two of your neighbors *were* burned out this afternoon: Greentree and Hamilton Hundred. Perhaps they'll serve as examples for the county."

His hostess had paled visibly at the announcement, but Dan could not regret his candor. He had been careful not to add that both plantation houses had bolted doors and windows, and made a desperate effort to drive off his men with gunfire. Naturally, their demolition had been a necessary warning to others. How could he promise that Selby Hall would receive better treatment after his dispatches reached headquarters?

"I can see there's no appeal from your orders," said Reen. "Is it possible you'll have some discretion in the matter?"

"We'll answer that tomorrow, Mrs. Selby. Meanwhile will you believe me when I say you deserve to survive?"

"I plan to survive, Major Carroll—regardless of what you do to Selby."

"May I also add that I hope to be your friend in peacetime— no matter what my orders are tomorrow?"

"How can we be friends when we live in hostile countries?"

"They can't be hostile forever. If our history has any meaning, it's vital that we contribute to each other's future."

"Look at this house," said Reen. "It was built by Georgians— and maintained by Georgians. Other Georgians will see it standing in the next century. We'll need no help from you."

"That's where you are wrong, Mrs. Selby. I'm devoting my life to proving it."

"Isn't that rather a large order, Major?"

"Perhaps it is, in these unhappy times. Fortunately, I have the resources to back it. I happen to be one of the three richest men in my state. For a Pennsylvanian that's saying a good deal." He smiled at his hostess: somehow the remark held no hint of self-esteem in this setting. "I take no credit for the fact my grandfather laid the foundation for those riches and my father expanded them. It's an accident of fate that both my uncles died in the war, making me the sole heir——"

"Forgive me, Major Carroll," said Reen, "but what's this to do with Georgia?"

"A great deal, I trust. Since this money comes to me by chance, I mean to plow it back."

"I'm afraid I don't follow you."

"Ever since this campaign was launched, I've been looking for a place to put down roots. Today I chose Cray County. I decided after our action at Indian Ford."

Yancey spoke from the table's head. "Does this mean you're turning farmer in our midst?"

"The moment it's feasible, I'm going to start buying land."

"Do you think the county will accept you?" asked Reen.

"I'll try hard to be acceptable, Mrs. Selby. It would help if I could call you my sponsor."

Reen had risen as he spoke, her eyes blazing. "I'm in no position to sponsor you, Major—whether you burn me out or pass me by. My husband would never permit it. Nor would my conscience."

"Time heals most wounds," said Dan. He saw that she was about to leave the room, and hastened to open the door for her departure. It was an easy way to detain her a moment more.

"Some wounds will never heal."

"Not even your prejudice?"

"I'll believe your plan to turn landowner here when I see it in action."

"That much I can prove in the spring—if the war's ended by then."

"It's my duty to warn you that you'll die of loneliness."

"There are worse ways to die, Mrs. Selby—if you're my antagonist."

They were eye to eye in the doorframe. Thanks to the wide bell of her skirt, she could not pass through without touching him— and, if Dan read her burning glance aright, she would refuse such contact. He held his ground. At that moment, the need to dominate was too strong to resist.

"I'll promise you still more," he said. "When I return I'll see that you sell every bale in your packhouse."

"How can you—if you're told to burn it?"

"To make a new crop then. Won't you believe that much?"

"No, Major," she said. Curiously enough, there was no anger in her tone now, though her eyes still smoldered. "I think you're baiting me with false hopes."

"I've spoken no more than the truth."

"Isn't this talk of a command decision at headquarters a trick to keep me on tenterhooks? Can't you destroy us—or leave us untouched, depending on your fancy?"

"No, Mrs. Selby. Believe me, I'm only an agent here. But I *will* be your friend tomorrow."

"Very well, Major. I'll leave you with the last word. And I'll remind you of that promise at a better moment."

The dark eyes burned Dan Carroll one more time—but her fingers were icy when they closed on his hand, forcing him to turn the doorknob and give ground. When she was gone, he turned to the plantation doctor. It was true she had given him the final word —but he could not believe he had scored a victory.

"First she insists we can't be friends," he said. "*Then* she dares me to prove my friendship. What does she mean?"

Yancey chuckled as he passed the port.

"Never ask a lady what she means," he said. "Not when the lady is Southern. You'll be no wiser than before."

13

Last night was the groundwork, Reen told herself. *Last night you took your enemy's measure. By and large, you managed well. Tonight you must hold him to his word.*

She had slept badly after Major Carroll had gone to work on his papers. Twice she had risen from her bed, certain she had heard the crackle of flames—but there had been no sound from the Union camp save for the thud of sentries' boots. In the morning she had started up one more time while the bugles blew reveille—fearful, at first, that the battalion was moving out. When Carroll's men had shown no sign of breaking camp after breakfasting around their cook fires, she had felt her heart leap. Selby had been granted a respite, however brief it might be: while these men in blue camped in her meadow, there would be no torches among her cotton bales.

All day long, she had forced herself to perform routine tasks.

With Sal beside her she had gone through the quarters to make doubly sure there had been no desertions. The major's men, she observed, were careful to stand aside from the Negroes while they worked. There had still been no incidents, and Reen had noted little real tension: even Luke had sullenly admitted that plantation business was proceeding like clockwork. For this she could bless the shrewd discipline of Saladin. . . .

Now it was night again. The occupation of her land was more than twenty-four hours old—but, from the snatches of information she had picked up, she did not believe it would last beyond the morrow. She could only pray that the 2nd Pennsylvania Cavalry would depart as it had come, and not leave a charred ruin in its wake.

She had punctiliously repeated her dinner invitation, but Major Carroll had sent his regrets. Lieutenant Keller would soon be returning from corps with his orders: meanwhile he would take pot luck with his men and receive reports from his patrols. Reen understood the message perfectly. This was her time of crisis, the enemy's moment to announce his decision. Remembering her encounter with that same enemy in her dining room door—and what she had read in his eyes—she felt sure there were trumps in her hand.

Reen dined from a tray in her room (it had seemed unwise to appear downstairs too soon). Afterward she dressed with care, in a gown of wine-red Chinese brocade that showed her figure to advantage. Tonight she was careful to lock her jewels away in the secret wall safe, along with her wedding ring. When she descended the stairs at last, she was glad that Ulysses had been sparing of candles. Shadows suited her mood—to say nothing of her impending meeting with Major Dan Carroll.

In the nearer of the twin parlors a lamp cast a warm circle of light on the table where he had spread his maps. Most of the charts were in their cases, and the major's greatcoat was folded neatly across a chair back. The proofs of his nearness made the room his own. Moving quickly into the glow of the lamp, she wondered why she did not resent it more.

Knowing his orderly might return at any moment, she did not

hesitate after she had turned back the flap of the dispatch case. A dozen posters were inside: thanks to Uncle Doc's description, she recognized them at once. Printed on heavy paper, embossed with the Great Seal of the United States, they bore facsimile signatures of the Secretary of War and the provost marshal on General Sherman's staff. Above them were three blank spaces. These, Reen judged, would contain the name of the individual whose property was to be spared, a description of that property—and, finally, the signature of the officer making the grant.

Today these posters were beyond price in Georgia. Uncle Doc had stated the case fairly: nailed to her gate, and backed by a corporal's guard, this square of paper could insure Selby's future. Reen's fingers trembled as she filched one from the case and slipped it beneath a pillow on the couch. She had barely time to seat herself there before she heard footsteps on the portico. She recognized Luke Jackson's dragging gait before he appeared in the doorframe—and sighed out her relief. It was far too soon to face Major Carroll.

"Come in, Luke," she called. "I'm quite alone."

The overseer had ridden out at noon on a special errand: she had expected him long before darkness fell, and guessed the reason for his tardiness. Even though he brought bad news he was welcome. She needed a touch of gaucherie to bring her back to earth.

"How far did you go, Luke?"

"Just to the turnpike, Mrs. Selby." Jackson came into the parlor gingerly—circling the map table with a scowl, as though it housed a nest of vipers. "Their army's *still* rollin' through the crossing."

"You reached Greentree then?"

"Yes'm. I stopped at Hamilton Hundred too."

"Is it true they're both burned out?"

"Greentree don't have a whole wall left: the fire did a job there. Miss Buell's moved into one of her slave cabins."

"And the Hamiltons?"

"They're campin' in one of the colonel's tobacco barns."

"I hope you invited both families here."

"They won't come, Mrs. Selby. Not after you broke bread with Major Carroll."

Reen smiled bitterly: she had expected this reply to her offer of asylum. "What else did you hear?"

"The Varnell place is still standin'. I don't have to say why."

"Are you suggesting that Yankee officers can be bribed?"

"All the Varnells are bombproofs, ma'am—with hard money in their pokes. They're white trash, and the whole county knows it. Now they're makin' the same talk about Selby."

"No money has changed hands here."

"Then why is our roof standin'?"

"First, because the house is Major Carroll's headquarters. Second, because he has a personal sympathy for the conquered. So he tells me, at any rate—and I've yet to think otherwise."

Luke's sallow face had gone white. "We can do without his sympathy."

"I'm trying to preserve my husband's plantation—and his workers. If I can save them by asking a Union major to dine I'll ignore the gossips."

"What makes you think he'll spare us, Mrs. Selby? Didn't he burn out the Buells—and the Hamiltons?"

Reen met the mutinous look without flinching. "At the moment," she said firmly, "I can't answer that question. I can only hope my estimate of the major's intention is accurate. Until I put that hope to the test, Luke, I'm asking you to hold your tongue."

The overseer was twisting his hat in silent fury. "I'll try, ma'am. But I can't take it kindly."

"If Selby goes, so will your job. Had you thought of that?"

"Maybe I don't want a job at that price."

"You'll stay on, Luke—and you'll keep your opinions to yourself. I think you owe me that much."

"I owe you plenty, Mrs. Selby—but I can't take back what I said." Luke departed with that pronouncement, still twisting his hat brim: Reen knew he could not trust himself to speak again. Turning to watch him go, she found that Uncle Doc was leaning in the doorframe, studying her with his familiar grin as he drew on his cigar. She met his stare with a toss of her head.

"Well? Do you despise me too?"

"You know better than that, I hope."

"How else could I act—and save Selby?"

"You did right," he said. "Never mind what's on the grapevine. What you feel in your heart's the important thing."

"I mean to keep my home, Uncle Doc. Nothing else matters."

Yancey flung his cigar into the night and came a step nearer. "Care to discuss your *modus operandi?*"

He did not stir as she lifted the pillow on the couch and brought out the poster. Nor did his expression change as he read it through to the last word.

"Where'd you get this?"

"From the major's dispatch case. Where else?"

Yancey returned the poster to its hiding place with something like haste. "What comes next?"

"If I understand you, all it needs is a signature."

"True—providing he has authority from above."

"Suppose he signed it regardless? Wouldn't it stand up?"

"It's quite likely," said Yancey. "But he hasn't done so yet."

"He will," said Lorena. "Will you leave that much to me and stop asking questions?"

The plantation doctor studied her for a moment before his lips curved into a smile. "Gladly, girl," he said at last. "In fact, I'll leave you the field."

Watching him cross the foyer and ascend the stairs with his slow, old man's gait, Reen fought down the impulse to call him back. When he had gone, she followed him—but only to the first landing, where she drew back into the shadow.

Ten minutes ticked by before she heard the foyer door swing open. It had been a small eternity.

Peering between the posts of the banister, she could just make out Dan Carroll's head as he hurried to his worktable, flanked by battalion runners. She heard the chair creak—and, leaning forward, could see his shadow in bold relief against the foyer wall. In the circumstances, she could only retreat to the landing and bide her time.

During the next half hour—to judge by the tramp of booted feet —he was busy with his dispatches. The series of couriers that entered and left the house, and the rattle of hoofs on her driveway, seemed to go on forever. Only when silence returned at last to both

foyer and portico did she abandon her fruitless eavesdropping and
rise from the stair on the landing. In another moment she stood
in the foyer arch—uncertain, even now, of her first move.

The major, still storing notes in the dispatch case, seemed unaware of her presence. She felt that his concentration on his work
was a bad omen. Somehow (in view of her desperate stratagem)
she had expected him to look up instantly—ready to resume the
argument where they had dropped it last night in the dining room.

"Do I intrude?"

Carroll rose abruptly. "By no means, Mrs. Selby. I was about to
send for you."

"Is it true you're leaving tomorrow?"

He smiled faintly then, with his eyes on the dispatch case. "I
hoped that was a military secret."

"I couldn't help overhearing——"

"We ride out at reveille, to join our brigade. There's no further
need for flank protection."

Forcing herself to the next, inevitable question, Reen felt her
heart turn over. "Have you received orders about Selby?"

"My orders just came through from corps. The matter has been
left entirely to my discretion."

Fear urged her forward, but she forced herself to cling to the
foyer arch while he flipped back the cover of the dispatch case, took
out a poster like the one she had just stolen, and offered it for her
inspection.

"This is a special warning from our provost marshal," he said.
"They were printed for this campaign by the general's order. Have
you seen one before?"

"Dr. Yancey mentioned them," she said. "I wasn't too clear as
to their use." Her voice was in perfect control as she uttered the
thumping lie. He would never guess that she needed all her
strength to keep back her tears when he slashed his signature across
the precious square of paper—then printed her name, and the name
of Selby Hall, in the space above.

"The purpose of this notice is self-evident," he said in the same
detached tone. "Now that it bears my name, it's official. When we
leave we'll attach it to your gate—and post a guard there to make
sure it's read. Which means, of course, that your plantation will

remain untouched until the war is over. Any scavenger who so much as lifts a pullet from your barnyard will answer a court-martial." He tossed the poster among his maps and smiled. "Don't look so dazed, Mrs. Selby. Last night I promised to do this for you—if my corps commander granted me the authority. Isn't the proof convincing?"

Laughter came at last, along with the tears—and Reen made no attempt to check them. Sinking into the nearest chair, she covered her face with her hands. Relief washed over her spirits like balm as she realized (for the first time) that this Union officer was sincere in his wish to protect her. At the same time (for a reason she dared not face), she felt curiously defeated. She did not risk meeting Carroll's eyes when he stood over her with a glass.

"Drink this," he said. "You've been under a fearful strain. I didn't mean to prolong it."

The whiskey cleared her head, but the numbness remained. The scene she had planned so carefully, it seemed, had already rung down its curtain: like an actress deprived of her great moment, she could only stand helpless in the wings. And then, through that fog of anti-climax, she heard Dan Carroll speak her name. Something in his voice told her that the play was not quite over.

"Mrs. Selby—Lorena——"

"Yes, Major?"

"May I call you Lorena, now I've shown I'm your friend?"

She raised her eyes at last (the tears were gone, as though they had never been) and studied the Yankee carefully. He still hovered above her chair, with one hand extended awkwardly. The gesture, she realized, was meant to cement the bond he now believed existed between them. Instinct warned her that it would be fatal to accept it. True, they had touched fingers briefly when she had welcomed him as a dinner guest. This would be a handclasp of another sort.

"How can we be friends, Major?"

"If someone won't make the effort," he said, "there's small hope for our country's future."

"Can't you see I *have* to be your enemy? That I can't take this protection as a gift?"

"Why not—when it's offered freely?"

She moved to the couch, found her own copy of the poster, and put it on the map table. Carroll had not stirred since she refused his hand.

"As you'll observe," she said, "this is a duplicate. I stole it in your absence."

"For what reason?"

"To persuade you to sign it, of course. At the first convenient moment."

"What means did you have in mind?"

"If all else failed, Major Carroll, I planned to offer—myself."

Once the words were out, she was amazed to find she could speak them so calmly. For one dreadful moment she was afraid he had not grasped her meaning. The slight smile that curved his lips infuriated her beyond all bounds, even before he spoke.

"Are you sure you know what you're saying?" he asked.

"Quite sure. I still intend to pay for that signature, if only to keep my self-respect."

Reen felt some of her resentment ebb away when she realized that she had shocked him at last. While the reaction lasted, she felt sure he would stalk from the room, leaving her with the last word. When he turned again to face her, there was something in his eyes that told her she had gained the initiative.

"Can't I protect you out of friendship?" he asked.

"I don't want your friendship, Yankee."

"No friend should be valued lightly. Not even when he wears an enemy uniform."

"I'd still prefer to settle my debt—in what I'm told is the traditional way."

"You're a strange woman, Lorena."

"Mind your manners," she said. "To you I'm Mrs. Selby."

"Even now?"

"Now more than ever." This time, there was no mistaking the light in his eyes. She pushed her advantage recklessly. "And don't pretend you haven't wanted me. I knew that much yesterday—the moment we met."

"Of course I wanted you," he said. "What man wouldn't?"

"It's a bargain then?"

"Go back to that meeting," he said. "It's rather important—for us both. I *did* want you when I saw you standing like a queen on the portico. But I wanted you for all the wrong reasons——"

"What do reasons matter tonight?"

"They matter greatly—to me. Yesterday I was prepared to hate you. I thought you were another parasite on the land—a leftover from the feudal age. I even fancied it might be a kind of revenge on the South, to take you on my own terms——"

"What changed your mind?"

"Selby itself. The things you've done here."

"Then you approve of my stewardship?"

"I felt I should honor that achievement," he said. "That's why I've promised you a guard. You might call it a gesture of atonement."

"Your motive does you credit," she said. "I'll accept it at its face value. It's more than I dared hope from a Yankee."

"Must you always use that word as a curse?"

"Shall I say what *I* expected, Major? I thought you were a beast from outer darkness—a monster in uniform I must appease at any cost. I haven't changed my mind, for all your fine words."

"If I were what you think," he said quietly, "I'd have taken you long since—*without* signing that poster."

"Why didn't you?"

He moved a step closer as their eyes met in earnest. "For just one reason," he said. "To prove I can be human. Is it too hard to believe?"

"I've made you an offer, Major. If you're leaving at reveille, it's time you accepted it."

She did not stir as he closed the gap between them in one long stride. When he took her in his arms, she was almost calm, though she shrank at first from contact with the blue tunic. Then, with no sense of yielding, a force beyond her control made her return his embrace. In another instant she gave back his kiss as fervently as he had offered it.

Her conscious mind still rebelled fiercely at the surrender. Then, as the high note of passion she had stirred so deliberately in Carroll found its savage echo in her heart, she ceased to think at all. There was no past and future while that mad music lasted, no reality but the hunger of her mouth on his.

"You can see we aren't enemies," he said at last, when he released her. "We never were."

Her mind groped for support in a sea without visible shores. She was drowning in that tideless bourn, with no wish to breathe again.

"What have you done to me?" she asked.

"Reminded you that you're a woman. Is the discovery more than you can bear?"

A sound of running feet on the portico, and a babble of voices outside, restored her sanity after a fashion.

Breaking free of Carroll, she drew back a portiere. She was in time to watch Uncle Doc cross the lawn from the back door: he was in his shirt sleeves, and left the Big House at top speed. Carroll joined her in the frame of the french window and pushed the glass wide. She could smell the smoke now, and hear the roar of flames behind the barns.

"The packhouse is burning!" The cry was wrenched from her throat. She hardly recognized the hoarse voice as her own.

A half-clad sergeant, his face black with soot, ran up the portico steps—snapping to attention when he faced Carroll.

"Will you come to the barnyard, Major?"

"What's up, Allen?"

"The gin caught first. Then the carpenter shed. They burned like tinder——"

"Are the horses safe?"

"Yes, Major."

"Back to your detail. I'll join you at once."

While this exchange took place, Reen had staggered from window to chair. She was still unwilling to accept the full impact of what she had seen and heard. And yet, when Carroll returned to her side, she felt strangely resigned—as though this, too, was part of a destiny she could not escape.

"Don't your men follow orders?" she asked. "Or was their timing bad?"

"There's been an accident, Lorena."

"Accident?"

"A fire started in the gin, and spread to your packhouse. You'll probably lose your cotton. Allen thinks we can save the barns."

"You call that an accident?"

"I do. Please believe me."

She moved to the map table and seized the official bulletin in both fists, shredding it to bits and flinging the pieces in his face. "You might have waited till morning to set the blaze," she said—and raised both fists to strike him as he continued to stand above her with the same granite calm.

"You don't think that for a moment. You can't——"

"What choice do you give me?" Reen turned as Yancey entered the room like a puff of brimstone. Both sleeves were charred, and his eyebrows seemed burned away. Yet he was calm enough, despite his heavy breathing.

"It's all right, Major," he said. "Things are in control."

Dan Carroll faced Yancey with the same firm poise. Even now he had the air of a man who had met worse crises than this and surmounted them.

"Please tell Mrs. Selby what happened," he said. "I'm needed outside."

The plantation doctor poured a drink and made no effort to speak. Reen went to watch the glare of flames. The fire was still bright, but she knew it was ebbing. Packhouse and gin were both at a safe distance; it was a still night, and there was little danger the blaze would spread. . . . Already, she saw, a score of Union cavalrymen had formed a bucket brigade at the barnyard well—and felt a hot blush of shame at her accusation. The shreds of the poster lay at her feet. She bent to pick them up—and drew back under the probe of Yancey's eyes.

"Did he promise what you want, Lorena?"

"So I thought."

"Get one fact through your head. The fire was an *accident*. One of the guards dozed off—on the porch of the gin. He had a lighted pipe in his hand."

Reen covered her eyes, though she felt no urge to weep: there were few tears left. "So I've misjudged Major Carroll one more time?"

"No one can blame you for that."

"I'll tell him I'm sorry when he returns," she said numbly.

"In your place I think I'd do that much." Yancey went to the portico and stared into the night. "Selby will be safe, once the fire's out," he said. "Dan Carroll isn't a man to forget a promise."

Both of them fell silent while Luke Jackson appeared on the lawn. The overseer was smoke-blackened, but the news he brought was reassuring. The fire was burning itself out, with the gin as its center. The Big House had never been threatened; the barns and quarters, save for a few pock-marks from falling embers, had escaped damage. The Yankees (Luke admitted) had pitched in with the field hands to put out the flames. A number had received burns: Yancey's help was needed in the surgery.

"Could you save the cotton?" asked Reen.

"Only a dozen bales, ma'am."

"Tell the major I'm on my way," said Yancey. He put a hand on Reen's shoulder after the overseer had hobbled back toward the barns. "Don't grieve too much," he said. "It's hard to see a fortune go up in smoke—but things might have been worse. With a northern breeze the house would have gone too."

"What good is Selby Hall without cotton?"

"There'll be other crops."

"I've barely enough to feed the hands for the next month. By the New Year we won't have a cent to our names."

"Don't tell me you've lost your courage over a packhouse fire. Think of Greentree and Hamilton Hundred. At least, you've a roof to shelter you—and protection until the war's end."

Reen nodded slowly, with her head still bowed. She had not stirred from the couch. Now, as Yancey turned to leave her, she shook off the choking hypnosis.

"When the major has a moment," she said, "I'd like to see him here."

"I'm sure he's aware of that," said Uncle Doc gravely. "But I'll convey the message."

She remained in the corner of the couch until Carroll crossed the portico. Her back was ramrod-straight—and the precise disposition of her skirts and folded hands would not have disgraced *Godey's Lady's Book.*

"Please come in, Major."

He did not speak at once—but she knew without turning that he had gone to his worktable.

"Your overseer told you what happened, I gather."

"I know everything. Will you forgive my stupidity?"

"Don't apologize. Your suspicion was only natural."

Without risking a direct glance as he settled at the table, she saw he was stripped to the waist, with a poncho tossed across his bare shoulders. Evidently, he had been part of his own bucket brigade. Somehow the absence of tunic and epaulets made him look much younger.

"I've a bit of unfinished business here," he said. "It will only take a moment."

Hearing the sound of pen on paper, she dared to look up. Carroll had spread another of the provost marshal's posters on the table. Reen saw he had written his name across it, beneath the carefully printed name of Selby Hall. She did not stir when he rose from his seat and dropped it on the sofa beside her.

"Please don't destroy this one," he said. "My supply is limited."

"Thank you, Daniel," she said in a whisper.

"I've promised to come back, Lorena," he said. "When I do, I'll offer you my hand a second time. Perhaps you'll find you can take it." Only the deep timbre of his voice betrayed him as he crossed the parlor, moving toward the archway that opened to the gallery and the guest wing. She watched him go with haunted eyes.

"Is this your idea of a good-by?" she asked.

"Won't it do, for now?" He turned in the archway to face her. For the first time she saw how much she had wounded him.

"Perhaps that fire was an omen, Daniel," she said. "Even though it wasn't your doing."

"At least you believe I'll keep my bargain."

"Of course. I've yet to keep mine."

Her voice had stopped him in time, in the shadow of the gallery.

"I think we should part as friends, Lorena."

"We may never be friends. But we can still be lovers."

She was on her feet with the words. In a single wild rush she was in his arms. This time when he bent to claim her lips, she offered them eagerly. They did not speak again as he lifted her in his embrace and carried her through the archway.

14

Lorena had risen in the dawn, a half hour before the Union bugles called reveille.

Dan Carroll was deep in slumber as she left the bedroom. She whispered a soft good-by: it scarcely mattered that he was unaware of her departure. He would understand the reason when he wakened fully.

At that hour, no one was stirring downstairs. She climbed the stairway unobserved: only Mammy Jo would know where she had spent the night. In her own room she studied her face in the mirror for a long time, marveling at her daytime mask. Its stern perfection would suffice—but she would never be the same again.

She had discovered the meaning of rapture in Dan Carroll's arms. It was her tragedy that the lesson had come too late, that she must go to an enemy's embrace to learn it. But she could not regret her night of love. Even though she must lock the memory away, even though she could share it with no one, it had served its purpose.

When the bugles sounded in the Union camp, she mounted the stairs to Selby's rooftree, and the widow's walk the Judge had built there. From this airy height she could look across her domain to the piney woods that boxed the horizon on the north and the turnpike beside the river. Bathed in the glow of sunrise, the land seemed untouched. It was only when the day brightened into morning that she could make out the fire-blackened shell of Greentree, the crumbled walls of Hamilton Hundred on the hillside beyond.

The 2nd Pennsylvania Cavalry departed while she watched, with a brave show of flags in its vanguard. Riding in a precise column of fours, the horsemen poured through her gates in a blue torrent. They had vanished in the cut below the riverbank before she could quite take in their going. At the distance, it was impossible to pick out faces. She knew only that Daniel was one of them—and that they could never meet again.

Far off on the horizon a dust cloud still marked the passing of the Union host—moving like a sleepy, all-devouring python across Georgia. Already it seemed a threat from another cosmos. Selby was hers again—and, come spring, she would find ways to make a crop.

In due season (this, too, was already more than a pious hope) she knew that last night's rapture would bear its own fruit as inevitably as the land itself.

Book Two

The buckboard's rickety wheels were patched with wire, but it was all his own. So was the mule between the traces, and the buggy whip in his hand. So, for that matter, was the bride on the seat beside him, whose brand-new store clothes matched his own in luster. Turning in at the gates of Selby Hall, flicking the mule's ribs to tease him into something resembling a steady gait, Sal controlled the urge to break into song. Instead, he smiled at Florrie and let his hand rest on hers.

"Doan' look so skeered, gal! We's jes' comin' home."

"Selby ain't home now, Sal. An' it ain't fitten to bust up de drive lak white folks."

"Honey, let yo' husband decide what's fitten."

"Maybe we doan' b'long to Miss Reen no mo'—but Ah'm still skeered."

"Miss Reen *say* we's t'let her know, minute we's hitched. She say come hyah t'help her make a crop. Dis way we do both." Sal smiled broadly—and clucked again at the mule. His voice, like his appearance, had taken on a new dimension in the months since the packhouse fire.

They had been eventful months—and each event had done its bit to strengthen a man's spine, to fill a man's head with the yeasty stuff of dreams. They had also been critical months for Selby Hall. Sal's heart had gone out to his former owner as he watched her face a bleak future and make what plans she could. Today Miss

Reen had summoned him to discuss the business of hiring field hands. If she meant to put her land to work again, he could hope the worst was behind her.

Sal closed his mind to surroundings while the buckboard rattled up the four hundred yards of driveway. Waist-high grass now blanketed the lawns, and untrimmed vines streamed from the arch of boughs above him; between the trees grunting porkers nuzzled untended. Last spring black gardeners had barbered those lawns and kept the live oaks free of parasites; black swineherds had penned the Selby hogs far from the formal grounds; Miss Reen's own house slaves had scrubbed that Grecian belvedere beside the lake until the marble gleamed as white as the swans that had floated there. . . . Today the belvedere had almost disappeared under wild grapevine, and the swan lake was choked with weeds. The swans themselves (despairing of further feedings) had gone to parts unknown.

Still, it had been right that Selby's former bondsmen should depart (like those swans) when Selby's chatelaine could feed them no longer. After Sherman's march it was impossible to evade the truth: the Negro was now free, though he had yet to find a meaningful use for his freedom.

Miss Reen and Sal had staked out the new domain between them —on a strip of bottom land beside the river. The spot was midway between Selby and the Varnells' land—an easy distance from other plantations that had been kept in repair. Appropriately, it was called Lincolnville, in honor of the dead President who had made such freeholds possible. Since the Selbys held title to the land, there had been no legal difficulties, once the Negroes were in possession.

Miss Reen had hoped her hands would find work elsewhere, now that her own funds had run out. Meanwhile the rich earth beside the river had produced abundant garden truck. Their former owner had insisted they share in the winter hog butchering. She had found ways to supply them with salt, corn meal, and other staples from her granary. . . . Since the exodus Lincolnville had grown by leaps and bounds. Other ex-slaves (returning from promised Edens that had given them only freedom to starve) had drifted into the bottom to add their flimsy dwellings to the rest. Not that jobs had been too plentiful so far—but no one there had gone hungry.

Today there was talk of better times, now that the war was past history. A military occupation would soon protect the black man's rights. Freedmen's bureaus (so they said) would help him to achieve his goal—if not the forty acres and a mule that had first been promised, at least a reasonable substitute.

Sal had been the leader of this trend toward independence, the motive force that kept Lincolnville in a state of health. Mayor of the settlement in fact if not in name, he had made its laws, arranged the wages of its inhabitants, and arbitrated the disputes. . . . Miss Reen was right, he told himself. None of this could have happened, had they remained at Selby. It had been essential that the hands move to dwellings of their own, to a way of life outside white supervision, however benign.

Sal had begged Miss Reen to accept free labor from Lincolnville, if only in return for her gifts of food. He had offered to work the land on a loan basis, with wages to come from future profits. The chatelaine of Selby had refused such help, though she had called in part-time workers to keep the house in repair. Castor and Pollux, the twin carpenters, were still in residence (and more than earning their keep odd-jobbing in the neighborhood). The Big House, thought Sal, had never looked more splendid, despite the brush-choked fields that surrounded it. It was he who had insisted on the usual spring painting. Following the diagrams in the Judge's study, he had clipped the boxwoods with his own hands; once again roosters and dragons and knights in armor stood in familiar green silhouette against the pillars of the south portico.

He had made no attempt to do more—until Miss Reen had sent word that she had put her hands on funds.

Looking back on the winter, Sal realized it had been a time of waiting, a kind of truce with fate. He had had no real news of Captain Selby: some said he had died in the last, suicidal defense of Petersburg; others insisted he was in Mexico. Sal's most startling discovery had been made on his last visit to Selby Hall (when he had announced his plans to marry Florrie). There was no escaping the fact that Miss Reen, at long last, had grown large with child. Mammy Jo, the only servant the Big House boasted now, had con-

firmed the observation in a whispered aside. Dr. Yancey expected
Selby's heir to arrive in August.

So far as Sal could tell, the chatelaine of Selby had taken her
altered state in stride. It was as though she, no less than her land,
awaited the change of seasons to renew herself.

"Whut yo' laugh at *now?*"

Sal looked up from his driving and chuckled at Florrie's frown.
"Cain't Ah laugh 'cause Ah'm happy? Fo' Miss Reen—an' us?"

"How come you think Miss Reen's happy?"

"She's havin' a son, Florrie. Ain't she wanted one?"

"Who say it gwine be a man chile?"

"Mammy Jo—an' Ah believe her. 'Course, havin' a son's jes' a
beginnin'. Now Miz Reen's got her hands on money, we's aimin'
to bring Selby back to what it was."

"Yo' aimin', Sal? Whut Marse Brad say to dat?"

"Maybe Marse Brad's stopped talkin'—fo' keeps."

"He's too mean t'die. We both knows it."

Sal dismissed the thought with a final flick of his whip and
steered the mule toward the carriage block. The day was too fine,
the prospects too golden, to permit the shadow of Bradfield Selby
to darken them. He sprang from his wagon and offered a hand to
his bride—laughing aloud when she shrank back in terror.

"Sal, we *cain't* use de front do'——!"

"Who stoppin' us?"

He crossed the portico and lifted the heavy brass knocker. When
he gestured, Florrie moved to join him. They were standing side
by side in the great, fanlighted doorframe when the portal swung
cautiously open. Luke Jackson, in his shirt sleeves, faced them with
hostile, incredulous eyes. A hibernating bear, surprised at its cave
mouth, could not have been more churlish.

"What's this mean, boy?"

Sal knew the overseer had been informed of his visit. He made
himself answer softly—in the singsong expected of the black man
when he is faced by the white man's anger. "Ain't you heard Ah'm
wukkin' hyah again Marse Luke? Keepin' Miss Reen's books—an'
roundin' up men?"

"I know she's usin' you to get field hands," said Luke. "*That*

ain't what I'm askin'. You lost your mind—knockin' at our front
door?"

Sal felt Florrie shrink against him. Again he answered quietly.
This time, he made no attempt to parrot an accent. In his wife's
presence he still used the speech of the quarters. Among the men
of the new South—when occasion warranted—he had learned to
speak their language.

"We're free now," he said. "Ain't you heard?"

"I've heard, all right," said the overseer. "I still won't believe it.
Take your woman to the kitchen stoop. I'll try to find Mrs. Selby."

"Miss Reen said we could go inside."

Sal held his ground while the overseer's fingers balled into a fist.
He waited until Luke Jackson's hand dropped to his side. Then
he led Florrie into the house, ignoring Luke's black-browed scowl.

Earlier visits had prepared him for stripped-down rooms, chandeliers drowned in cheesecloth, and parquets innocent of carpet.
As her servants dwindled, the mistress of Selby had saved her home
as best she could: the fact that her famous twin parlor now served
as an office was eloquent testimony of the change. Plantation ledgers lay face open on a long trestle table, the pages bathed in the
sunlight that poured through uncurtained french doors. Since the
New Year (when her last hard money had vanished) these parlors
had served as auction rooms. Army contractors had swarmed here,
along with scalawags from Atlanta, while the Big House finery was
knocked down to the highest bidder.

It had been a touch-and-go time, but Selby had endured—even
when stripped to the bone. Now, if Sal could believe Miss Reen's
summons, it was time for the upturn.

Asking himself what had brought the change of fortune, Sal had
no clear answer. Rumor insisted that Miss Reen's brother had sent
help—since he was making another fortune in Mexico these days,
as a go-between for Maximilian and the Confederate *émigrés*. It
was logical that Quenten Rowley should send cash to Selby from
that distant El Dorado. . . . Sal shrugged off the enigma. Miss
Reen had said there were funds on hand. It was enough for now.

Settling at the account books, he understood the reason for Luke
Jackson's peevishness. The overseer's attempt to balance the ledgers for the first quarter of 1865 had foundered in a swamp of bad

arithmetic and ink-stained erasures. It was still apparent that the sale of plantation furniture and other items had fetched a tidy sum. Checking bills of sale against the ledgers, Sal wondered if Miss Reen had stripped her house deliberately, to finance her first post-war planting. . . . A closer look revealed another picture. The mistress of Selby had paid panic prices to feed her slaves before the mass exodus. There were still a few hundred gold dollars in the cashbox. But it would take thousands to make a crop in these dog-eat-dog times.

"Looks like you turned sto'keeper, Marse Luke," said Sal. "You done right well."

The overseer hovered in the foyer with a fist on each hip. "So it's still Marse Luke," he snarled. "What do I call *you*—Mr. Saladin?"

"Sal will do—an' we got no cause to fight. Ain't we worked for Miss Reen all through the war? Ain't I always balanced her books?"

"You're welcome to those damned accounts," said the overseer dourly. "I'll admit I can't make head nor tail of 'em. I'll also admit there's no one else in Cray County who can bring two hundred hands to work tomorrow——"

"Sho' can, Marse Luke. I got 'em waitin' now——"

"Assuming, of course, we can strike a bargain."

"We'll do that thing," said Sal. "Doan' let it fret you. Cotton-seed's as good as planted, if Miz Reen can pay us wages."

"She's prepared to pay. But see you keep your place, boy. Even if you *are* workin' in the parlor now, I can still skin you alive." Luke stalked out with that ponderous threat. A moment later Sal heard his feet on the uncarpeted stairs, and knew he had gone to summon his employer.

Florrie had retreated to the frame of the nearest window like a bird poised for flight. Sal leveled a finger at the couch, one of the few set pieces the room still boasted.

"Set there, gal," he ordered. "An' fold your hands like a lady. How often must I teach you?"

"You been uppity enough, Sal. I got no call t'*set*. Not in Miss Reen's house."

"Jes' do what I say—an' quit shakin'."

He had made himself comfortable behind the trestle table while he continued to argue—not so much with Florrie as with an unseen antagonist, whose name he could not quite spell out. Now, checking the last of the ledgers (which stood open at the current month), he drew in his breath sharply, forgetting his own fears at the sight of the figures before him.

"Fifty thousand dollahs, gal! They ain't that much money!" But the figures were still there (in rich black ink) when he looked again. Fifty thousand in gold, deposited to the credit of Selby Hall, at the brokerage firm of Curtis and Barton, London. . . . Curtis and Barton were the plantation's agents abroad: they could market a crop on any exchange the moment it was baled.

Quenten Rowley, it seemed, had backed his sister in good time. Only one thing was puzzling—and Sal admitted it was none of his affair. The check that Curtis and Barton had deposited to Selby's London account had come from a Philadelphia bank. Why would Quenten Rowley—who was still in Mexico—work through so remote a source?

Sal was still brooding happily over the splendid black-ink entry when he heard footsteps in the hall. He sprang to his feet as Miss Reen swept in. Her smile told him he was welcome here—even as it convinced him that she had risen above Selby's current crisis. . . . Today, in a loose housecoat that concealed her figure perfectly, she seemed at peace with herself and the world. Sal wondered if this was part of expectant motherhood—a hedge against fate while her child grew within her.

"It was good of you to come so soon," she said warmly. "You're both looking well. Better than *I've* dared to look since the war ended."

Florrie, Sal observed, had not quite checked a mechanical curtsy —but she found her voice. "Does we look diffrunt, ma'am? Ah sho' feels diffrunt."

"Are you married at last?"

"Yes'm. Since mawnin'."

"Let's hope it's a new day for us all then," said Miss Reen. "At least, we're putting the land to work."

Flanked by the ledgers, Sal answered promptly. This was a language he could speak with ease.

"This cash in London, ma'am. Is it in yo' name?"

"It is indeed, Sal."

"Reckon yo' can raise fifty thousand mo'—on the house?"

"Easily, in Atlanta."

Sal felt his heart expand with pride as he sensed the dimensions of the gamble and the vital role he would play in it.

"Miss Reen, can I say what I think?" (Already the mere act of addressing her on an equal plane had smoothed his English.)

"That's why I asked you here."

"They'll be bad trouble—if Cap'n Selby gets home befo' the crop's ginned."

"Why?"

"'Cause I cain't keep *all* our folks in Lincolnville. They's work turnin' up at the Varnells'. When we start here, we'll have strange hands——"

"There's no avoiding that, Sal. I understand."

"Yo' understand, Miss Reen. Will he?"

"We needn't worry too much about my husband."

"Is he dead then?"

"Far from it," said the mistress of Selby. Listening to that dry tone, Sal could detect no emotion.

"Folks say he's gone to Mexico."

"He plans to join the Emperor's army."

"Ain't he comin' back at *all*, ma'am?"

The flash of fire in Miss Reen's eyes told Sal he had gone too far. He waited breathless for her answer.

"Dr. Yancey has just returned from Atlanta," she said tonelessly. "For the past three days, he tells me, Captain Selby has been visiting there with brother officers. He has stated his plans, both publicly and in private. My guess is that he'll soon be on his way to New Orleans—and Vera Cruz. If he does pay Selby a visit, he won't linger."

"Can we plan without him then?"

"Yes, Sal. In fact, I think we must."

Sal kept his eyes on the ledger, feeling a great weight lift from his mind. "I got two hundred hands ready to break ground. Can we use that many?"

"Easily."

"Trust me, ma'am, when I say they's good workers."

"I trust you, Sal. I always have."

"We can buy seed cheap in Macon."

"Good. I was worried about that."

"I got carpenters in Lincolnville too. They'll build us a new pack-house in jig time, with the twins to show 'em how. An' we'll be needin' a new gin, come August——"

"One is on order now. From Heath's, in Baltimore."

Plunging into familiar routines, making rapid notes while Miss Reen spelled out her wishes, Sal felt he was home again. The last trace of awkwardness left him: he smiled across the room at Florrie, who continued to stare blankly, as though she could not quite believe this smooth-talking man of affairs was her husband. As always, Miss Reen's confidence in his judgments had restored his self-respect. It was only when he thought of Captain Selby that he felt the familiar rage constrict his heart—and with it those searing doubts for the future.

When they had finished the inventory of their assets, Sal laid down the pen and gathered the account books. "If you like, ma'am, I'll finish at home. Can I say one thing mo'?"

"Of course."

"Take back the Jedge's study for yo' office. Soon's I get the books in shape, I'll work out of Marse Luke's, same as always. Take my word, Miss Reen, yo' held yo' last auction."

The mistress of Selby nodded soberly and settled on the sofa— a move which brought Florrie to her feet. "You're right, Sal," she said. "We must begin to keep up appearances. Are you sure you'll have time to help—now you're in charge at Lincolnville?"

"I'll make time, ma'am."

"Is it true you've built a house there?"

"Yes, Miss Reen—it's free and clear."

"I wish I could give Florrie something for your home. But you see how things are here."

"We got all we need, Miss Reen," said Florrie. "Sal bought hit— 'long with dese sto' clo'es."

Sal sighed—and took his wife's arm. Some gulfs were still too wide to bridge—but he could not regret bringing her to this meeting.

"Time we left Miss Reen in peace," he said. "An' you got no call to act boastful."

"Ain't boastin', Sal. If Miss Reen want, Ah'll staht wuk hyah tomorra——"

Lorena shook her head firmly. "You've a home of your own now, Florrie," she said. "And a husband. You'll find that's a full-time job. Mammy Jo will look after me until Selby can afford servants again." The words were spoken calmly. It was the matter-of-fact tone that cut Sal to the heart—the admission that the great tide of change would never be reversed. . . . *We'll work for you in other ways*, he told her silently. *We'll prosper again, if all goes well. But we are no longer a part of Selby.*

On the drive again, clucking the sleepy mule awake, Sal looked hard at Florrie.

"Why'd you say you'd come back, gal? You knew she wouldn't let you."

"Sal, Ah couldn't believe we's free. Not till Ah heard *her* say hit."

"Believe it now?"

"Reckon so. But Ah's still skeered. Whut if she's wrong 'bout Marse Brad? S'pose he *do* come home—an' give black folks de whip again?"

Sal turned on her furiously—but found he was without words. Instead, they continued to stare at each other for a silent moment while the buckboard rattled across the rank fields of Selby. There was but one answer to the problem of Captain Selby. He dared not speak it aloud, not even in this high moment.

"Marse Brad's got to mind the law, same as anyone," he said at last.

"Y'mean, he doan' own me now? You *sho'*?"

"You b'long to yourself, Florrie. Cain't you understand?"

"An' to you, Sal."

"An' to me—cause you want to belong. Marse Brad's ownin' days are dead and gone."

2

Alone in the empty parlor, Reen sank to the sofa and covered her face with her hands. The wave of hysteria was brief: in a moment she was herself again. Still, she was glad to collect her thoughts before she summoned Luke.

She had planned this meeting with her two former slaves—if only to prove, however inadequately, that it was possible. The effort had been made, the bargain established. Now, thanks to Sal, two hundred hands would swarm into her fields tomorrow, ready to take orders from her overseer. With hard cash to pay their wages, she could put Selby on its feet again. With that end in view, she had dared today's fumble at democracy.

Reen knew her name had been cursed throughout the county for her treatment by the Union cavalry during the invasion. The fact that she had kept her rooftree standing after they had ridden on, the still more damning fact that a provost guard had protected her gates, only added fuel to the fire. She would be damned anew tomorrow, when she hired back her Negroes on Sal's terms—but there was no alternative if she meant to survive. With a child to support, a heritage to secure, she could bear her neighbors' hatred.

Thinking of the child, feeling the stir of life within her, she smiled at the secret she had refused to share with a living soul— even with Uncle Doc. It was a secret that made any compromise worth while.

Luke Jackson appeared promptly when she called his name. Aware that he had hovered outside the door to listen to her talk with Sal, she did not risk a reproach. Luke's loyalty had been badly shaken—but it was still alive.

"Sorry, ma'am," he said. "Reckon I should of stayed. But I couldn't swallow that black boy's sass."

"Freedom is a heady drug, Luke," she said patiently. "Perhaps it's gone to Sal's head a bit. But he's on our side."

"Do we have to take him back?"

"I already have—as bookkeeper and labor boss. We'd best call things by their right names."

"Who'll give the orders? Him or me?"

"You're in charge, Luke," she said wearily. "He'll see your orders are carried out."

"I've told you I don't need help, ma'am."

"Many of our people are working elsewhere. You won't know the new hands. Can't you let Sal back you?"

"My whip's all I'll need. No black man says no to it."

"Not when they had no choice. Today they're wage earners. If you mistreat them, they'll go elsewhere."

"So this boy calls the tune—just 'cause he's boss Nigra?"

"What if Sal *weren't* on our side? Could we make a crop?"

"Miss Reen, I've admitted he's ridin' high in the county. How did he build the best house in shantytown?"

"I know that answer too," she said. "Sal's the leader in Lincolnville because he saved his wages."

"All through the fightin'—when he had no right to wages."

"He earned them, Luke—as much as you."

"*I* didn't quit—when you couldn't pay me."

"Sal left the quarters—and took the others with him—because I ordered it."

"I'm still askin' why, ma'am."

"I had no right to keep Negroes on the land when I couldn't support them. Now they've settled in homes of their own. They can take work at a dozen places——"

The overseer spoke thickly, with his eyes on the floor. His voice seemed to issue from his own grave. "Does this mean you're behind your black boy—all the way?"

"It's cost me a great deal to admit it," said Reen, "but Sal calls the tune today. Perhaps he's grown into power too fast. It could make trouble later—for us all. The fact remains he has a labor force and a will to survive. With his loyalty, we'll be solvent in six months. I can even pay your back wages."

"I'd rather work for nothin'."

The mistress of Selby got to her feet. Luke (she thought) had always been faithful for the wrong reasons—but she could not afford to dismiss him now: her position in the county was already precarious enough.

"Give this new system a fair trial," she said. "Remember we're making a crop—even if we're late in planting it."

"Thanks to your brother's money," Luke said grudgingly.

"Do you resent that contribution too?"

"No, ma'am, I don't. But I can't take it kindly that you've made Sal my equal here. It won't last, and you know it."

"Promise you'll make no trouble—or we must part company today."

"I ain't leavin'," said the overseer. "At least, not now."

"May I ask why?"

Luke's tanned cheeks turned scarlet. "You're carryin' your husband's child, ma'am. You need a white man's protection until he settles here again. Doc Yancey's done what he could—but he's gettin' old." The overseer swallowed the rest in time as Uncle Doc stumped down the portico, his jaw clamped on a contraband cigar. "If you'll excuse me, I'll go about my business. I've said my piece —twice over."

The two men exchanged curt nods when they passed in the doorframe. Observing the exchange, Reen could understand Luke's resentment well enough. Since the burning of the packhouse the overseer had been a caged tiger: with no outlet for his strength, he had simply exploded in temper. Today Sal had been the inevitable target. The plantation doctor was also a focal point for his choler, since he had recently offered his services at a hospital in Atlanta which cared for Union and Confederate wounded impartially. Nor could Luke forgive Uncle Doc for serving the Negroes from Selby, without charge, at their new settlement. In his book it was unthinkable that a man could keep a foot in both camps—that he could pardon both and hate neither.

Thanks to his new schedule, Uncle Doc was much afield these days, though he slept at the Big House when his work permitted. Today he had gone on a special errand at Reen's request. The twinkle in his eye told her that he brought the news she expected —and feared.

"It's true then? Major Carroll is back?"

"He moved in at Four Cedars yesterday," said Yancey cheerfully. "Bought the whole shebang outright—and paid what I'd call a fair price, in these times. When he gets clear title he's taking over the Varnell land as well."

Reen drew in her breath as the import of the statement sank home. The rumor of Dan Carroll's return had reached her yesterday—and even then she had guessed it was fact, not gossip. Outsiders had already begun to take up land in Cray County—usually at their own figures, now the plantation economy was prostrate. The sale of Four Cedars, however, was by far the largest of its kind. If Carroll could also acquire the Varnell land, his boundaries would touch her own.

"Don't pretend you're surprised," said Uncle Doc. "When he promised to come back he meant it."

"Why must he come now? He couldn't have chosen a worse time."

"With Brad in Atlanta? There's no reason for them to meet."

"Brad is sure to hear the major was quartered at Selby during the March. How can I explain his return? What can I say to *him* —if he tries to call here?"

"I'll answer the first question," said Yancey. "What an absent husband don't know won't hurt him."

"Then I'm to tell Brad nothing?"

"Nothing whatever. Including the fact that his forthcoming heir was sired by a Yankee. *That's* a fact we'll share with no one."

Reen closed her eyes as the plantation doctor continued to study her with his good-humored grin. Had she met that level gaze she would have burst into a crazy peal of laughter—and Uncle Doc's news was not the sort to inspire mirth.

"So you think the child was Daniel's," she said at last. "It's something you can't prove."

"True enough," said Yancey resignedly. "Just remember Brad must never suspect. As the Bard of Avon remarked, it's a wise father who knows his own child."

"And what do I say to Daniel?"

"He's a neighbor now. Isn't it good form to receive him when he calls?"

"I *can't*, Uncle Doc!"

"You might even thank him—for keeping your head above water."

"You've guessed then—about our London money?"

"Naturally—the moment you told me."

"That fifty thousand dollars came from *Quent*," said Reen. "The county believes it—and you're backing the story."

"I already have," said Yancey. "In my opinion, you showed rare good sense in taking it."

"I'm in a corner—and I must fight my way out. Try not to enjoy my suffering."

"Why should you suffer?" asked Uncle Doc. "Because you spent a night with Dan Carroll? Your reasons were better than most."

"It was a sin. Don't pretend it wasn't."

The plantation doctor shrugged. "Have it your way, girl. But in your heart you're glad he's back in Georgia."

"Give me one good reason."

"He's in love with you—isn't that something?"

"He *said* he loved me, the night the packhouse burned. I wouldn't listen then—and I won't now."

"How can you help it when you're using his money?"

"He's a rich man who's made me a loan. In the circumstances, I'm forced to accept it."

"Sure you don't love him a little in return?"

Reen did not stir when she answered: she was proud of the smoothness of her lie. "Very well, Uncle Doc—since you insist. I'm grateful to Daniel for giving me a child. There's no deeper feeling."

"Why not?"

"Because I'm a Selby. Call it my cross, if you like. I'll bear it for my son's sake."

"Surely you owe Dan more than gratitude."

"What are you suggesting?"

"I'm making no suggestions, Lorena. I'm stating your problem. You belong to one man legally, and you're loved by another. What comes next?"

"Nothing. I mean to go on as before."

"Brad's hell-bent for Mexico. Suppose he leaves Georgia without meeting Dan?"

"In that case I'll restore Selby. Once that's done, I'll raise my boy and await my husband's return."

"What becomes of Dan?"

"His future is his own concern. I'll have no part of it. Tongues have wagged over me enough. I'll give them no further cause."

"In that case it's only fair to send him back to Four Cedars. He's waiting outside now."

So far, Reen had heard Yancey in a kind of helpless limbo. Expecting such an attack, she had been prepared with her answers. Now, faced with Dan's imminent appearance, she felt nothing but a glow of anticipation. It confused her far more than the fear she had expected, once this moment was upon her.

"Can't he come back tomorrow?"

"It would only be harder then."

Reen drew herself up proudly. Uncle Doc was right. This was an inevitable meeting: it was futile to postpone it.

"Is this his first stop?"

"Naturally, since you were his hostess during his previous visit to the county," said Yancey with the widest of grins. "He's leaving cards tomorrow at Hamilton Hundred and Greentree. Not that he hopes to be received."

"What if I side with the county—and say I'm not at home?"

"Is that the message I'm to convey, Lorena?"

"Of course not. Just stay where you are: I'll need someone to fall back on."

Uncle Doc shook his head. "Sorry, my dear. I'd give a great deal to witness this reunion—but it's something you must handle alone." He strode out on that pronouncement so quickly she could not call him back.

Once she had forced herself to stand her ground, Reen discovered she could control the urge to flight. Memory was another matter: it had already turned traitor at the very moment when she needed poise so desperately. The flaming impact of Dan's first kiss returned to her—and took her breath away. . . . She had made a bargain with this Yankee, she told herself. There had been a fixed end in view, and it had justified the means.

Her hands closed fiercely on her swollen body and the precious freight it housed. Once again she insisted that she did not regret her temporary surrender, since she had made it for the good of Selby. Later she would repay the money Dan Carroll had loaned her. Now that he stood a second time on her doorstep he had no right to expect more.

Braced as she was for Carroll's appearance, Reen could not avoid staring as he crossed the lawn.

She had expected him to be in uniform. In white linen, with a flowered waistcoat and riding boots, he seemed a stranger. Outwardly, at least, he was a Southern planter—but the effect of costume remained. Wondering how many eyes had watched him enter her drive, she forced herself to take a demure step forward.

"So you're back in Georgia, Daniel," she said calmly. "I could hardly believe it when I heard. That's why I sent Uncle Doc to make sure."

"You knew I'd return, Lorena—the moment I could."

He moved toward her slowly, as though aware that she needed time to adjust to his presence. Welcoming him again with a small, grave gesture, she offered him the sofa—the only comfortable seat the room boasted.

"Tell me about yourself," she said—pleased that her hostess tone was still flawless.

Carroll ignored the invitation as their eyes held. For one giddy moment she feared he would take her in his arms. So far (thanks to her loose housecoat), he could hardly have guessed her condition. She wondered if she should announce it at once: the knowledge she was with child might force him to keep his distance. Try as she might, she could not force out the words. . . . *Once and for all*, she told herself, *this must be a matter-of-fact parting, a sundering without pain. You can never ask for his pity.*

"Surely you knew the date of my arrival," he said. "Or did my letter go astray?"

"That could hardly happen, Daniel. It came by Army courier."

"You read it carefully, I trust?"

She nodded. "Including the fact you'd deposited fifty thousand dollars with my London agents."

Carroll let his glance sweep the empty parlor. "I'd have told you that much long ago," he said. "Unfortunately, there was no way to get news through the backwash of the war. I might have saved your furniture if Lee had surrendered a month sooner."

"Furniture doesn't matter—if one's house still stands."

"Dr. Yancey told me what you've gone through," he said. "There's no need to make light of it."

Again Reen nodded slowly. "I'll accept your loan and thank you for it," she said. "As you can see, I've little choice. Why did you settle on that particular amount?"

"It was the book value of your cotton. And it isn't a loan—it's a recompense."

"You owed me nothing for the cotton," she said. "And nothing for what came after. Selby was spared—that was our bargain. Fifty thousand seems high pay for one night of love."

She had hoped to shock him with her boldness—to destroy, however crudely, the web of tenderness he had cast about her. It had been a long time since she had known tenderness, or yielded to his soft compulsion: she would be lost if she yielded now. . . . When he shook off the import of her words (as easily as a man smiling at the tantrum of a child), she knew she had failed.

"I didn't seek you out that morning," he said. "There was no time for a proper good-by. Otherwise I'd have asked for an understanding. That's why I'm here now."

"What's left to understand? I shared your bed—and you protected Selby. The bargain ended when I left your arms."

"Is that all it meant to you?"

"How could it mean more to either of us? Was it your first wartime affair? Are you that much of a Puritan?"

Again she had sought in vain to shake him with a callous disavowal. When he took her hands, she snatched them free and put the trestle table between them.

"Look at me again," he said. "Tell me it was just a bargain to save your home. I'll try to believe you."

She met his eyes then, with the cashboxes between them, narrowing her own eyes a trifle to make the words convincing. "I told you as much at the time," she said. "I won't say I regret the bargain. If that makes me a hussy, so much the worse. But there'll be no aftermaths—even though I *have* been forced to accept your money. If that's why you're in Georgia, your mission is accomplished."

She was glad he turned away after her barefaced lie: she was fighting for her life, and could hardly have continued the deception a moment more. Settling at the table, cupping her chin in her hands to stop their trembling, she watched him closely while he surveyed the room a second time. The inventory was a thorough one: she knew he was collecting himself while he checked on the visible evidence of the auctions she had held here.

"I said I'd believe you," he told her at last—pausing at a great bare spot above the mantel where an Adam mirror had once hung. "I'll keep that promise. But my mission here is only beginning. As it happens, I've returned for several reasons. Your welfare is the most compelling—but the others are worth mention."

"Dr. Yancey tells me you've bought Four Cedars."

"That's just a start. Our land will have a common boundary in a few months' time. Next week I'm putting in the first crop Four Cedars has produced since '61. With fallow land, I may outbale Selby."

"Is this a new challenge?" she asked with a flashing glance. Now she had carried off her falsehood she felt she could fence with him on equal terms.

"Call it a friendly rivalry between neighbors," he said—and moved at last to the sofa. With his long, white-clad legs crossed, and his riding crop tapping a varnished boot top, he seemed more Southern squire than ever.

"Do you mean to turn cotton grower here—because of a quixotic argument we had last autumn?"

"Don't give yourself too much credit," he said quietly. "It was a promise I made myself long before we met. I feel it's my destiny to bridge a gap in our country's growth—by turning farmer in the midst of what you'd call my enemies. I intend to teach those enemies to be my friends. If that sounds pompous, forgive me. As a former lawyer I'm apt to speak rhetorically."

Again Reen produced a model hostess smile. "Could this be a guilty conscience speaking?"

"My conscience is at rest," he said. "I won't even apologize for helping to win the war. Not if I can do my part to win the peace."

"You've loaned me the cash to put Selby to work again. Isn't that more than enough?"

"For the last time, Lorena, it was repayment for damage, not a loan. And it was only a beginning for us both. Give me time: I'll show you how good a neighbor I can be. Don't forget you'll soon need help in other ways."

"Then we're to have a military occupation?"

"It's inevitable, with the Radicals taking over Congress. I think it's a ghastly mistake to saddle the South with a peacetime army. At least, I can make sure Cray County's occupation is managed fairly."

"Are you in charge of that too?"

Carroll lifted his eyes from the flick of his riding crop. "Not yet. But I'm confident I'll be assigned as military commander of your district, since I'm a landholder."

"You mean you've arranged it, don't you?"

"Such things are simple, if you've funds to pay for them, and friends in the War Department. In any event, I'm here to stay, and quite alive to your best interests. We'll have ample time to work out our plans."

"We've no plans to share, Daniel. Haven't you heard a word I've said?"

"I've listened carefully, Lorena. It's my words that have fallen on deaf ears. First of all, I love you. Surely that gives me the right to speak."

"Not if I don't return your love."

"You will in time," he said. "I'm staking everything on that belief."

"For what reason?"

"Because you're a woman starved for love. Not that we need labels for this thing we've shared. I'm aware you've problems here— and they won't be solved easily. As I say, I've no wish to press you."

"Thanks for that much," she said with the faintest of smiles.

"I'd go tomorrow if I felt you'd be happier without my presence. But you'll need friends when the Army moves in. You *must* see I'll be useful."

"Of course I do, Daniel. Don't think I'm not grateful."

"Rebuild here, by all means. Make Selby flourish once more. The job will be done eventually. We'll knock down our fences then, and join hands."

"You do take things for granted, Major Carroll."

"No, Lorena. But I can hope. I think you should grant me that much."

She kept her voice steady with a last effort. "My husband is in Atlanta. When he returns, I'll ask him to give you a mortgage." It was a futile attempt, and she knew it: she could never tell Brad the truth about that fifty-thousand dollar draft in London. Brad would let Selby rot before he accepted a Yankee loan.

"The transaction is between you and me," said Dan. "Your husband has no part of it."

"My husband owns Selby."

"He doesn't own you—he never could. You're free to choose between us. I'm asking for the woman Brad Selby never knew, the one I brought to life."

Carroll got up from the sofa. Had he so much as touched her hand, she knew she would have yielded. Instead, he bent to pick up his hat and riding crop with the air of a man who has made his point and refuses to press his advantage further. The pause was her salvation. When he moved toward her, she had regained her poise.

"You're asking for a great deal, Major."

"Perhaps. But I'll not settle for less."

"I'm afraid I must wish you good morning then."

"As you wish, Lorena," he said. "But there can be no real peace between us—until we finish what we began here."

When she found an answer, her voice was low and taut. "Can't you face the facts, Daniel? I'm married to this land—and the man who owns it. I belong to both, like any beast of burden."

"That isn't true. It can't be."

"Until I know my husband's wishes I can't even think clearly."

"I understand he's about to take off for Mexico, and another war."

"I'm not at liberty to discuss Captain Selby's plans," she told him stiffly.

"Have it your way," he said. "It's unlikely he'll trouble us in the immediate future. Meanwhile I'll do my best to turn into a Georgian."

"Georgians are born, not made."

"That's another myth I intend to disprove."

She did not stir as he took her hand and kissed it before he left her. It was the briefest of contacts, but she could feel her resolve turn to jelly while it lasted. . . . Only when she stood alone once more did she realize that she had won her desperate struggle for survival. Major Carroll had left the field—after what had been, at best, an intense skirmish. To continue the martial metaphor, he had retired to a prepared position while he awaited her next move. This was an armistice—and she knew he would maintain it faithfully.

While that truce lasted, her two great secrets were safe. The Yankee invader had not guessed she was carrying his child. Nor did he know that she loved him—and would go on loving him to the day she died.

3

If you want a good time
Jine the cavalry . . .

Riding down the river road that led to his domain, Captain Bradfield Selby sang in time with the drumming hoofs of a mount that (like its rider) seemed rather the worse for wear. The song ended in doleful cacophony after he had reined in briefly at the entrance to Hamilton Hundred and stared at the fire-gutted façade beyond. *You must still be drunk,* he told himself. *Only a fool would sing in the midst of ruin.* Yet he still felt lighthearted as a schoolboy as he urged his horse into a gallop and covered the last mile to his own gateposts.

Selby had been spared—save for the gin fire: Reen had kept the house intact. That much he had heard in Atlanta—and he had rejoiced in the knowledge as a signpost to the future. Even today, when the scalawag was king in the South, his house and land represented a solid value. Now that his plans were set, now that his star shone bright again, he could afford to ignore the catastrophes that had overtaken less fortunate neighbors. The race, as always, was to the swift. Old Hamilton was too feeble (and too haunted by the past) to go with him to Mexico. Mary Buell had no choice but to wear her widow's black in the ruins of Greentree. It was a different story for Captain Bradfield Selby—and the captain's wife.

He reined in once more at the crossroad, aware that his piebald mount (ridden at a killing speed from Atlanta) showed signs of collapsing beneath him. The wretched animal had earned a breather

—and he needed a moment more to choose the best way to broach his plan to Reen.

Perhaps he should have written her from Atlanta—or, at the very least, sent some word via Yancey. Of course, it was beyond belief that she would oppose his will: from their wedding day his word had been law. History was to blame if he had been forced to give her this taste of independence during the war years.

One thing was certain: he was leaving Georgia until the balance righted. His wife was part of the bright future he had visioned, if not an outright essential. Recalling the champagne-gay evening he had passed with his brothers in arms, he felt a profound sense of mission invade his brain. While it lasted, it was strong enough to blot out externals—including the morning-after headache that sounded its anvil's chorus behind his eyeballs.

A glass of Selby's famous brandy (decanted, as only Ulysses could, from a keg in the cellar) would dispose of the headache. It would also restore his *amour-propre* before he put Reen in her place. The tired horse trembled under his hard cavalryman's knees, but he roweled it mercilessly until it broke into a gallop. Beyond the bend the gateposts of Selby rose unscarred in the bright spring sun. Even this tottering Rosinante would bring him safely to his portico.

Brad had expected to find his lawns a jungle, and his rose gardens gone to brambles. It did not shock him unduly to observe the chasm among the work buildings where the packhouse had once stood. But he was unprepared for the sight of strange black men in his fields— for the purposeful labor that had already laid out a good hundred acres of cotton rows in his first quarter section, and had begun to break ground in another. So great was his astonishment, he did not roar out a protest when several of the field hands stared at him blankly—apparently unaware that the master of Selby had ridden in. He had noted many such cases of insolence on the road home— and had grown weary of flogging the wrongdoers into servility.

In the old days his house slaves had been ordered out en masse to greet his home-comings. There was a boy to catch his reins—and another to brush the dust from his shoulders. Ulysses, if he was warned in time, would be ready at the carriage block with a mint-sprigged glass. . . . Today the drive was empty—and the tall house (new-painted though it was) seemed empty as a mausoleum. He felt his fingers itch for the whiskey in his saddle boot—but he resisted the need for a bracer until he had ridden into the horse barn. After he had drained the flask, his spirits lifted a trifle. It had been a long ride from Atlanta—and the road had been thick with memories.

His spirits rose still higher as he crossed the lawn and mounted the south portico. Here, at least, was the Selby he remembered: the lush spring grass was a green carpet, the antic roosters and dragons in the box hedges were pruned to their accustomed shapes. The glimpse of Reen in the parlor gave his home-coming dimension and meaning—and an instant focus for his wrath.

His wife was bent over an account book—and wore the loose, homespun cotton work dress he had cursed a thousand times. The room behind her was stripped to the woodwork—he had expected that. Hard times beyond belief had stalked through Georgia in Sherman's wake: it was too much to hope that Reen had escaped entirely. What he could not forgive was her appearance. Come what may, the chatelaine of Selby Hall had no right to show herself downstairs in a crokersack. . . . Or so Brad thought as he stalked into his home at last, via one of the wide-open french doors.

He had intended to stand before Reen with quiet dignity, letting his battle-scarred presence announce his return. He had promised himself that he would not speak—until she had apologized for the icy reserve she had shown him on his last leave. Now he had the uneasy conviction that he must shout to gain her attention. . . . The wall between them was invisible, but he felt its presence keenly.

"Is this your best greeting?" he demanded.

Reen looked up from her account book. When their eyes met, her calm acceptance of his arrival enraged him even more. Holding his anger on leash, he circled the trestle table warily.

"Welcome home, Brad," she said—and dropped her eyes at last.

"Thank you for that much, my dear," he growled, sweeping off his sun-faded campaign sombrero in the deepest of bows. "For a moment I thought you didn't quite remember me."

"I heard you were wounded," she said in the same oddly withdrawn tone. "Is it true?"

"I was a casualty at Petersburg," he said, forcing himself to match her manner. "It was only a Minié ball—in the shoulder. But it was a long time healing."

"I also heard that you've been in Atlanta since Friday," said Reen. "Couldn't you have sent me some word?"

"I was busy—making plans for us both."

"At least your wound is healed. And you're home again."

"Would you call *this* home?" He found he had roared the question.

"I've kept your roof standing, and I'm putting in a crop. It's more than most Georgians can say."

"How? With your two hands?"

"I have money—from Quent. I've hired two hundred workers from Lincolnville. You must have seen them in the fields."

Brad dashed his sombrero to the floor and ground it under his spurs. Atlanta had buzzed with the news of Reen's windfall: he knew she had proceeded with spring sowing without awaiting his permission. Faced with the actuality, he let his temper rip out of control.

"Damn Quent Rowley's charity! And damn those hands you've brought in for hire! Selby isn't worth rebuilding. Certainly not on such terms."

"We're putting in a new packhouse," she said as calmly as though she had not even heard his outburst. "And I've ordered a new gin from Baltimore. They'll ship it by way of Mobile. We can run off twice the bales——"

"What right have you to buy a cotton gin without consulting me?"

"The money is mine, Brad. I'm using it as I see fit."

"Not when I've made other plans. Not with strangers moving into the county and slaves calling themselves our equals. I'm going to take you away from this debacle. How soon can you be ready?"

"Away from *Selby?*"

"Packets are leaving New Orleans for Vera Cruz each Tuesday. I've already booked a cabin. We can use your precious brother's cash to pay for it."

"Are you out of your mind?"

"We mean to continue the war from the Rio Grande," he said. "Whole regiments are moving through Texas now to join forces with Maximilian. We've generals to spare, and a battle plan. There's land in Mexico, for those who wish to settle. And titles in the Emperor's court, if you have the price."

"I've heard those fables too. Don't tell me you believe them."

"Ask Quent, if you want a witness. He's down there now, making a killing in land deals. I mean to do likewise when I'm not in the field."

"Would you really desert Selby?"

"What does Selby mean to me—with no son to inherit? I put it on the Atlanta market yesterday. The scalawags will grab anything that's still whole—and pay well."

"This land has belonged to your family since Oglethorpe. You *can't* give it up."

"Don't think the sale will be permanent. We'll win Selby back in a few years' time—just as we'll win back Georgia."

"The war is lost, Brad. Why start another?"

"To my friends the surrender of Lee and Johnston is only an armistice. I tell you, a new day's dawning south of the border. Maximilian is hand in glove with our cause, and I'm told his court is second to none in Europe. He welcomes men of parts. With Quent already in Mexico, and with what I get for Selby, I'll soon be back where I belong. Frankly, I don't intend to settle for less than a dukedom. With my battle record, I think I deserve one." He broke off triumphantly as she turned away with a helpless lift of her hands. He knew the gesture well. In the past it had meant his will had prevailed one more time.

"You and Mexico should suit each other perfectly," she said.

Brad recovered his sombrero from the floor and stroked the worn felt into shape. He regretted his tirade a little. It was natural that Reen should be thunderstruck by his scheme. Obviously, her limited imagination needed time to take in the horizons he had opened.

"I knew you'd see things my way," he said. Now he had driven home his point, his voice was almost kind. "We'll re-create the true South in Mexico—and remake history, too. More than a hundred men from my company have pledged their help. There'll be thousands more by the time we arrive. My guess is we'll control the country in six months."

"What then? Will you cross the Rio Grande and reconquer the South?"

"Stranger things have happened, Reen. My brother officers are bringing their wives. We've arranged a meeting place in New Orleans——"

She turned to face him, her head high and her shoulders set. "Join them by all means then—if it's what you really want. There's cash on hand for your steamer fare. And Quent will help you, if he's still in Mexico. But don't ask me to be part of this insane scheme. I'm needed here."

Brad stared at her blankly—positive he had not heard aright. "You said you grasped my reasons for going."

"I do, perfectly."

"I'm ordering you to share the journey. You're my wife—or doesn't that mean anything?"

"It means a great deal, Brad. So much, I refuse to give up your land."

"Even if I swear to win it back—along with Georgia?"

"Do you honestly believe you can do that?"

"The Confederate States Army is the greatest fighting force the world has known. We can still win this war, once it's reassembled."

"After your own leaders have given up?"

He lifted a hand to strike her. "Whose side are you on, Reen?"

"The war is over, Brad. Our only chance is to stay where we belong—and rebuild."

"And knuckle under to Yankees?"

"Why not? They're the winners."

"I'd die first. So would you—if you'd kept your pride."

"My pride is in my land and my heritage. I'm defending both."

He gave up the argument for the moment, and stormed to the cellaret that held his decanters, only to find it empty. The discovery that Selby was bone-dry was the straw that broke him. Flinging himself on the couch (like a child who has just been scolded), he felt tears of frustration sting his eyelids. When he raised his head he was glad to see that Reen had left the room. She was standing on the portico, watching a procession of field hands take the short cut from fields to barn, as the work bell sounded the nooning.

"Where's my brandy?" The question was shouted at an enemy

who refused to take shape. He hardly expected his wife to answer—
and faced her in some confusion as she returned to the room.

"Really, Brad. You should know better than to ask."

"Old Yancey said he'd bury the kegs."

"We dug them up last month and sold them at auction. Along
with the Selby silver and china. And your three hunters."

"You had no authority——"

"You left mortgages in Atlanta. When the bank closed, they
were bought up by land jobbers. What could I do? Refuse to meet
interest payments—let everything go for a song?"

"Very well, Reen," he said between clenched teeth. "You needn't
hit a man when he's saying good-by to all he holds dear."

"Don't you want a true picture?"

"Damn your true pictures! Where are my house slaves? Why
wasn't a boy at the carriage block to catch my bridle?"

"The slaves left the quarters when I could no longer feed them.
You must have heard they've settled at the Forks."

"The shantytown they call Lincolnville?"

"Today the people in that shantytown hire out as wage earners."

"Is it true one of our own slaves is their ringleader?"

"Without Sal, I'd be unable to start a crop. So would every landowner in the county who can afford to plant this spring."

"You'll never make a crop here. I've told you Selby's on the
block."

"Suppose I advance you the passage money—and deposit ten
thousand to your account in Mexico City? Will you leave Georgia
quietly? Let me manage Selby until you've had enough of swash-
buckling?"

"I won't be bribed," he said sullenly. "You're coming with me."
His hand closed on her wrist with the command—but she broke
free easily. He had forgotten her strength: it had always seemed a
trifle indecent in a woman.

"Look at me!" she cried. Her voice matched his in fury. "Even
you must see why I can't leave Selby."

"Give me one sound reason."

"Don't you want your heir to be born an American?"

He stared at her then, as though he could not get enough of
staring. With the hot noon sun behind her, he saw her (perhaps

for the first time) as a woman, not merely as a blind resistance he must beat down. There was no mistaking the opulence of her figure, despite that shapeless dress.

"Are you sure, Reen?"

"Of course I'm sure."

"When d'you expect the child?"

"Uncle Doc says it will come in August."

"You're quite right," he said slowly. "The boy must be born on Georgia soil. All Selbys were—since our first land grant."

"You won't sell out then?"

"How can I—now?" Brad had recovered both his spirits and his aplomb. Seizing his wife's hands, he whirled her into a quick waltz step before he went capering across the room—leaping high above the bare parquet with a series of heel clicks like pistol shots. The rebel yell he loosed set the chandeliers dancing.

"*Yaaaaaaaaaaaaaaaaah!* A boy at last, by God! Where the devil's my brandy? I want to drink his health."

"And mine, Brad?"

He recalled his wife's presence a trifle belatedly. She was standing where he had left her, in the bath of light from the garden. Her feet were planted firmly, and one hand rested on her hip. In a fit of pique he had called it her "peasant's pose." At the moment, it suited perfectly. . . . Rummaging in his cellaret, he came up with a dusty goblet, which he lifted to her in solemn homage.

"And *your* health too, Reen—even if I must toast you with an empty glass. Thank you for making me a father."

"I'm glad you're proud of *something* I've done."

"Proud? I haven't been prouder since I killed my last Yankee." He leaped high in another *entrechat*, a second, earsplitting yell. "*Yaaaaaaaaaah!* I've something to come home to now."

"You still plan to go to Mexico?"

"Naturally. Don't think I'd deprive my son of a dukedom."

"No, Brad. I'm sure you wouldn't want to do that."

Some of his exultation seeped away. Reen's level eyes, her dry-as-dust tone discouraged hilarity. Anger was the quickest escape: he took it by rote.

"How long have you known you were pregnant?"

"Since early December."

"Why didn't you write me?"

"How could I? When I wasn't sure you were alive or dead?"

She had all but screamed the words. Prepared for anything but wrath, he fell back a step.

"Which did you hope for, Reen?"

"God help me, I don't know." Her fury had gone as abruptly as it came. Before he could challenge her again, she ran from the room.

Brad considered following her—if only to pin down the terms of their agreement—then shrugged off the need. Reen, after all, had earned that explosion of nerves. A woman with child (he reflected) was seldom her natural self. He could rely on her backing when he took off for Vera Cruz next Tuesday, thanks to that bank balance in London.

He had returned to the plantation only to announce his plans. Now that she had refused (for good reason) to accompany him, he would meet his destiny alone. In a way, he could not help feeling a sense of relief—and gratitude to Reen. Brad Selby had always cut his widest swath alone.

It was imperative that he return to Atlanta, to confer with friends who had promised to share his voyage to Vera Cruz. Before he turned to go he scribbled a New Orleans address on the first blank page of the ledger. He left it open where Reen could not fail to see: she would understand the hint, and send him funds before his sailing date.

For a moment more he stood in the stripped-down parlor, fighting the conviction that he was the only living thing in an open tomb. The nightmare had haunted him of late: a change of air would cure it fast enough. . . . No useful purpose would be served by lingering at Selby—with a pregnant wife who lost her temper at the first touch of the spur.

He thought of seeking out Luke Jackson, and decided against it. There would be time to spare in New Orleans: he could send the overseer his orders by mail. Clapping on his hat, Captain Bradfield Selby prepared to quit his domain with no regrets.

Halfway down the portico, remembering a locked cabinet in the study that had once held a cache of brandy and cigars, he returned on the off-chance it had escaped the auctioneers. The tobacco was gone—but two cobwebbed bottles were tucked away behind the secret panel. With a load of this sort to balance his saddlebags, the ride to Atlanta would be a pleasant one. He was humming again as he turned to the parlor door.

On the threshold he realized he was no longer alone downstairs.

The blackamoor who stood turning the pages of Reen's account book had come in unannounced. The neat linen coat he was wearing had come from a white man's store. So had his riding breeches and boots, and the hat he had tossed on the table. Even his manner, thought Brad, was borrowed from his betters. There was no mistaking his air of ease as he settled in a chair, tore out the page that contained the New Orleans address—and, folding it between the covers, began making busy entries.

Brad knew it was Sal, though the fellow's back was turned. His bellow of protest was instinctive.

"What are you doing here?"

Sal rose from his chair. He did not speak at once—and there was something in his poise that suggested Brad, not he, was the intruder.

"Mornin', Captain Selby," he said at last. His voice was drily polite.

"You black ape, can't you *speak* like a Nigra?"

Sal's eye did not waver. "We speak the same language now, Captain."

"I've told you to keep out of my house——"

"Miss Reen hired me as her labor boss."

"Get out of Selby—and stay out!"

Sal did not budge when Brad charged the table, remembered in time that a bottle was cradled in each arm, and paused to set down the burden. Had his fists been free, they would have fastened on the Negro's throat—but the act of safeguarding the brandy gave him pause to reflect. *This is Reen's doing,* he thought. *And you put the reins in her hands.*

"Who said you could work here?" he barked.

"Miss Reen, Captain. It's only till we move her books to the study. Then I'll be usin' Marse Luke's office, same as before."

"Very well," said Brad. His rage was in control now—enough, at any rate, to permit him to fire thunderbolts at will. "I won't countermand Mrs. Selby's instructions. Not when I'm on my way to Mexico——"

"I wish you a safe journey, sir."

"I wouldn't," said Brad. "Not if I were in your shoes. When I come back to stay I'll probably kill you. Maybe I should do the job now."

He had let his hand fall on his pistol. Drawing it from its holster, cocking the hair-trigger hammer, he felt his self-respect return in a great, hot flood. Something in the black man's eyes told him the threat had registered—though he continued to stand his ground.

"Can't you be done with killin', Captain?"

"Not while your kind's aboveground." Brad had spoken solemnly, with a heavy emphasis on each syllable: the fact that he was retrieving the brandy at the moment (he felt) did not lessen the threat. It was only when he stood at the carriage block outside that he realized Sal's thin-lipped smile had been as scornful as his own. . . . Was it possible the burrhead failed to realize he had just signed his death warrant?

Dropping a bottle into each saddlebag, Brad vaulted to the horse's back as lightly as he had done in his first action. The animal seemed winded despite its rest, but he spurred it into a headlong charge down the driveway. Today it was essential that he leave Selby at a gallop.

He looked back just once at the gate, though he was positive that Reen had failed to witness his departure. Not that it mattered if she was sulking upstairs—so long as she awaited his return with the proper blend of respect and fear.

On the turnpike he permitted his mount to slow to a jog trot. His hand closed on the saddlebag, and he felt his last tension melt away as he breathed deep of the Georgia spring. Not every barn was burned on the highroad. With two bottles for company, he could rest the horse at the next haymow, doze away the afternoon in the shade, and finish his ride in the cool of evening.

As a veteran he had learned to take his rest where he found it. As a man of destiny he could afford a nap, now he held the future in his hand.

4

Andrew Selby was born in the dog-day heat of August, when the fields were a white foam of bursting cotton bolls—and the new gin from Baltimore (bedded firmly on its stone foundation) waited to process a banner crop.

Uncle Doc (who enjoyed these guessing games with nature) had written down the tenth as Reen's delivery date. Considering the mother's eagerness, he was glad that the child had arrived on schedule. The birthing had been announced at the day's end, when Sal's workers streamed in from the rich green furrows. At Reen's behest Yancey himself had gone to the balcony outside her bedroom to shout the news. His ears still echoed with the roar of joy that had risen from two hundred throats as the tidings spread. . . . It had been fitting, he thought, that the mistress of Selby and her workers should rejoice together.

That night, they had lingered beneath the portico to serenade the new arrival—until Uncle Doc had been forced to dismiss them so the mother could sleep. Reen's man child had received the tribute in silence. Then, like infants the world over, he had responded with his own wailing cry—a salute to life no less instinctive than the pagan music from the lawn.

Now it was over (Yancey told himself) he had been sure the child would be a boy. Just as he had known that Reen would name him Andrew, after the Judge.

From his first cry, Andy had been in lusty health—and Reen, like mothers everywhere, had gloried in his beauty. Standing at her bedside that evening, Uncle Doc had realized the true meaning of fulfillment. Cynic though he was, his eyes were wet. So were Mammy Jo's when she came forward to take the infant and dress him in his swaddling clothes.

In the three days that followed the accouchement, the plantation doctor had studied child and mother narrowly. Strangely enough— since boys so often resemble their fathers—Andy seemed to favor Reen rather than Dan Carroll. The resemblance, Yancey thought, harked back (by who knew what mystery of inheritance) to the earliest Rowleys—perhaps to the pirate forebear who had given the family its first push toward riches. The child's head was crowned with black ringlets; even now Uncle Doc guessed that the large, wide eyes would be as dark as Reen's. Eight pounds at birth, the boy was wonderfully formed. What heartened the watching physician most was the way he pulled at his mother's breast from the first day—so fiercely that pain and delight were mingled in Reen's face as she looked down at him with adoring eyes. . . .

On the fourth morning after the birth, Yancey came into Reen's bedroom a half hour before the great brass bell on the overseer's porch could signal the start of another workday. Even now, in the dew-wet cool of morning, the day promised to be a scorcher. *Ideal cotton weather,* he thought, *after the drenching rains of July.*

Though he slept badly as a rule, he had snored through eight full hours. His wakening had been brisk with purpose—and he had come here to make sure his plan was carried out. Now, finding the new mother deep in slumber, he had not the heart to waken her.

Mammy Jo (who slept on a cot in the dressing room) stirred in the shuttered darkness when he called her name. At his nod she lifted the baby from his cradle and took him to his morning bath. Uncle Doc sighed as he looked down at the sleeping girl on the bed. Never had Reen seemed younger, never more defenseless—and more content. He knew she had earned this moment of happiness. She also deserved to rest, if this were a season for resting. It seemed a needless cruelty to remind her that she must be up and doing—but the time had come to speak. Downstairs a score of decisions waited: only the mistress of Selby could make them.

Yancey opened the double doors on the portico balcony. The early sunlight flooded the room—but Reen did not waken. He shrugged and moved to the balcony rail. As he had expected, the lone horseman already waited on the drive. Each morning since his son's birth Dan Carroll had ridden over from Four Cedars for news —and each morning Uncle Doc had stood here to give it.

"How is she?"

"Flourishing, Dan. I'm getting her up today."

Carroll rode across the lawn, into the shadow of the portico. "Isn't it rather soon?"

"Not for Lorena."

"What of the child?"

"Growing faster than any boy has a right to grow."

"I'd like to see him," said Carroll. "I don't suppose that's advisable."

"Not yet, Dan."

"Could I call later—as a neighbor?"

You know he's yours, thought Yancey. *Even if you haven't put the thought in words.* "Of course you can call," he said. "Our fences join now, so that's only good manners. And don't fret about Lorena. She's the mother of a son; she'll fight for what's hers—and his."

"I wish I could help."

"Stay on your own land, Dan. When she needs help she'll send for you——" Yancey turned back toward the bedroom with a finger to his lips: Reen had just wakened, and was calling for the child. The rider below, understanding the signal, lifted a hand in farewell and rode off as silently as he had come.

"Where are you, Uncle Doc?"

"Coming, girl."

When he re-entered the sunlit bedroom, Reen had begun to yawn her way to wakefulness. Wisps of a dream clung to the corners of the great four-poster. Guessing its tenor, Uncle Doc maintained a careful silence while he mounted the steps to take her pulse.

"Were you speaking to someone on the lawn?"

"I was alone on the balcony," he lied.

"I thought I heard your voice."

"I was muttering to myself. It's an old man's privilege." He spoke easily—glad to note that her heartbeat was normal to the second. "I was also testing the weather. It seems perfect for growing things."

"Cotton and babies both?"

"And mothers. After breakfast you're getting out of bed."

"So soon?"

"You've lazed long enough on an overstuffed mattress and crowed over what you've done. It's high time you started earning your keep again."

There was silence in the room, broken only by Mammy Jo's humming as she finished bathing Selby's heir. Reen's eyes strayed toward the sound. Yancey could read her thoughts clearly.

"I'd be the first to agree I'm heartless," he said. "But it's the only way. I won't have you brooding a day longer."

"Who says I'm brooding, Uncle Doc?"

"In your place I'd brood plenty."

"Why?"

"Are you still denying you've had a child by one man—while you're married to another?"

Reen did not answer at once. When she spoke, the words seemed to drop into a soundless void.

"You're right," she said. "I must earn my keep, with a son to raise—and a husband in Mexico."

"Mammy Jo will help you dress."

"I can dress myself. Will you forgive me for stealing three whole days to dream?"

"Can you share the dream, girl?"

"No one can really share a dream—but I'll give you the essentials. For three days I've pretended I was like other women. I even thought the world owed me protection, now I've given it a child. It was a happy illusion, while it lasted."

"D'you know better now?"

"Yes, Uncle Doc."

"Sorry to be the one to remind you."

"I've always known better," she told him. "Today I meant to ask whether it was safe to get up."

"You'll be glad you made the effort, once you're on your feet again."

"I'll take that as a compliment," she said. "Was it so intended?"

"It was indeed. Earth mothers who are also earth molders are rare in any culture. Today the South needs them badly."

He looked down at her for a moment more, wondering if he should confess the secret of Dan Carroll's visits. In the end he left her without taking the risk. Reen had always been strong enough to fight the world alone. She would never be alone again, now she had given Selby its heir.

Book Three

"Georgia is an armed camp, Mr. Rowley," said Dan Carroll. "I needn't repeat the reason."

"Not to a visiting Charlestonian," said Quent. "Naturally, the coming winter of our discontent springs from the same cause."

"You don't blame me then—for patrolling every road in Cray County? I assure you, there's no other way to keep the peace."

"My dear Major, after four years of war and three of Reconstruction, I've ceased to blame anyone."

After a business meeting at Four Cedars (which had been both revealing and profitable) the two men had ridden out in the late afternoon. Bound for Selby Hall—and Quent's first visit in over two years—they had followed the road along the river. . . . Now, on a spot of high ground, they had reined in for the view. The vast checkerboard of fallow fields (weeping, at the moment, in autumn rain) illustrated the tragic subject of their discourse all too vividly.

The red-brown river wound from west to east, through a landscape desolate beyond belief. It had inundated its banks for miles on end. Silted as the current was, it offered testimony of leached lands upstream, of idle fields that bled their topsoil with every rain. Dan could have named each of those fields as accurately as though a map lay on his saddle. Once again the Yankee major (who could now call himself a Georgian by adoption) sighed deeply as he reflected on the stubbornness of a conquered land that still refused to admit defeat.

Hamilton Hundred and Greentree were not the only plantations that had turned their backs on the present. More than three full years after the end of armed resistance a score of estates in the county remained unworked. Save for a few Negroes too decrepit to leave their former masters, they were totally unmanned—and yet, by a financial legerdemain that defied analysis, nearly all of them had fought off foreclosure. It had been a senseless defiance—and, for that very reason, all the more rabid. Slaveholders before surrender, these landowners meant to bring back slavery on their terms. While they continued their scheming they would hire no Negro labor—and they refused to face the existence of an army of occupation on their very doorsills. Nor would they admit that the aftermaths of the violence they plotted could be far worse than the ills they sought to cure.

The encampment under Carroll's command stood on the next bluff—two companies of mounted infantry, a highly mobile force that could reach any part of its bailiwick in a matter of hours. So far, he had trained his men rigorously and used them with the utmost discretion, relying on their presence to hold trouble in check. The camp stood on his land, at a corner of Four Cedars, the vast acreage he had spent three years in restoring—both as a labor of love and as an example to the die-hard secessionists that surrounded him. Here the land was good for little but wood lots and grazing. The rest, nurtured by his careful farmer's hand, awaited only a change of season to bring forth its abundance.

Dan's campaigner's eye surveyed the neat rows of tents, the timbered cookshack, the covered corral that would keep the horses healthy through the winter. Constant maneuvers had kept the men from moping at their thankless task—and, since it was obvious to all Cray County that these military police had the power to enforce their will, there had been no real clashes so far.

True, a dozen crosses had been lighted in the past week—mostly in the yards of isolated Negro cabins, or as warnings to poor whites unpatriotic enough to sell produce to Carroll's quartermasters. But there had been no direct assault on Lincolnville. And Sal's work bands, trooping in force to their tasks all through the hot, taut months of harvest, had yet to be molested.

It was no basis for complacency, since the fundamental issues remained unsolved. Until blacks and whites could find a way to live in peace, the irritant of an Army occupation would continue—to enforce the Reconstruction edicts passed so hastily in Washington. Major Dan Carroll could only pray for better times with the year's turning.

The causes of the deadlock were many: the root cause was simple. A Georgian by residence if not by birth, Carroll pondered the events that had brought so much of the South to the brink of rebellion, reduced its politics and its economic pattern to chaos, and created an undying legacy of hatred. *The word is greed,* he thought. *What else could bring the locust swarm into this conquered land?*

With former rebels denied the vote, with bayonets at every polling place to protect the Negroes' own grotesque fumbles at citizenship, there had been no chance for a meeting of minds before the looters took over. Inevitably, the conquered had fought back. The provocation had been dire—especially in areas like Cray County, where slaves had been most numerous. Just as inevitably, the Negroes' evil mentors had gone beyond all bounds in their hunger for spoils. And yet sanity had already returned to the border states. It might have come to Georgia too—had Georgia been spared the constant agitation of the Klan.

At first the Ku Klux Klan, for all its terrorist trappings, had seemed a necessary counterstroke to beat the carpetbaggers down, to convince the brand-new freedmen that a prostrate land was not theirs for the taking. Had the Klan taught its enemies these lessons and then disbanded, it would have written a proud footnote to history. Instead, it had continued to mushroom in its own right, until its anonymous members seemed to revel in killing and burning for their own sake. Now (in this bitter autumn of '68) Carroll feared the passions these night riders had aroused could only be quenched in blood. Certainly the gulf that divided the races was deeper than before—and the will to destroy had long since replaced reason.

Thanks to his vigorous patrolling in Cray County, the local Klan had remained largely a hidden menace. It was still his duty to stamp it out. This could be done only by head-on contact with the night riders—a form of military action far more difficult than conventional battle.

Stern measures had been carried out elsewhere in Georgia: in every case, the Klan had fought back with furtive savagery. Carroll was now en route to perfect his own battle plan. Reluctant to waste lives needlessly, he had half decided to leave a final warning at Colonel Hamilton's door. (The hero of Shiloh was known to be a county leader, and orders for new violence were said to be on hand from the Klan's headquarters outside Atlanta.)

Carroll hoped to prevent hostilities in time—but he had his strategy ready: obviously, the chances of invading the colonel's brain were slight. . . . He threw a sharp look at the horseman beside him. Quenten Rowley seemed lost in a brown study of his own.

"Speak your mind, Mr. Rowley," he said. "It will go no further."

"The name is Quent, now we're business partners," said Lorena's brother. "As for my thoughts at the moment, they're highly unoriginal. I was despairing of the human race. How does one combat its cussedness when it refuses to obey the right orders?"

Dan found he was laughing as they resumed their jog trot on the muddy highroad. After their conference at Four Cedars he had felt that Quent was his ally—even though the alliance was offered from mixed motives.

His visitor had come up from New Orleans at his request. Last night, over brandy and cigars, Quent had agreed to continue the fiction that it was he who had given Selby its famous loan. In return for this pretense Dan had promised to ship his current crop (along with Selby's) on a steamer Quent had just acquired in Mobile. The agreement would be mutually profitable. Lorena's brother had friends in every way station on the long, bribe-haunted road to the cotton-hungry milltowns in Britain and New England. If he was charging top prices for his transport he could assure quick sales, at prices that could only be described as astronomical.

Since he had taken over at Four Cedars (and bought the Varnell estate as well) Dan had found a planter's life could be a rewarding one—providing the planter was buttressed with hard cash, and a will to survive. His position as military commander in the district had assured his immunity. It had been only natural to extend that immunity to Selby Hall—since he used Lorena's gin to bale his crops and shipped from a shared warehouse at the railhead.

Thanks to such circumstances (and the fact their acres now joined), he had created an island of peace for them both, in a sea of troubles. So far, the sea had broken on their boundaries. He could hardly hope their luck would last forever.

Carroll had worked hard to make friends among his neighbors. He had offered crop money at prewar rates—and the offer had been rejected by all the large landowners. He had found a few takers among former sharecroppers—and the smaller, non-slaveholding farmers. Some of his debtors had fared well enough to buy extra acres with the profits from their first crops. Some of the sellers had been the very nabobs who had refused Dan's help. More often the owners had preferred to sell their unworked quarter sections to Selby—hard though it was to admit that Lorena had succeeded where they had failed.

The county's attitude toward Selby Hall had hardened to one of watchful waiting. Reen, the county noted, had been financed by her brother in the year of surrender—so no one condemned her good fortune openly. Nor was she blamed for sharing her gin with Major Carroll. He had been careful to pay the highest rates: her neighbors admitted that Reen had done right to drive a hard bargain.

It would be another matter when the Buells and the Hamiltons learned that he planned to court her openly. Her neighbors had not yet accepted the fact that Lorena Selby was a widow. Perhaps they never would. Brad Selby's name was still a legend, in death as it had been in life.

Dan had kept personal matters from the conversation during last night's conference with Lorena's brother. On his rare visits at Selby Hall he held his feelings on an iron rein—but he had also set a time limit on his patience.

His years at Four Cedars had been long and lonely: he had earned the right to make plans. Once the threat of the Klan was put down, bitterness would subside, in some measure. Was it too much to hope that the county would accept the union of the Selby and Carroll names?

As for Reen herself, instinct told Dan that she could not drift forever in limbo—that her heart, if not her stubborn mind, was ready to receive him. Obviously, he must defer a formal proposal until the question of the Klan was settled. Meanwhile he could at least force her to admit her husband was dead. The rest must come naturally, once she had cleared that mental hurdle.

With friends in Mexico City, Dan had checked closely on Brad Selby's progress there. The rebel hero had been a firebrand in the war party that had strutted and wheedled its way through Maximilian's court. As a brevet colonel in the Emperor's army he had fought brilliantly against the insurgent forces of Juárez, while that peasant leader threatened to make a clean sweep of the comic-opera kingdom. Finally, he had been killed in action near Córdoba.

Brad, it was said, had fought gallantly in the defense of a crossroads farm. With his officers dead, he had repulsed a last assault almost singlehanded—until a lucky shot had finished him. Even then (and this was his best tribute) his attackers had held back until the farmhouse could be put to the torch. It was only when fire bombs had demolished the walls that the enemy made a concerted rush. The dead and dying had been dragged from the charred redoubt. Some of the bodies were already burned—but there was no mistaking the insignia of the commander.

Ten days ago the official news that Dan awaited had arrived from Washington: Brad's demise was now a part of history. Maximilian was dead, and relations of a sort were established with the new government—enough for dispatches to filter through. . . . One of the first diplomatic pouches had contained the death certificate of one Bradfield Selby, *extranjero*, volunteer in the Emperor's cavalry —and, if one could believe the note of commendation, a military man of the first caliber.

The sequence of events, Dan reflected, was simple, stark—and in character. Having lost one war, Brad had simply moved on to a second, even more hopeless battleground. Long before his arrival at Maximilian's court the Confederate officers there had realized it was impossible to continue their futile struggle from this base of operations. Beset by his own woes, haunted by a fading star, the Emperor had offered them rhetoric, asylum—and little more. As time wore on, the former rebels had drifted to other climes. Some had tried gold prospecting, or turned native among the peasant farmers. Others, like Brad, had served the Emperor—until their stars had sunk together.

Brad's ending had been a fitting one—a part of the bizarre coda to the long and dissonant symphony called the Civil War (or the War between the States, depending on the historian). The rebellion smoldering in the South today was war of another sort—impossible to put down with bayonets, impossible to control without them. . . . Carroll pushed the problem aside as Quent leaned over his saddle to address him.

"When is the wedding, Dan? I should have asked sooner."

Now the question was in the open, Dan found he could accept it naturally. "That's up to your sister."

"Don't pretend you haven't asked her."

"I predicted we'd join forces someday, when I bought Four Cedars. At the time, she refused to listen. Her husband was still alive—and en route to Mexico."

Quent considered the answer as they approached the entrance to Hamilton Hundred, a pair of neo-Gothic gateposts deep in ivy that suggested the portal of some mystic shrine. Untouched by Sherman's invasion, the gates gave no hint of the desolation they inclosed.

"Surely Lorena realizes that Brad's death is on the records."

"Last week I sent her a copy of the dispatch."

"Why didn't you deliver it in person?"

"I felt it was unwise to intrude. Brother officers wrote from Mexico, nearly a year ago, announcing Selby's death—but she sent me no word that she had heard the news. I learned of those letters only by chance."

Quent's too-handsome lips curved in the saturnine grin Carroll had begun to recognize as his trade-mark. It was the smile of the born satyr, who understood all appetites and the masks that concealed them.

"You aren't too impetuous a wooer, my friend."

It was Dan's turn to smile (one secret at Selby, he perceived, had been well kept). "Your sister is well aware of my affection," he said. "For the past three years I've given her ample proof."

"So you have. In my book you qualify as a saint. I can't believe that even a saint will wait forever."

Dan hesitated before he answered—though he knew Quent could be trusted. "Yesterday Lorena sent her overseer to Four Cedars with a check for seventy thousand dollars. Repayment for cash I advanced in '65—plus the standard interest scalawags charge in Georgia. I tore the check in half, put the pieces in a second envelope, and returned them—with a note saying I'd call this afternoon to explain."

Quent chuckled. "I'm beginning to catch your drift. Evidently, I arrived at a providential moment."

"You'll speak in my behalf then?"

"Gladly, if you feel it will help."

"I hope I merit your endorsement."

"Put it this way, Dan. That check was a symbol to Lorena. Now she's proved she can pay the last of Selby's debts, she has also proved she's a free woman. The prescribed time of mourning is behind her; she has left Brad's shadow—with legal proof that she's a widow. In your place I'd strike, and strike quickly." Quent dismounted in the shadow of the Hamilton gateposts. "As I say, I'll plead your cause—the moment I've paid this call."

"*I'd* planned to call on the colonel too."

"Let me go in first—and wait on the portico. You may learn more."

Quent tethered his horse to a sapling that had taken root in the wall of the abandoned gatekeeper's cottage, an example which Dan followed. The two riders approached the wreck of Hamilton Hundred on foot, the man in Army blue a pace behind the man in riding clothes.

The house, as Dan recalled all too vividly, had been mostly demolished by the fire that had followed its owner's armed refusal to surrender three years ago: the crumbling walls, clothed in a shroud of wild grapevine, still towered gauntly against the rainy sky. The Hamiltons lived in what they had salvaged from the holocaust, a portion of the eastern wing the fire had spared. It contained the colonel's library and a den that housed his lawbooks. Curiously, this fragment of a once-great mansion was virtually intact. High, glass-fronted shelves still held the classics, bound in calfskin and blue morocco. Busts of the poets looked down from niches in the ivory-white walls—and the portraits of Hamilton and his lady filled the two overmantels. In the den a lamp above the worktable beat back the threat of the lackluster afternoon.

All this Carroll observed while he followed Quent into the shelter of the portico—or rather the remnant the flames had missed. Here, partly to shut off this undamaged fragment of the house (and partly to provide additional living space), was a lean-to built of cypress boards. Its sloping roof was crudely shingled, but it was a shelter of sorts. Since the Hamiltons were too poor to paint (and far too proud to whitewash), the makeshift addition to their dwelling had taken on a gray-green, mossy patina. It blended naturally with the wreck of a mansion that had once been a show place for all Georgia —much as a shepherd's hut might seem part of the Grecian ruin to which it clung.

"The colonel has callers," said Quent. "Look down in the stable yard."

Dan nodded. He had recognized the wagon—and the work horse cropping grass between the traces.

"The wagon is Sal's," he said. "The horse belongs to Luke Jackson. I'd heard they were coming here today to take final title to a quarter section."

"The one that adjoins Selby, of course," said Quent. He frowned, and moved a step closer. "Lorena's done a good bit of land trading lately."

The tall windows of the wing (most of whose panes were broken) gave the unannounced visitors a perfect view. In the colonel's den the lamp had been lighted for a purpose: Sal was seated at table with a lawbook at his elbow, making careful additions to a document spread before him. He had closed the door to spare Colonel Hamilton a view of his labors. In the library the colonel sat stonily in an armchair, dressed in his best broadcloth. Luke Jackson roamed restlessly before the shelves, pretending to consult volumes at random. When the owner of Hamilton Hundred spoke, his voice reached the portico clearly. From the first words, Dan realized he had no choice but to eavesdrop.

"Don't fidget, Luke," said the colonel. "I'm quite resigned. Beggars can hardly be choosers."

"There's no call to take that tone, sir. Sal would step lively enough if we told him you're in the Kl——"

"None of that, Jackson!" Hamilton had used his parade-ground bellow. "*You* aren't even supposed to know—remember?"

"Have it your way, sir. But I'm still honored to be calling here again. Even on so sad an errand."

The colonel's chest had puffed at the compliment. Listening without compunction at the broken pane, Dan was glad he had not tried to force an entrance. It would have been worse than useless to appeal to Hamilton—now he had confessed his connection with the night riders.

"I swore I'd never communicate with Lorena Selby again," said the colonel. "Now I've broken my vow—long enough to ask help through her overseer. It isn't a pleasant admission, Jackson."

"Don't blame us because we've cash on hand, sir." Luke's voice still dripped respect—but the listener at the window knew he meant every word. "It was Quent Rowley's money, as you know, that saved Mrs. Selby in '65. She's used it since, as best she could."

"*Your* principles are sound, Jackson. Why d'you stay on there?"

"I've my reasons, Colonel."

"I suppose your devotion does you credit," said Hamilton. "Still, it can take a man too far. How can you work side by side with a Nigra?" He bounded to his feet in a sudden burst of rage. "Is it true he's top dog at your plantation?"

"Mrs. Selby's in charge. And I'm still her overseer."

"But Saladin sells the cotton—and pays the bribes?"

"No, Colonel. Her brother does the bribin' now."

"That would be my entrance cue," Quent whispered. "Stay where you are, Dan." He swept into the house with the debonair flourish of a man who had just heard his name mentioned. "Guilty as charged, Colonel," he said—and held out his hand.

Hamilton, in the act of pacing his carpet with his arm raised in a silent imprecation, had frozen in his tracks—but Dan guessed that he was not too startled at the abrupt appearance. News of Quenten Rowley's arrival in the county had surely reached him—plus the fact that Quent had spent last night at Four Cedars. After a short hesitation he took the visitor's hand.

"I make no charges behind a man's back, Mr. Rowley," he said coldly. "I'll repeat it to your face—it's bad news when you turn up in Georgia."

Quent shrugged off the words. "It's always refreshing to hear a man speak his mind. Go on speaking it, please. Why should the fact that Lorena's a rich woman disturb you?"

"I don't begrudge Lorena her success. As a hero's widow she deserves it—if only to raise Brad's son properly. It's her means I can't condone."

"Where would you landowners be without help from Selby?"

"I'll grant you we've been forced to take her loans. I still call your sister's methods a disgrace."

"Would you prefer to get your money from Atlanta—at three times the rates she charges?"

"That's an insulting question, Rowley."

"Then stop insulting Lorena. She bought up county land when owners like you were starving. And sold it back—at the same price— when the owner was in funds again. You can't accept cash from her with one hand and make a fist with the other."

"I have but one fist left, sir. While I draw breath I'll use it to defend the Confederacy."

"As of October 1868?"

"Forever, if need be."

"Must you also use it to threaten my sister?"

"Your sister bears a proud Georgia name, Mr. Rowley. For her son's sake I pray she'll be worthy of it in future. I denounce her present methods bitterly."

The contending voices hushed: Sal had come in quietly from the den. On the portico the eavesdropper saw that the Negro's manners were perfect: thanks to that careful serenity, it was impossible to know if he had heard the last exchange. Bowing to the three white men, he spread the red-sealed deed he carried on a taboret at Hamilton's side.

"Sorry to be so long, Colonel," he said. "Mrs. Selby insists on a repurchase clause in all land transfers. That's what delayed me." He offered his pen with the words, and a pocket inkpot. "If you'll sign beside the seal——"

Hamilton, whose face had taken on a wine-red hue, waved the offer aside. "Stand back. I've my own pen."

"As you like, sir."

No one stirred while the hero of Shiloh scrawled his name across the deed. Sal tucked the new owner's copy into his pocket with the gravest of bows. Only the watcher at the window could see the sad half-smile on his lips as he turned to go. There was no malice in that smile—only a touch of pity.

"Thank you kindly, Colonel," he said. "I'll wait in the wagon, Marse Luke."

He went out with the same unforced dignity. Passing Dan on the portico, he offered a nod of recognition, but did not speak. In another moment, he had crossed the stable yard and climbed to the seat of the buckboard—where he settled patiently, hunching his shoulders as rain began to fall again from the leaden sky.

In the library Colonel Hamilton still sulked in the armchair, his copy of the transfer forgotten on the table. Quent had moved to the doorframe, as though to take his own leave—then leaned there, his eyes veiled. Luke (who had stood rooted in the shadows like a brooding ox) moved forward dutifully.

"Don't take it too hard, sir——"

"The thing's done," said Hamilton. "I've no wish to discuss it."

"It's only a quarter section, and we gave you top price. Most of it's only good for fox huntin'."

"That quarter section was half my present estate, Jackson."

"We'll sell it back when you make your next crop."

"How can I make a crop without my slaves?" The colonel shook his fist at the door Sal had just taken. "I'll never hire hands from *him*."

"I can't blame you for that, sir. But——"

"Strutting in store clothes like some Indian nabob! Lording it in his own house at the Forks with his woman and his two picka-ninnies! His thumbprint's on the air we breathe. What's to become of us, Jackson?"

"We'll win the county back," said Luke soothingly. "And you'll make a crop someday—on your own terms."

Hamilton sat bolt upright in his chair. "D'you endorse that sentiment, Rowley?"

Quent's eyes were still far away. "Sorry, Colonel. I'm a busy man, with no time for daydreams. You and Sal must do business someday—or the Yankees will buy you both out. There's no other way."

"I won't ask you to leave my house, sir. You are still Brad Selby's brother-in-law, God rest his soul. But I *will* wish you good day. It's obvious which side you favor."

"There's only one side now."

A door slam was Quent's answer: the ancient warrior had vanished into the murky region where house and lean-to merged. Still lingering on the portico, Dan shook his head in numbed disbelief. *He needs that arrogance to exist,* he thought. *If he admitted Quent was right he'd cease to be.*

Still lounging in the door, Quent gave Dan a solemn wink. Again it was the watcher he addressed, though the words were thrown at Luke.

"Don't let Hamilton deceive you," he said. "Sal is only his whipping boy. I'm the chief villain—and I'll tell you why. As a Southerner in good standing I should have let Selby fail with the others. In that event the Hamiltons could pity my sister today—instead of envying her."

"Maybe you've a point there, Mr. Rowley," said the overseer dourly. "She *still* had no call to pay white man's wages to Nigras."

"No. She could have starved like a lady, along with Clara Hamilton and the others. And then sold her land, to keep up the role of martyr. Instead, she's shown an honest profit—even if I *have* paid a few bribes to clear her cotton. No wonder the colonel hates her."

"It still ain't fitten, Mr. Rowley."

"It's poor weather for pride, Luke. Until we can drive the rascals out we must buy and sell on Yankee terms—or go under."

"The Klan thinks different."

"It would—with men like Hamilton under the nightshirts."

Luke came closer. His voice was a hoarse, wheedling whisper. "Make her throw Sal out, Mr. Rowley. Make her use white men in the fields—before it's too late." He pulled his slouch hat level with his ears and stepped into the rain. Dan had just enough time to retire behind the corner of the portico: he had no wish to meet the overseer now. In another moment Quent strolled out to join him. Together they stood on the rotting floor boards and watched Luke and Sal drive off together.

"Sal needs a bodyguard," said Dan. "But I can hardly assign one without making a bad matter worse."

"Luke won't let him be hurt. Not while he's working for Lorena."

"Luke can't go on serving both the Klan and Selby."

"True enough, Dan. Divided loyalty can be a heavy burden. Especially for a man with an angry heart and a limited brain. Perhaps Lorena should dismiss him."

"In my opinion," said Carroll, "she's keeping him on for just one reason. He'll surely warn her in time—if the Klan does plan to hit Selby Hall."

Quent nodded as they moved toward the gatehouse—and his lips curved into their familiar grin. "Did you figure that out for yourself, Major? You're by way of becoming a Georgian."

Between the Hamilton acres and Selby the road followed the riverbank, shadowed for most of the distance by giant oaks. Dan was still deep in talk with Quent when he felt his horse shy and brought the animal up sharply. The two riders had just rounded a turn. Hanging from an outthrust limb ahead was the body of a man, twisting slowly with the endless patience of death.

"Good God, Dan!" exclaimed Quent. "What is it—a lynching?"

"So it seems." Carroll's wartime experience had inured him to such scenes; he was the first to put the spur to his mount. "Hurry, will you? He may still be alive."

Neither of them could see the victim's face in that uncertain light, but it took only a moment to reach him. The horses continued to shy away as both men held them to the road.

"Cut the rope," Carroll directed. "I'll catch him."

The body sagged across the saddle as Quent's pocketknife slashed through the rope; holding the limp burden steady as he dismounted, Dan lifted it to the riverbank. One look at the blue-black face and the protruding tongue told him the man had long since ceased to breathe. It was obvious that his executioner had not intended that he die mercifully, with a snapped neck as in a proper hanging. The noose, expertly tied, was meant to strangle the victim while he kicked and fought against it.

Quent had already led both horses up the road and tethered them. When he returned, Dan had placed the dead man on his back. Pinned to his shirt was a square of white sheeting. "KKK" had been slashed on it in bold red letters. Beneath it (and barely visible, thanks to the pelting of the rain) were three words: "Death to Traitors."

"Do you know him?" Quent asked.

"It's Jed Peters. A tenant farmer on what used to be Varnell land."

"Which means he's working for you now."

"For more than a year," said Carroll. "I was pretty sure he was a Klan member, but I never questioned him. Yesterday he came to Four Cedars to tell me he'd quit."

"Did he turn informer too?"

"No. I have other sources of information."

"The leader must have thought he revealed their secrets."

"One particular secret, unless I miss my guess." Carroll got to his feet. "Only a state officer of the Klan can pass sentence of death. Even then Colonel Hamilton would hardly have the courage to carry it out on his own."

"Meaning that this order of execution came from above?"

"Exactly. I've already had word that our local Klansmen were expecting a Kleagle from Atlanta. *He* did this."

"As a warning to you?"

The Army major turned somber eyes on Quent. "Hardly. They must realize by now that I don't scare that easily. My guess is this was a way to keep the local night riders in line."

"By making them partners in murder." Quent nodded thoughtfully. "Will it turn the trick?"

"I think not," said Carroll. "I've lived among these people for three years. If my experience means anything, this sort of violence will have the opposite effect. The Klan has a wide membership in Cray County: I can give you most of the names. But it's never been able to muster a very large percentage on its rolls. Most of our night riders are riffraff. With a few extremists like Colonel Hamilton to give the orders. I can't believe the others will condone this lynching. I'm positive they had no part in it."

"In that case Peters' hanging could sound the death knell for the Klan in the county."

"The death knell's sounded already," said Carroll grimly. "I'll see to that, now they've shown they're ready for real violence."

"Where will they strike next?"

"Probably at Lincolnville. We've been expecting an attack there for the past month."

"Or at Selby Hall?"

Dan studied Quent narrowly, then shook his head. "I'd guess Lincolnville. They hate Lorena enough—but she's still Brad Selby's widow. And he's a local hero."

"At least for the present," said Quent drily.

"What d'you mean? He's dead, isn't he?"

"Oh he's dead, all right. I was there the day after they burned out his command post. But I fear that Captain Bradfield Selby died as he had lived—without too much regard for his fellow man."

"Is there a blot on his record then?"

"Put it this way," said Quent. "He was in Córdoba on the Emperor's business—with a patent giving him title to some estates confiscated from Mexican patriots. Later he tried to run off rightful owners as well. That's what stirred up the hornets' nest."

"Are you going to tell Lorena?"

"Suppose I leave that up to you."

Carroll spoke without hesitation. "I fought against Selby once. He sacrificed a whole command needlessly, but he was a brave soldier. I think we should leave it at that."

Quent shrugged. "What do we do about Peters?"

"I'd appreciate it if you'd wait with the body until I can send a wagon. Now I'm sure a Kleagle is giving orders here, there's a lot to be done."

"Do you plan to arrest Colonel Hamilton?"

The major shook his head. "No jury would convict him on this evidence. Dr. Yancey will tell you the only way to save a man with a gangrenous leg is to amputate. If I'm lucky, that will happen to the whole Klan tonight. Or at least the Cray County branch."

2

The nursery was on the second floor at Selby Hall, a wide, airy apartment joined to Reen's own room by a connecting door. Standing beside the bed (she had insisted on a real youth bed years before her three-year-old was tall enough to fill it), the mistress of Selby smoothed the counterpane with careful hands.

The bed had not been slept in for some time. Andy had gone to relatives in Asheville that August to escape the summer heat, with Mammy Jo as his nurse companion. Until local tensions were resolved, they had been told to remain: once again Reen could not regret that decision. It was her first separation from the boy since his birth, and she had made the break at no small cost to her feelings. Even now she could not quite believe he was gone. . . . When she wakened she caught herself listening for his laughter next door. Each noon (after her inspection tours to the ends of an ever growing domain) she was sure he would come running across the lawn to greet her. At the end of the workday she still visited the nursery, even though it was empty.

The snug white room was quiet. She studied its familiar contents —the huge rocking horse, the playhouse in the alcove, the rabbits and gnomes that frolicked on every wall. This was a time of day she loved. In the nursery it was easy to remember that life held meaning, to regain the serenity that eluded her in working hours.

Reen moved to the armoire that housed Andy's spare clothes (the inspection tour was ritual). Here was the Indian suit she had ordered from New York. The dress coat from Atlanta (for his third birthday). The Confederate uniform she had accepted, after long hesitation, from the same tailor. At the dresser she arranged her son's silver-backed brushes and studied the row of photographs. Here was Andy as a baby. His first steps on the portico, with Mammy Jo in the background. His first ride on his mother's side saddle. . . . Finally, in a separate frame, was the picture taken on Andy's last birthday. Reen had saved it for the end. It was a delight to note, for the hundredth time, the increased depth in the boy's fine, dark eyes, the manly lift of his chin.

He was still her living image. Sometimes it was hard to force her mind beyond, to admit that part of him was Dan Carroll. With each passing day it was clearer that she could not postpone the effort.

When she had sent her overseer to Four Cedars with her check she had been sure Daniel would return it: the attempt to settle their three-year-old account had been a kind of testing. Not that she could have blamed Daniel had he taken the money and turned his back on Selby Hall—yet she had hoped and prayed he would understand her long hesitation. Caught as she was between hostile forces, she was still fearful to make a move that would commit her.

She had been almost giddy with relief a year ago when friends in Mexico had written that Brad was dead—but the sense of freedom had been short-lived. Loved or unloved, her husband had died a hero. Her code insisted that she mourn his loss—and a year of widow's black was the least Cray County would allow. All that year, while the menace of the Klan worsened throughout Georgia, she had not dared to face her true feelings. Could she face them today —when Dan Carroll made his promised call to ask her hand in marriage?

Unsure of that answer, she moved into one of the dormers to look down on the driveway.

The rain had slackened with the closing in of evening, and a weak sunset haloed her live oaks. On either side of the freshly raked drive her lawns were velvet-smooth again. Beyond the wings of the house her work buildings shone with new paint: in the carpenter shop sparks geysered from the forge, where Castor and Pollux were mending a broken trace chain. Selby was in complete repair again, and prospering as never before in its history. She could thank her own determination for that, and her own patient industry.

Of course, there had been lively assists from her neighbor at Four Cedars—to say nothing of the expert business hand of Quent Rowley. . . . Thinking of her brother, she was pleased to note that he had ridden through the gate astride a horse from the Four Cedars stable. His head was sunk in thought—an unaccustomed pose for Quent. Nor did he look up when he dismounted at the portico.

Reen knew he had spent last night with Major Carroll, to discuss business arrangements that would prove profitable to both Dan and himself. She could not help wondering if the talk had included more personal matters—and was sure that it had. Her brother could not help liking Daniel, she reflected. Despite the difference in their environment, both were gentlemen. Besides, both were united in their devotion to her welfare.

When she descended the stairs, a house boy was taking Quent's bag to his usual quarters. Quent himself was in the first parlor with a glass in his hand and his back to the fire. Chatting with Uncle Doc, and leveling an imperious finger to stress a point, he had never seemed more at home.

The plantation doctor, lolling in the deepest of Reen's new armchairs, struggled to his feet at her entrance. His gait had slowed this past year. Of late she had often caught him dozing in the same chair before the dinner hour.

"Stop cursing our friend Hamilton, Quent," he said. "Greet your sister as she deserves."

Quent held out his arms to Reen and gave her another of the half-friendly, half-mocking kisses she could remember from her childhood. "How is my favorite relative these days?"

"Tired, but flourishing," she said—and took the hassock beside Uncle Doc.

"I won't question your prosperity," said her brother. "Where did you acquire the parlor suite?"

"At a London auction. My agents bid it in for me."

"It's real Chippendale, I take it."

"Yes, Quent."

"What did it cost?"

"Enough. I wasn't cheated."

"Lorena, d'you think such ostentation is proper?"

"I want this house to look its best—with Andy almost old enough to notice. None of his ancestors knew want here. Why should he?"

Reen felt the probe of her brother's glance while she made her pronouncement—and wondered how much that keen mind had guessed of Andy's real origin. Not that Quent Rowley's guessing mattered. . . . She continued in the same steady tone, describing the boy's recent progress and explaining her reasons for sending him away.

"Asheville, eh?" said Quent. "You *are* splurging. Don't you deserve a vacation too?"

She met the look squarely. It was important that he realize her courage had never been higher. "I can't leave now. Not while the county's swarming with bullies in nightshirts."

"You just said that's why you've kept the boy in Asheville. Why aren't *you* afraid?"

"I've no cause—with Uncle Doc on hand."

Yancey spoke from his armchair. "Uncle Doc is an old dog who's lost his teeth. You need a man here, Lorena."

"Don't tell me the Klan would burn the home of a Georgia hero." She had not meant to sound so bitter—but even today she could not dismiss Brad's image without a surge of rage. For a moment she let the talk go on without her. She was remembering (too vividly for her peace of mind) the way her head had spun with giddy gladness when the news had reached her. When she had realized she was a widow, that she need take orders from no man alive. . . .

"Don't gamble on the Klan's next move," Quent said. "They might decide to teach the hero's widow a lesson."

"I can defend myself."

"Not against cowards who burn and run. Make sure you're protected all the way. Marry Major Carroll."

"Are you pleading his cause now?"

"He's a good man, Lorena. They're a rarity in these parlous times."

"You'd have me marry a Yankee?"

"Yankee is a silly word. So is rebel. It's time we stopped using them both."

"The South has suffered in Yankee hands, Quent. As much at this moment as it suffered in the war."

"Major Carroll's had no part in the torture. As a military commander he's run things fairly. It isn't his fault so many of you refused his aid. Can't you set an example?"

"I tried to repay what I owe him. He returned the check. Can I do more?"

"Call him what you like, Dan Carroll turned planter for your sake. Night and day for over two years he's patrolled your fences to head off the Klan. All that time, he's waited for you to notice him—while you've gone on honoring a worthless husband. A rakehell, praise heaven, who is now buried in Mexico."

"Must you speak ill of the dead?"

Yancey entered the argument quietly. "Selby was yours, Lorena, long before Brad deserted you. In your place I'd rejoice in my freedom. I'd also remind myself that it is not good for man to live alone—and far worse for a woman."

"You're a fair-to-middling healer, Uncle Doc," she said. "Don't turn mind reader too."

Yancey chuckled, and winked at Quent. "I think she's weakening," he said.

"And not a minute too soon," replied Lorena's brother. "Dan's on his way here now. Shouldn't she receive him alone?"

"Well, girl? Shall we go about our business?"

Reen shrugged off the teasing and clung to her place by the fire. She had need of its warmth as she admitted a strange chill at her finger ends. "This much I'll tell you both," she said. "I can decide on my own future, with no help from matchmakers. And if Dan is courting me this evening, I don't need chaperones."

"You're right, Uncle Doc," said Quent. "She's weakening—definitely. Come help me unpack. I've a present for you in my saddlebags."

Yancey raised a hand in benediction from the foyer arch before he followed in Quent's wake, and Reen acknowledged the gesture with a wordless smile. Outside, she saw, the sullen day had closed in again, blotting out the sunset. It was time to light the lamps, to give orders for dinner. But she sat on unstirring, holding thought at arm's length while she fought for some measure of control.

She had said she could plan her own future, with no outside aid. Why had she never felt colder, never more alone—while she awaited the arrival of the one man who could make that future secure?

The chill of foreboding had not left her when Sal appeared in the study door with a document in his hands. She recognized the transfer deed to a quarter section of Hamilton Hundred.

"It's all yours now, ma'am."

"Only until the colonel buys it back."

"Colonel Hamilton's done with buyin'. All he can do now is sell his medals."

"If I were you, Sal, I'd keep that thought to myself."

"Don't you worry, Miss Reen. I stopped thinkin' aloud for white folks—'cept in this room." Their eyes met, and she could guess the unspoken query on his lips. He would never utter it, she knew: she had trained him too well for that. "I checked the account from your Mobile broker," he said, moving smoothly to a subject closer to the everyday. "Will you read it now?"

"Tomorrow will do, Sal. And I don't blame you for hoping I'll marry Major Carroll."

"So does all Lincolnville, ma'am."

"Speaking of Lincolnville, you'd best be on your way. The turnpike isn't safe after dark—even with the patrols."

"I got my own patrol, Miss Reen. Fifty hands are waitin' at the stable now. I told 'em I'd work late today."

"I'd still feel safer—if you brought Florrie and the children here. At least, until the Klan and the Army settle their quarrel."

"We got strong shutters at the Forks, ma'am. Once we close 'em we sleep sound."

"I wish I could say as much, Sal."

"When tomorrow comes, Miss Reen—maybe you can."

He, too, was gone now—with the cat-foot tread whose velvet precision still troubled her. She understood the hasty departure when she turned up the first lamp and realized Luke had been hovering on the portico steps, waiting for Sal to leave. Over the years, the two men had learned to work together smoothly—but Luke had steadfastly refused to meet the young Negro halfway. Joined as they were in selfless dedication to Selby Hall, they were allies who could never be friends. To this day, the overseer refused to enter the Big House when the labor boss was present.

"Can I speak to you in private?" he asked.

"Of course, Luke." *You are the last,* thought Reen. *Once you've given me a piece of that slow-moving mind, I'll be free to make up my own.* Not that she resented the intrusion. However mixed his motives, Luke had served her long and faithfully. His opinions—as she had learned to her sorrow—were a faithful echo of the county's.

"The major's here, ma'am. Countin' his bales in the packhouse."

"I know, Luke. I asked him to stop by. I hope you said he was welcome."

"I've yet to give him the time of day, Mrs. Selby."

Reen smiled up into the man's equine stare. "Can't a lady choose her friends, Luke?"

"Not Cap'n Selby's widow."

"The major has every right to call. He's paid us well to have his cotton baled."

"Why don't he take his bills of lading to the railroad—same as any farmer?"

"Tonight he's here for a special purpose. Or should I say, to ask a special question?"

"I hope I can guess your answer."

"Don't try too hard," she said quietly. "I'm not sure of it myself."

"You'd never marry a Yankee, Mrs. Selby. You *can't*."

"Does that mean I wouldn't dare?"

"That's just what I mean—if you'll give me leave to say it."

Reen's voice hardened. "Who put those words in your mouth? Colonel Hamilton?"

"It's what the whole county's sayin'. You can't go on like this—givin' Sal the leeway you do. Payin' top money to Nigras when white folks are starvin'——"

"I offer work to all who'll take it. There aren't enough white hands trained to chop cotton. What there are refuse to work here."

"Can you blame 'em?"

"I blame no one. People are always slow to outgrow their taboos."

"What's a taboo, ma'am?"

"In this case the belief a man's color is proof of his worth."

"But it *is* proof. The Bible says so. Are you tellin' me that Sal's as good as me? That he's got the same rights?"

"Naturally not, today."

"The Yankees have settled an army in Georgia to see he gets the vote. The major says it's the law."

"Major Carroll agrees that law was ill advised, that it came far too soon. You can't pluck an aborigine out of Africa, work him like a pack animal, and expect him to behave like a citizen overnight."

"They'll *never* be citizens."

"Never is a big word, Luke. Meanwhile the law remains. It's the major's duty to enforce it."

"Miss Reen, you know it's made nothin' but grief, givin' black cotton-choppers the ballot."

"So it has," she said. "And so it will—until they're educated to use that ballot properly. We've paid for that mistake all over the South. There's no need to pay in blood. Not if we keep our heads."

"Maybe that ain't so in Cray County," said Luke darkly. "Like I told you, most folks think you've joined the enemy. They'll be sure of it if you marry the major."

"He wants to be our friend, Luke."

"How? By provin' a field hand's better than his overseer?" Luke's tone changed to one of pleading. "I'm only tryin' to save you from bad trouble, ma'am. Marry this fellow, and you'll have to pay the price. The Klan might even attack Selby. I ain't promisin' they won't."

The threat was in the open now. She had known he had sought her out for something other than an argument over Sal and the major. "How long have you been a member, Luke?"

She saw that the question had shaken him and put him on the defensive. "I joined two years ago."

"From the start then?"

"Yes, Mrs. Selby—the minute the Klan organized the county. For just one reason—so I'd be on the inside lookin' out. So's I could warn you if you went too far."

"And you think I've gone too far now?"

He nodded, still defiant. "Everybody says it."

"I'll tell you your real reason for joining, Luke. You needed something to hate—that's why you're a Klansman. Something you could cow with fiery crosses—night riding—death in the dark." Realizing that her voice had become shrill, Reen made a great effort to pull herself together. "Doesn't it shame you to hide behind a bed sheet —and torment innocent people just because their skins are black?"

"The Klan has been the savior of the South." The overseer's head lifted with the pronouncement.

"At first, perhaps. Today it's killing what it set out to save. In the end it will only kill itself."

"Then you agree with Major Carroll?"

"Of course I do. At least, you must realize he's in complete command here. He knows your ringleaders by name—including Colonel Hamilton. And he has three hundred dragoons camped on the river bluff. If the Klan dares to attack Lincolnville or Selby Hall, he'll destroy you."

"Maybe he won't move fast enough this time."

"What does that mean?"

"I'll tell you a little secret, ma'am. A Kleagle's come from state headquarters with a posse of brand-new men. He's brought secret orders, and we're waitin' to ride tonight. Suppose we're told to move on this plantation?"

"Plenty of your Klansmen would like nothing better," Reen said bitterly. "Especially the ones who owe me money."

"'Tain't the only reason, Mrs. Selby. You got to believe that much."

"I believe you, Luke," she said wearily. "And I appreciate the warning. Go out tonight and take orders from your Kleagle. Call yourself an archangel, avenging the shame of the South, if it will ease your mind. But don't waste time trying to frighten me. And be ready for work in the morning."

After Luke had gone, it seemed to Reen that she had sat for hours in the darkened parlor. The wall clock told her that barely five minutes had passed before she heard Dan Carroll ride up from the packhouse. She moved to the portico to meet him, feeling a great weight lift from her heart.

"Come in, Daniel," she called. "Did you find your shipping list in order?"

He smiled up at her from the bottom step. "Of course." As he spoke he bowed with careful formality, without venturing closer. "I wanted to thank you again for the use of your gin. This promises to be a record crop—for us both."

"You may speak freely," she said with a smile. "We won't be disturbed—or even spied on. Luke has just warned me against you, so his conscience is at rest."

She studied him carefully while he crossed her threshold, paused to lift her fingers to his lips—then went to warm himself at the hearth. *You're as calm as I*, she thought swiftly. *In your heart you know this meeting was ordained.*

"Did you heed the warning, Lorena?" he asked with his eyes on the pine-knot fire.

"No, Daniel."

"May I ask why?"

"For the simplest of reasons—I can't outgrow the habit of fighting my own battles."

"I'm glad I'm numbered among your allies then," he said—and turned to face her. "As it happens, I've a new offer of collaboration."

Knowing just what was coming, she did her best to answer lightly. "A *new* offer, Daniel?"

"Will you come to Four Cedars as my wife?"

So the proposal was in the open at last. She answered it quickly, with no pause for thought. The words had been waiting a long time.

"How can I?"

"How can you refuse?"

"I've a son to raise, on his own land. As a widow I've my rights to protect——"

"You've finally admitted Captain Selby is dead?"

"Last week I filed petition in Atlanta to exercise my dower rights —and take over the plantation. The right has just been granted."

"I've no wish to deprive you of that heritage," he said. "Selby can be held in your name. When the boy's of age, we'll arrange for him to inherit. Can't you see I've made this offer for *all* our sakes?"

"You've done too much now."

"I've done nothing, so far—beyond helping to restore what the war destroyed."

"As you know, I'm prepared to repay that loan."

"It was never a loan. Call it an investment in your future—and in mine."

"Selby needs help from no man, Daniel. I've proved that much."

"Even the strong need love, Lorena. You, more than most—since there's so much unrequited love within you."

"Your sentiment does you credit, Daniel," she said, making her voice bitter with some effort. "Unfortunately, I'm a cynic who's paid a high price for experience. Considering everything, you can hardly blame me for being wary of new investments."

"What sustained you here before we met?" he demanded. "Work and more work—nothing more. With your eyes fixed on the furrows, you'd forgotten the stars."

"I've my own lodestar today—my son. My work has brought its

own recompense. Selby is all mine now. Until I pass that inheritance on to Andy, I couldn't ask for more."

"How can you settle for so little? When you've so much to give—to me, and to the South?"

"Why should the South's agonies concern me?"

"Think only of us then. You've loved me from the moment we met. Three years ago you denied it—and I took the lie at face value. Tell me it's the truth, and I won't trouble you again."

She wrenched away from the attack without meeting his eyes. "Suppose I do love you—a little? Suppose I'm hussy enough to confess I'll always remember what we shared the night of the fire? Does that excuse me from my duty to Andy? My debt to the Judge—to keep Selby as it was?"

"You can't keep things as they were. Not with the war lost and the Negroes free. Except for Selby and Four Cedars, the county is a rubble heap that cries out for rebuilding. If we join forces, Lorena, we can be the architects of that new day."

"How—when my neighbors hate me? And they'll never take help from you."

"Not while the past clouds their judgment, I'll admit. But that can't go on forever. The South has what the North needs. Eventually, they'll meet as partners. Just as you and I must meet."

When she spoke again, her voice seemed faint and far away—like an echo from a dream. "Don't press me, Daniel. My first duty is to my son."

"*Our* son, my dear."

"His name is Selby."

"What do names matter? We created him."

Her hands were in his now: she could not remember when he took them. With a great effort she forced herself to break free.

"Very well, Daniel. He's your son too. But I can never acknowledge it."

"I don't ask for that. The boy will carry on the Selby name: he belongs here. Selby is his fulfillment. But where is *your* fulfillment, if not in me?"

His voice had flooded her soul with the greatest longing she had ever known. If she turned to him now, she felt she would be lost.

"Ask me tomorrow," she whispered. "I may have the answer."

"I'll ask you tomorrow," he promised. "And the day after. Until you remember you're a woman in your own right."

When she dared to lift her eyes she thought at first that he had left her. Then she saw that he was standing in the farthest doorframe, where the lamplight did not reach.

"There's another reason why I came tonight, Lorena," he said. "The troop will almost surely see action before morning. If anything happens, I want you to know how much I love you."

It had never occurred to her before that the Klan posed any threat to him. The thought gripped her heart with dread. At last she could understand her chill of foreboding all too well.

"Luke warned me they might attack Selby," she said.

"I think not. According to my information, Lincolnville's the target."

"But the Negroes are helpless there."

"Not quite," he said quietly. "We'll be ready."

She said the first thing that came into her mind. "Please come back, Daniel."

When he moved toward her again, she was sure he would take her in his arms—and knew she could not resist. Instead, he lifted the edge of the lace shawl she was wearing and pressed it to his lips.

"I'll be back," he told her in a whisper. "Depend on that." Then he turned and stepped through the doorway, into the encroaching dark.

She leaned out to call him back, to answer his proposal now, so he could take the assurance of her love with him. Then—realizing she had already given it—she moved back into the house. Her eyes were swimming with tears as she clung to the newel post in the foyer. *Three years after Appomattox*, she thought, *you've made your separate peace. Pray God it endures.*

3

The fire in the parlor hearth had died to embers when Yancey came downstairs. He did not see Reen until she moved in the shadows that half hid the sofa.

"Why aren't you dressing?" he demanded. "Quent is soaking in a hot tub—but he'll be down soon."

"I've been sitting here thinking," she said.

"Did I see someone ride away just now?"

Reen smiled as he added fresh pine knots to the embers. "You know perfectly well Daniel was here, you old fraud. I'll wager you were watching from an upstairs window."

"Guilty as charged," Uncle Doc admitted. "From the set of Dan's shoulders, I'd say he didn't hear bad news."

"I've promised to give him a decision soon."

Studying Lorena for a moment before he spoke again, Yancey was pleased with what he saw. "Let's hope you told Dan you love him. He's entitled to know that much."

"He knows I love him, Uncle Doc. He's always known."

"So far so good then. Giving yourself to him can come later."

"I've done that much already," she said with a wan smile.

"So you have—in the hope that *he'd* give you a child. That was purely selfish."

Reen bowed her head in a wordless affirmative. "You're right, of course," she said slowly. "I can see it now."

"This new giving must be different," he told her. "If you marry Dan you must settle for being a woman. No more attempts to dominate."

"As tired as I am now, Uncle Doc, I'll welcome not having to make decisions."

"You won't be able just to sit back," he warned. "Not while the South relies on violence to settle its problems."

She looked up sharply at the words. "Daniel spoke of seeing action tonight. Will the Klan dare to attack Lincolnville?"

Again Yancey found himself hesitating. Reluctant though he was to spoil her mood, he realized he could not hold back his news.

"Quent thinks so," he said. "Apparently, the Klan's Atlanta headquarters feels that Cray County needs a strong dose of terror. For a starter a man was hanged today near Brandt's Crossing."

Reen drew in her breath. "Why wasn't I told sooner?"

"Your brother felt we should spare you."

"Who was it?"

"Jed Peters—one of Dan's tenant farmers. He resigned from the Klan yesterday."

"Was it a warning to Dan?"

"Quent thinks it was Atlanta's way of keeping our local membership in line. They've sent a Kleagle here to enforce discipline. Unless Dan hits back fast, there'll be murder and burning all over the county."

"With Selby as a target?" she asked quickly.

"It could well be—after Lincolnville. So far as the Klan is concerned, the two are joined together."

"Because I hire Negroes through Sal?"

"That—and the position he fills here."

"Would it help if I let Sal go?"

"It might. After all, you're a Confederate hero's widow."

"Suppose I gave up all the way and married Daniel?"

"First, you *wouldn't* give up. Second, the future of the South has to be settled before it crucifies itself again. That issue is bigger than any of us, Lorena. We can't continue slavery under another name. It was doomed when steel was born in Pittsburgh and the machine came into its own——" Realizing that he was growing oracular, Uncle Doc broke off. "A few people still shut their eyes to the truth. They'll have to see it soon or be destroyed."

"There's been so much fighting. Why must there be more?"

"To pave the way for the bloodless revolutions that will come later. Take my own field of medicine. Someday we'll find a real cure for childbed fever—a man named Semmelweis may already have found it in Europe. Removing that and surgical pyemia will save more lives than we lost in the war." Warming to a favorite topic, the plantation doctor let his credo pour out unchecked. "Soon there'll be machines to pick cotton and pull a dozen plows. Slavery couldn't exist in such an economy. If Southern statesmen had foreseen *that* revolution, we'd never have seceded. Unfortunately, too many thought like old Hamilton——"

"And Brad?"

"And Brad," he said. "Thanks for finishing my sermon."

"Brad was always a natural leader of men," Reen said thoughtfully.

"So he was—more's the pity."

"If he'd known how to lead them right, there'd have been no limit to what he could have done."

"With you to help him."

"I wanted to help, Uncle Doc: you know that."

Yancey nodded. "At least, you've no cause to reproach yourself. The past's over and done with. It's the future you must work on now. Yours and Dan's——"

Intent as he was, he had not heard the sound of footsteps on the lawn outside. He turned to the french doors only when his eye caught the spurt of a match in the dark. The tinkle of breaking glass followed instantly: Yancey had barely time to spring to his feet when an object bounded into the room through the shattered pane —a paper-wrapped stone that rolled between them and struck a brazen note from the firedogs on the hearth. Startled though he was, Uncle Doc was glad to note that Reen's eyes were riveted on the symbols emblazoned on the paper. She had not yet noticed the tall white silhouettes just beyond her portico—or the flare of a second lucifer, igniting the tar-soaked cross planted in her best flower bed.

"*What is it?*" He saw that, caught off guard, she had reacted as any frightened woman would. This was not the Lorena Selby who had faced a Union cavalry battalion—or used her own body to bargain for her home.

"Judging by the calling card," he said, "we're being visited by the Klan."

The cross outside hissed into flame. Perhaps a dozen men were grouped about it. In ground-length robes of dirty white and tall, cone-shaped hats, they were figures from a ghouls' sabbath. Knowing they would not leave until he had picked up the stone, Uncle Doc turned the missile over with his toe and unwrapped the paper that covered it. He had seen those three blood-red K's on other warnings. This time, there was a sketch of a gibbet beside them, with a body dangling from the rope. Beneath it, a message was printed in block letters:

HIRE WHITE FOLKS TO CHOP YOUR
COTTON, LORENA SELBY. AND FIRE
YOUR BLACK BOOKKEEPER, OR YOU'LL
WISH YOU HAD.

Yancey read the words aloud, then moved to Reen's side. The watchers on the lawn must detect no sign of panic.

"Pay it no mind, girl," he said. "I'll send the rascals packing."

He had tried to shield her from the view outside, but it was too late: the reflection of the burning cross was already picked up in the mantel mirror. Yancey could feel rage pulse from her—as tangibly as though an electric charge had passed between them.

"How did they get this far?" she cried.

"It doesn't matter. Now they've left their message, they'll go——"

Lorena moved to the door and threw it open. "*You skulking cowards—get off my land!*"

The words were shouted. Even as she flung them into the night she had rushed to the mantel and snatched down one of the two matched shotguns that hung above it. Then she charged out to the portico, with the muzzle leveled at the nearest Klansman's heart.

"Wait, girl——!"

"Don't shoot, for God's sake!"

Yancey and the man beneath the white robe had bellowed in unison—but the plantation doctor made no move to stand between gun and target. He smiled grimly as the other raiders scuttled into the dark. When the blast came, the Klansman staggered but did not go down: at the last moment, Reen had lifted her sights. The man's hood, as though released by a spring, was blown clean off his head, revealing the ashen face of Colonel Hamilton. The second barrel of the shotgun, Yancey noted, was still unfired, and the hero of Shiloh was framed in the sights.

Reen spoke crisply. "If you call again, Colonel, use the back way. And take your card with you."

She flung the stone, so accurately that it struck Hamilton's shoulder a punishing blow. Then she charged out to the lawn, swinging the gun like a bludgeon. Hamilton, regaining his senses when he realized he was unwounded, took to his heels—a monstrous, faintly comic figure, the skirts of his robe lifted above his fast-pumping shanks.

Yancey gained the lawn as the flailing gun butt demolished the cross in a single blow. He was in time to catch Reen in his arms before she crumpled in a dead faint. There was no need to check on the retreating Klansmen. The drum of hoofs on the work road and the flare of a single torch told how quickly they had departed.

Quent met Yancey in the upper hall while he carried Reen through her bedroom door.

"I witnessed the finale from my balcony," he said. "Did Lorena do any damage?"

"Only to Hamilton's dignity."

"Is she hurt?"

"No. She'll come round in a moment."

Together they made Reen comfortable on a chaise longue. Her swoon, Uncle Doc realized, had been only a natural withdrawal, vis-à-vis the invaders of her domain. Once she had routed them, there had been no need to wear a mask of courage.

"Stay with her, Quent," he said. "I'll make sure the night-shirts have gone."

"I'll do the scouting, if you like."

"You'd only get lost in the dark. Tell Lorena to dress for dinner as though nothing had happened. I'm sure they won't trouble us again tonight."

In the foyer downstairs he dispersed the frightened knot of servants and lighted a lantern to explore the rose garden, and the path the raiders had trodden there to reach their horses. It was evident that they had used the plantation work road to approach the Big House from the north—leaving the river road to cut across the bottom lands, where only coon hunters knew the trails. Departing by the same route, they had avoided a clash with the Army patrols on the turnpike. Such an approach had needed daring. There were quicksand bogs beside the trails: only picked horsemen could have managed it.

Returning to the parlor by way of the shattered glass door, Uncle Doc was convinced that the enemy would not return since he had registered his point. Now the hooded phantoms had vanished, he could not help chuckling at the memory of old Hamilton's precipitate departure. He had taken the second shotgun from the mantel for his tour of inspection. Still carrying it hunter fashion on one shoulder, he permitted himself a detour to the study door. Lorena kept a cellaret there between the bookcases: he felt he had earned two ounces of brandy to warm his bones.

Sal had left the lamp burning above the big worktable, but the rest of the room was in darkness: Yancey found his way to the cellaret by instinct rather than sight. Over the years, the Judge's study had lost its air of aloofness: it was frankly an office now, rather than a scholar's retreat. . . . Aware that he was poaching, Uncle Doc leaned the shotgun against a shelf and dropped to one knee to open the cellaret. Only then did he realize that he was not alone.

The figure that detached itself from the shadows had seemed part of the wall, a white blur that blended with the bookshelves and the ordered stacks of records. When it took shape in the lamplight it seemed to fill the whole room. Yancey would have sworn that the pointed hood just missed scraping the ceiling as the visitor gave him the travesty of a bow.

The gun was in his hands now—and the barrel was rock-steady as he drew a bead on the man's chest. He had expected the warning on the lawn. Invasion of the Big House itself was another matter.

"Drop that hood, or I'll blast you to hell!"

The intruder spoke in a high falsetto, obviously intended to disguise his true voice. "Don't shoot, Doctor. I'm your friend."

"You're a trespasser. And a dead one, if you don't follow orders."

A roar of mirth escaped the hood as the man spoke in normal tones. "Put down that gun, you old fool, and pour me a drink. I'm home again."

It was the voice of Brad Selby.

4

Brad knew he would always remember the way Yancey's jaw had dropped—and the gasp that had escaped his lips, like the sigh of a broken bellows. Pushing him aside, and taking the nearest bottle from the cellaret, he told himself that he had earned that burst of laughter.

He had planned this home-coming for months, down to the last detail—including the *danse macabre* about the fiery cross and his own wait in the study, in full regalia. At first he had hoped that Reen would find him there—but he was not too displeased when Uncle Doc had blundered in. He needed this chance to catch his breath, to think aloud—and to ask questions. For a long time now, he had moved too fast for conscious planning.

"Let's go into the parlor," he said. "This room has a stink of field hand about it." He kicked the side windows open, letting a gust of air make a shambles of Sal's neatly stacked invoices. "Tomorrow we'll see it's aired properly. March—and pull all the drapes. I don't want patrollers spying."

Leaning in the doorway while Yancey put down the shotgun and closed the curtains, Brad felt his heart swell with triumph. He drank again from the bottle to preserve that surge of happiness at concert pitch. "Try not to look so bug-eyed, Uncle Doc," he said. "I'm very much alive."

Yancey shut the last of the drapes. "Take off that bed sheet," he said—and Brad was glad to observe that he looked every year of his age as he dropped into a chair. "Stop posing as a ghost, since you aren't one."

"Your welcome is quite in character," said Brad. "Fortunately, I'm an obliging soul." He flung off the robe, spinning the white fabric with a practiced toss of the wrists. The reverse of both robe and hood was dead black, a trick he had invented to approach a victim undetected. When the robe was nearly folded, he offered it for the plantation doctor's inspection, including the blood-red insignia.

"D'you recognize the initials?"

"So *you're* the Kleagle from Atlanta," said Yancey. "I might have guessed."

Brad stretched full-length on the new divan that was now the centerpiece of the parlor, careless of the punishment the silken fabric was taking from his spurs. He found that he was enjoying the aura of new money that surrounded him. It was sweet relief to be home again—and even sweeter to bask in the fire of Uncle Doc's hate.

"Keep right on," he said. "You're doing fine."

"You brought orders to Hamilton, and the local Klan?"

"Of course."

"Including a cross on your own lawn?"

"The burning of the cross was the colonel's idea," said Brad. "I agreed—if only to teach Reen a lesson. Judging by the way she collapsed, it's sunk home."

"Were you part of the group?"

"Naturally not. I was watching from the drive. While you were carrying Reen upstairs, I slipped in by the cellar door." Brad reached for the bottle. It was amusing to deal out information in small doses, but his time was limited. "I've a whole half hour to spare, before attending to some other business. You may entertain me in your usual style until I take off."

"I trust this departure is permanent," said Yancey.

"The job I do tonight will be my last for the Klan. At least, for the time being. Starting tomorrow I plan to turn country squire again."

"Here at Selby?"

"Where else, damn it?"

"You realize, I hope, that you're officially dead? The estate has just been transferred to Lorena."

"The report of my death was based on wrong evidence. I chose to keep up the fiction for reasons of my own."

"To get out of trouble in Mexico?"

"Have it your way," said Brad serenely. "I won't argue."

"Isn't it true you failed in land speculation at Carlota? That you invested in the Mazatlán gold fields and lost your shirt? Didn't you fight a duel with your principal creditor—and skedaddle when his heirs pressed for payment?"

"Your detective service is excellent, Uncle Doc."

"If Quent has the facts in order, you were still in uniform when they sent you to Córdoba to burn out a nest of rebels. My guess is you pretended to die there to escape your debtors. Am I still right?"

"To the last detail," said Brad. He drank again from the bottle, warning himself to stay reasonably sober. Trust the old fool to rub open a half-healed wound—to suggest, on the basis of rumor, that Bradfield Selby was born to fail. Drowsing in the deep comfort of the sofa, he let his mind go back to those raffish years in Mexico. The fever of hope that had sustained him at first, after his interview with the Emperor's chief of staff. The splendor of his new uniform. His first victories against Juárez's rabble in arms. The slow realization that his roaring cavalry charges into the mesquite were only dress parades—that *this* enemy could slither from view as easily as a dusty snake, only to coil and strike again. . . .

Little by little he had found himself forgetting his plan to liberate Georgia, while he became enmeshed in Maximilian's own hopeless struggle to survive. Year by year he had fumbled for wealth and glory, only to lose his path in that strange, sun-baked land.

The expedition to the gold fields had brought back only a few nuggets. At Carlota, struggling to recoup with sales of confiscated haciendas, he had been outmaneuvered by courtiers whose influence was far greater than his own. (As he had said, Yancey's diagnosis of his troubles had been painfully accurate. But he had proved—at least, to his own satisfaction—that a true soldier never surrendered, regardless of odds.)

Brad had gone to Córdoba to replenish his fortunes and burnish a star that was sadly in need of polish. He had thought his name in the court gazette would win back his lost favor with Maximilian. How was he to guess that the Emperor was about to face a firing squad? Or that those wretched hill bandits would swarm down upon him by the hundreds—until even a veteran of the Confederate States Army could no longer beat them off?

He had made his last stand in a bullet-pocked farmhouse, after his scouts had told him the deathblow would come with dawn. Pepe Ortega, his second-in-command, had been ordered to take over—while *el coronel* Selby slipped down the ravine in the darkness to bring help. It was not Brad's fault that the enemy struck at midnight, with a salvo of fire bombs to assure its success. Or that Ortega, flushed with his first command, was wearing his commander's coat and epaulets when he died. Naturally, the scorched body had been mistaken for his own.

Brad himself had prudently donned civilian garb for his escape —in this case the second-best suit of one Esteban Salazar, the owner of the farmhouse, who had died in the first day's fighting. Since he had taken Señor Salazar's papers along with the coat, Brad had also decided (for the time being) to assume the identity of that worthy *hacendado*. In Vera Cruz he had been bold enough to present himself at Don Esteban's town house—where he had thrown himself on the mercy of Señora Salazar and begged for asylum until he could put his affairs in order. It had been part of his luck that she had welcomed him, quite literally, with open arms.

The Salazar union, Brad gathered, had been the usual Latin marriage of convenience between an old man and a young woman. It had amused him to repay Inez's hospitality with some of love's livelier counterfeits. The fact that he had uncovered a sleeping wildcat did not trouble him too much: if he bore her claw marks still, he had earned the scars honestly. Not too honestly, he added —remembering how he had borrowed his passage money when brother officers (like himself, fleeing the shape of disaster) had urged him to return to his native state and offer his services to the Klan. . . .

Brad came back to what Uncle Doc was saying with a contented sigh. He had enjoyed that interlude with Inez Salazar. It was true he had left her penniless. Considering his service in Mexico in its time of troubles, he felt no pang of conscience.

"I won't deny I picked another loser," he said complacently. "Nor do I give a tinker's dam for the lies my enemies told Quent Rowley. I've nothing but good marks on my records—and I'm home to stay."

"Did they hang Jed Peters at your order?"

Uncle Doc's impudence amused Brad—so much, that he decided to be truthful. "Peters was executed as an informer," he said. "That's a capital offense in any army: the Klan has the same disciplines."

"If you're a Kleagle," said Yancey, "you were also the hangman."

"What happens in the Order is the Order's secret. I'll tell you this much, however. Tomorrow—when I've put away my robes and the patrollers come calling—no one here will say I'm a member. You least of all."

"Don't be too sure."

Brad shrugged. "You aren't a free agent at Selby, old man. Reen will close your mouth after I've talked to her."

"Don't be too sure of Lorena either."

"She proved her devotion when she gave me an heir. For three years she's held the fort against the scalawags. Why should she fail me now?"

"Does it matter that she no longer loves you?"

"What's love got to do with marriage?"

"Or that she plans to marry Major Carroll?"

Brad snorted with laughter. Yancey in a temper was always a prime diversion. "I heard of that fellow, even in Mexico City. I can't think Reen would be a traitor to her class."

"When will you stop hiding behind phrases? Can't you see your world of make-believe is dead? Lorena will never let you plunder Selby again."

"What happens at Selby is my affair. And don't start making trouble, or I'll kick you downhill to the poorhouse." Brad had spoken mildly, much as he might have addressed an ancient house pet that had misbehaved. "What you call make-believe is still very much alive. Men like Colonel Hamilton and I have seen to that. We're making sure it stays alive when the Yankees leave."

"Using what means—the hangman's rope?"

"Why not—if it silences the troublemakers and helps to put our slaves in their place?"

Yancey tossed up his hands. "Even your vocabulary belongs to yesterday."

"Who gives a hoot in hell if *slavery's* illegal? There's a way to bypass any law. When the courts are on our side again, we'll call 'em peons, or sharecroppers. Any word will do, so long as they work on our terms. And they'll work, damn 'em—now we've thrown the fear of God into their hearts. Old as you are, Yancey, you'll live to see the day."

"Heaven spare me from it."

"Why are you complaining? You've had a good life at Selby—with a boy to bring you drinks, and another to pull off your boots when you were drunk. Keep a civil tongue, and you can still have it."

"I suppose that means you've already taken over here—in your mind."

"I'm home again," said Brad. "A war hero, with medals to spare. Beginning tomorrow I'll show you how to run Selby."

"After you've attacked Lincolnville?"

"Don't try to trap me—we're operating under secret orders."

"The whole county knows you're riding tonight."

"And the county's on my side. I'll tell you this much, for the record. In just an hour a hundred Klansmen will rendezvous at a spot I'm not at liberty to disclose. We'll be joined there by a special posse from Atlanta. Both units are under my command."

"As Brad Selby?"

"Of course not. I'm a Kleagle from headquarters, performing my last tour of duty. No one will ask my name. Tomorrow I'll have earned my retirement."

"Luke must know who you are."

"Luke—and old Hamilton. I needed two friends on the spot to keep me informed." Brad sat up with a cavernous yawn. It had been a rewarding visit—and he had thoroughly enjoyed Uncle Doc's fuming as he outlined his plans. But it was time for a bit of discipline he anticipated more keenly. "My wife should be recovered by now. Tell her I want to see her."

"Is that all you have to say to me?"

"I've already told you too much. Follow your orders." Brad had intended the command as a dismissal. To his annoyance, Uncle Doc spoke again from the foyer door.

"I suppose you plan to kill Saladin?"

"That much you can count on. In fact, I won't rest until I do."

"Don't forget the Army considers murder a hanging matter."

"That wonder-boy major can't hang a nameless killer. Will you stop jawing and tell Reen I'm downstairs?"

Brad was deep in the bottle, and careless of his spinning head, when he heard his wife's steps on the stairs. Swaying to his feet, he was careful to draw back into the shadows before she entered the parlor: it was a purely defensive move, to measure her reaction.

He had expected a tear-stained face—or a mask of terror. The look she gave him as she crossed the room could hardly have been more casual. Had he just returned from a spree in Atlanta (he thought furiously), she would have greeted him with those same long-suffering eyes, with the martyred mouth he knew by heart.

"Come into the light," she said. "Show me you're real."

Brad stepped into the glow of the lamp above the mantel. "You might counterfeit a little surprise," he said bitterly.

"Uncle Doc told me a ghost had returned to haunt us," she replied. "It seems you actually exist."

"You're damned right I exist!" he shouted. "Must I prove it?"

"You already have."

"Not *this* way!"

He had already swept her into a brutal embrace. When he released her he knew that her lips had neither received nor rejected his kiss. They had merely submitted.

"Nothing is changed, I see," he told her.

"Surely you didn't expect it to be."

"Forgive me, Mrs. Selby," he snarled. "I was carried away by your beauty." He turned from her contemptuously as she continued to study him with the same weary air of resignation. Even as he had uttered the bogus compliment, he had sensed his error. Clearly, he must find ways to dominate this vixen. He would never succeed if he revealed the depth of his hate.

"Don't ask me to pretend," she said. "You're a bit late for that."

"I'm home, Reen. Home to stay. Doesn't it mean anything to you?"

"I've done well in your absence," she said. "Would you care to look around? Even in the dark you can see what I've rebuilt——"

"Selby's prospered," he admitted. "I'll grant you the success—you always had the knack. But I value my neighbors' opinions too. Is that too hard for you to grasp?"

"By no means." Her voice—unlike his own—was in complete control. As the silence grew between them, Brad felt that his wife was staring through him, without seeing him at all.

"Does a man's good name count for nothing?" he demanded. "Is money all that matters?"

"Saving your home wasn't easy, Brad."

"Don't pretend you saved it for me. You thought I was dead. It was your chance to remake Selby in your image, and you seized it."

"I rebuilt for the boy."

"Not that your motives matter," he said. "What concerns me now is the county's respect. I must earn it back."

"Uncle Doc has told me your plans."

"We're riding to Lincolnville tonight—two hundred in all. We're gutting it as thoroughly as Sherman gutted our plantations. I'll kill its black mayor myself, if I have to roast him alive. Then we'll see about rebuilding here. In *my* image, for a change. Do you follow me, so far?"

"All too clearly." Neither her voice nor her eyes had wavered. "Naturally, I'm going to warn Sal."

"You'll have no chance. Luke's on guard now, to make sure no one stirs from the house. Not that I'm afraid you'll talk, Reen. You're too good a Southerner—even if you have been flirting with Yankees." She colored at that, for the first time: Brad thought she was close to tears. He was obscurely pleased when her head lifted in the old, arrogant fashion he remembered so well. Even when he hated her the most, he could grant Reen her pride.

"Sal and his work force kept this plantation alive," she said. "Surely you can forgive him his success."

"Nigras were meant to be used. When they step out of line they pay the price."

"If you burn Lincolnville, where will the planters get hands this spring?"

"By spring our slaves will be hungry enough to come begging. The quarters are still standing. I'll let 'em move back. They can work for their keep again—as God intended."

"You *can't* kill Sal in cold blood."

"The subject's closed," he said. "Where's my son?"

"Mammy Jo took Andy to Asheville. I told her to stay."

"There'll be no more trouble in Cray County, once we've leveled that shantytown. The child can start home tomorrow."

"I'll send Luke to the crossing with a telegram," she said. This time, he was positive she was near tears—and gloried in the sudden sense of power it gave him.

"*I'll* send the telegram," he cried, banging the table with his fist. "Can't you understand your rule here is ended?"

"I'm trying, Brad," she said. "I'm trying hard."

Taking her tone for weakness, he pressed his attack. "Beginning tomorrow you'll be in charge of the kitchen. You'll plan dinners for my friends, pour our wine—and come to my bed when I wish it. Don't frown, my dear—it won't be often. Otherwise you'll keep clear. I'll manage things, with Luke's help. Just as I'll manage my son's raising."

"That's a mother's job."

"No, Reen—not after your record here. I'm raising the boy to respect my ideals and my code. Teaching him to be a leader in Georgia. Not a Yankee-lover like his mother."

She flung at him then, so violently he spun away from her by instinct: the hands she had raised were arched like claws. Putting the couch between them, he laughed aloud when he saw how deeply he had roused her.

"Don't force me to go on hating you," he warned her. "It could be right sad for us both."

"Can't you spare me anything? I've given you all you've ever wanted."

"All but yourself, Reen."

The taunt fell between them like a stone. Her voice was in control when she spoke again.

"I tried to make this a marriage, Brad. You know that."

Brad shrugged. Having established his authority, he could yield a point or two. "I've no complaints, now you've given me a son. You're a useful ornament here—and my boy needs a mother who can take orders."

"Do you expect me to be grateful for that dispensation?"

"I think you should, Reen. Don't forget, I've had a thorough sampling of opinion in the county. In your place I'd walk warily."

"I'll behave as I please."

"Not after tonight." He picked up his robe, flaring the wide skirts with a rotary motion of the wrists, enjoying the way his wife's eyes followed the gesture. "I'll be back in a few hours," he told her. "Try not to worry. As you know, I'm hard to kill."

"You've gone too far this time, Brad. If there's a God in heaven, you'll learn that much before morning."

"Allow me to rephrase your pious thought. With God on my side, I'm coming into my own at last."

"I can leave you when I like. The bank accounts are in my name."

Brad shook his head. "I know you better than you know yourself, Reen. You wouldn't leave Selby and my son. Not if I horse-whipped you before the whole county."

"I can have you hunted down—as an arsonist and a murderer."

"You can—but you won't."

"Why are you so sure?"

"I've told you, Reen. Perhaps you *would* have married Major Carroll—if I hadn't turned up tonight. But you'll never betray the master of Selby Hall to a Yankee." He was ready to leave at last. If he lingered a moment more (donning his snow-white robe with a flourish, preening himself at the mantel mirror before he lifted the hood), it was only to drive his lesson home.

"Where are you going now?" Reen asked.

"First, to our rendezvous at the ford." Now he was sure of her, he saw no harm in rehearsing his strategy. "The enemy is watching the turnpike: we'll cross to the north bank, to throw him off scent. Then we'll swing back to Brandt's Crossing. There are trails in the swamp even Hamilton doesn't know. With me to lead the way, we'll reach Lincolnville by midnight."

"Quent is here," she said. "And Uncle Doc. Aren't you afraid they'll warn Major Carroll?"

"I've told you Luke's outside. He'll shoot on sight if anyone attempts to leave."

"Even me, Brad?"

He was in the doorframe now—and turned to smile blandly. "Even you, my love."

Reen rushed forward to bar his path. Her hand was on his arm, the first time she had touched him of her own accord. Brad flung her aside—so savagely that she fell to her knees. Deliberately (since he was on the point of departure) he opened the portieres, pair by pair. Then, without a further glance at his wife, he lifted his hood and stepped outside into the darkness.

A horse waited at the block, with Luke at the bridle. Brad mounted with the running leap he had made famous, lifting one arm in a final, sardonic salute to the portico. Reen, he observed, had staggered out to watch him go. The rebel yell that ripped from his throat was pure animal release as he galloped toward his revenge.

5

When Brad had gone, Reen lingered outside a moment more, to assure herself that the silhouette of Luke Jackson on the driveway and the gun cradled in his arm were both genuine. Returning to the parlor on lagging feet, she felt her head swim. *You cannot faint again*, she told herself. *There's far too much at stake tonight.* Yet she had no memory of her near collapse on the couch.

Once her head had cleared, she found she could face her dilemma squarely. Not that she could plan coherently as yet. The threat of the silent watcher outside, the fact he could observe her slightest move in the brilliantly lighted parlor, still numbed her brain.

What if she walked boldly into the foyer, ran down the back stairs, and escaped by the cellar door? She abandoned the idea after making a tentative move in that direction and noting that Luke had stepped closer to the portico. Instead, she marched through the open door to the study and began to put together Sal's invoices, scattered to the four corners by the wind.

It was a melancholy task, but it kept her hands busy. Returning to the parlor, she found Uncle Doc seated in his usual chair. The old man's rocklike repose cheered her somewhat.

"Were you listening?" she asked in a whisper.

"Heard every word," he said loudly. "Pay no mind to that renegade outside."

Reen caught his purpose when she saw that Luke had stiffened at the label. Now they were two against one, she felt less forlorn.

"Where's Quent?"

"Still upstairs," said Yancey. "And unaware, as yet, that we're in a state of siege." He beckoned to the sentinel. "Come indoors, Luke. There's no need to catch your death out there. When Mr. Rowley appears, you can guard the three of us in comfort."

The overseer shambled into the room with a hangdog air that was almost comical. The gun he carried was cocked and ready. Reen saw it was an Army carbine, one of the English models known as a repeater. Brad's preparations, she reflected, had been thorough indeed.

"I won't ask if you're ashamed, Luke," she said. "It's obvious you've gone beyond that."

"Don't blame me, Mrs. Selby. I'm only followin' orders."

"Do you feel it was honorable to turn against me?"

"The cap'n is right, ma'am. We got to fight fire with fire."

"Then you approve this raid on Lincolnville?"

"I sure do."

"And my husband's plans for Sal?"

"We put it to a vote at the last Klan meetin'. Eight out of ten wanted him dead. I was one of 'em."

"At least, it's a relief to learn what you really think."

"If you ask me," said Yancey, "Luke's given precious little evidence he thinks at all." He addressed the overseer directly, with a coldness that transcended mere contempt. "You voted Sal's death for just one reason. In your heart you know he's the better man."

Luke's face darkened. "You got no call to say that, Dr. Yancey. This is my duty as I see it."

"Duty to what? Law and order, or mob rule? To a lady who's given you everything? Or to a man who's gone mad?"

"Ain't no use arguin'," said the overseer. "Mrs. Selby's had some mighty bad advice, but that's over now——" Luke broke off abruptly and flattened to the parlor wall. All of them had heard the rattle of hoofs on the drive.

Waiting in a corner of the divan, wondering if the first shot would come from the darkness (or from Luke's carbine), Reen gasped her relief when the rider arrived unmolested. After the man had secured his reins at the horse block and moved into the light-spill from the french doors, she saw it was Lieutenant Andrews, one of Dan Carroll's youthful aides. Dan had used the boy before to send messages.

She addressed Luke in a whisper while the overseer continued his grotesque crouch against the wall.

"Put down that gun, you idiot—and show yourself. He's bringing word from the major."

Luke babied his carbine a moment more, then leaned it in a corner and took his stand before the mantel with folded arms. Slow though his brain might be, he had grasped the folly of armed resistance to an Army messenger—when the messenger's comrades were probably in earshot.

"Just watch your tongue, ma'am," he warned. "I can shoot first, if need be."

Keeping the overseer in the corner of one eye, Reen moved to greet Andrews. For an instant she debated a dash for freedom, with the Union officer as a shield—but the hazards were too great. Andrews might be alone, after all. It would be safer to permit him to deliver his message.

"Come in, Lieutenant," she called. "You know Dr. Yancey, of course. And my overseer."

Andrews moved slowly from the shadowed foyer to the blaze of lamplight in the parlor. He was obviously bursting with tidings and uncertain of the best way to convey them. Reen spoke again, before he could note Luke's all-but-drooling interest. Once again she felt that the fate of Selby might hang on her next utterance.

"I suppose you've heard a group of Klansmen passed this way," she said. "We drove them off easily enough."

"We've flushed more than one small party tonight, Mrs. Selby," said Andrews. "They cut for cover—before we could trade shots. Seems this new Kleagle sent 'em out to cross us up."

"I'm afraid I don't follow, Lieutenant."

Andrews looked at the other two men. "May we talk in private?"

Luke picked up the cue promptly. "I'll be goin', ma'am." He turned to the study door, picking up the carbine almost as an afterthought. "I'll take the short cut, if you don't mind."

Reen watched him narrowly as he went through the study door with a properly resentful glance for Andrews. She knew he would listen behind the half-closed portal: to her eyes it seemed the grossest kind of ruse. Yet she realized it had convinced Dan Carroll's messenger, even before he spoke again.

"Please forgive my bluntness, Dr. Yancey," he said. "The request does not apply to you."

Uncle Doc exchanged a glance with Reen, then lumbered into the study, to return with a decanter and glasses. "May I give you a drink, Lieutenant?"

The aide declined the offer with excellent manners. "I didn't mean to sound mysterious," he said. "But my report is confidential.

The major isn't too sure of your overseer. To be frank, Mrs. Selby, he felt you shared his doubts."

"So far, I've had no cause to complain of Luke," said Reen. "Good field bosses are hard to come by these days."

"I'm not questioning your judgment," said Andrews. "And I'll make this brief. The Kleagle I just mentioned is a clever fellow. In fact, he's been almost too clever for his own good. Right now he's holding a powwow at the ford to make us believe he's riding clean out of the county. Actually, we're sure he'll strike at Lincolnville around midnight."

Reen chose her words with care—and wondered what Luke was making of this exact breakdown of Brad's strategy. "May I ask how you're so well informed?"

"You knew they'd hanged Jed Peters, I gather—it's all over the county by now. If the Kleagle ordered it—and the major says he did—the man's an idiot." Andrews spoke with the harsh certainty of youth. "He meant it as a warning to local members. Actually, it's driven a lot of good citizens clean out of the Klan."

Uncle Doc snorted a hearty affirmation. "That was my guess too. I'm glad to have it supported. Scaring Negro voters from the polls is one thing. Murder's quite another."

"The major wanted you to be the first to hear," said Andrews. "Nearly fifty vigilantes joined us tonight: there'll be twice that number tomorrow. Most of 'em are former Klansmen. When that Kleagle rides down on Lincolnville, we'll have help to spare."

Reen felt her heart contract at the news. It meant the tide had turned, that her war-weary neighbors, spurning the incitements of such firebrands as Hamilton, had finally come to their senses. No less surely, it insured Brad's doom—unless he chose to turn back. . . . Knowing this would be Luke's advice the moment he could reach the ford, she pulled her eyes away from the half-open study door.

"Will the attack still come, Lieutenant?"

"The major's sure of it," said Andrews. "They'll be swimming the river downstream—so they'll approach by way of the crossing. We'll have a reception committee waiting where they'll least expect it. The Klan won't ride again in Cray County—not after tonight." He looked down at his gloves, smiling at his boast. "At least, that's

Major Carroll's opinion. He wanted you to know—so you'd rest easy about Lincolnville."

"How did you learn their plans so soon?"

"It wasn't hard, Mrs. Selby. Not with fifty men changing sides. Lots of 'em were friends of Jed Peters."

"You're sure this Kleagle won't give up?" Even now Reen could not bring herself to speak Brad's name.

"Not tonight he won't," said Andrews. "A chance like this won't come again. He brought down nearly a hundred bullies from Atlanta—and he's mustered another hundred out of the piney woods. The sort of rednecks who'll shoot *anyone* to avoid hard work."

"It's a fight to the finish then?"

"Rely on that, ma'am. What the Kleagle don't know is that the local Klan has always been more bluster than brawn—until today's hanging. Tonight the stay-at-homes are fighting with the Army."

"I see, Lieutenant. Thank you for coming."

Andrews smiled. "The pleasure's mine, Mrs. Selby. If you'll excuse me now, I'll be on my way."

Reen spoke for Luke's ears. "I was hoping the major had sent you to guard us."

"Sorry, but we can't spare a man. My platoon must make a feint at the ford. We want the Klan to think we're fooled by their dodge."

Uncle Doc, still watching Reen, moved into the foyer with Andrews. "It seems the Army thinks of everything," he said. "Please wish the major success, in my name."

"Of course, Doctor—if I can reach the field in time. In any case, he'll come here when the action's ended."

Uncle Doc, Reen observed, was careful to keep in clear view while he saw Andrews to the door. Luke was in the room instantly, almost before the courier could mount and ride away.

"Thanks, Mrs. Selby," he said in a conspirator's whisper, though there was no need. "It was right smart, the way you drew him out."

Bringing Uncle Doc into the room with a gesture, Reen spoke quickly. "*You* were the spy, Luke—and you held the gun. What else could I do?"

"You didn't give him the Kleagle's name."

"Why should she?" asked Yancey. "Captain Selby is already riding to his death."

"There ain't enough Yankee bullets to kill the cap'n," Luke said confidently.

"Does that mean you're going to warn him?"

"D'you think I'd run out on Brad Selby now?"

"You might," said Uncle Doc. "If you stopped to think, that is. Major Carroll knows your plans. You *must* see the Klan's number is up. Hold your tongue tonight. You'll save your own neck tomorrow."

"And let the cap'n die?"

Yancey shot a glance at Reen. "Brad Selby is legally dead, Luke," he said. "Within the hour, another nameless Kleagle will be shot down outside Lincolnville. Stay where you are, and you'll avoid arrest tomorrow. It's as simple as that."

"Not to me it ain't," said the overseer. "I'm goin' to warn him, and you can't stop me."

Yancey could move fast for his age. The shotgun above the mantel seemed to leap into his hands, and the twin barrels had centered on Luke Jackson's back before he could clear the doorway. The overseer turned toward Reen with a stunned look in his eyes.

"Mrs. Selby, you ain't goin' to let your husband be shot down like a dog?"

Lorena had not spoken during that lightning change of fortune. Her gaze was fixed on the portrait of the old Judge in the gallery beyond—and she could almost believe that those wise, shadowed eyes were reading her heart, that they were telling her she was a Selby now, in every sense. *Brad was right*, she reflected, *I can't betray him now. While he lives, we're on the same side.*

"Let him go, Uncle Doc," she said.

"Lorena, you don't know what——"

"I can't let Brad die."

Slowly Yancey lowered the gun. Luke was through the door in a flash. She could hear the drum of his heels outside as he raced toward the horse barn.

"You've just signed Sal's death warrant," said Uncle Doc. "If Brad escapes tonight, he'll come back. All of Lincolnville may be destroyed. Innocent people who've trusted you and worked for you."

Reen seemed to hear the words from a distance: she did not answer directly. "Do you believe in a God of vengeance? If he exists he must be punishing me tonight for my sin with Daniel."

"Right now I don't even believe in a God of justice——" Yancey paused abruptly. Both of them had heard the pistol crack from the direction of the stables. "Or maybe I do."

Reen was on the plantation doctor's heels in their dash across the barnyard. Just inside the open doors of the horse barn she could see a writhing shape sprawled at the entrance to the nearest stall. The figure of a second man bent above the stall door. Even at the distance, she knew it was Luke and Quent. Her brother straightened and thrust the long-barreled pistol into his belt.

"Don't look so concerned, Lorena," he said—and stood aside to permit Yancey to kneel beside Luke. "He was a perfect target. I'm much too good a shot to kill a man unless I mean it. Is he hurt badly, Uncle Doc?"

Yancey had already cut away the blood-soaked cloth above the overseer's knee. He was now in the act of lashing Luke's belt about his upper thigh as a temporary tourniquet. "The bullet went through clean," he said. "We'll take him to the surgery and locate the bleeding vessel."

"Just make sure he doesn't ride a horse tonight," said Quent. "There's liable to be shooting—and he might get hurt."

Luke did not speak while they bore him into the surgery: fighting the pain of his wound in tight-lipped silence, he refused to meet Reen's eye. Quent did not linger as the plantation doctor went about his task with dispatch. Grimacing at the sweetish smell of blood, he guided Reen into fresh air again—then leaned back against the surgery porch, lighting a cheroot and blowing a smoke ring at the slowly clearing sky.

"Ten minutes ago," he said, "I almost blundered into the parlor. Fortunately, I heard Luke's voice in time. I went down the back stairs, and waited in the gallery. When he bolted for the stables, it was a simple matter to trail him."

"You were taking quite a chance," she said. "Brad might have posted other guards."

"My guess is that he left Luke as an observer only," said her

brother drily. "Your husband can have little doubt of your loyalty—
as you've just proved."

Reen's brain steadied: she was remembering why she had spared
Luke just now. Her own hunter was in his stall: once he was away
from Selby, nothing could catch him. But Quent's hand had closed
on her arm before she could start toward the horse barn.

"It's no use, Lorena. Even if you were twice the rider you are—
you'd never reach Brad in time. If you could, I don't think he'd
believe you."

"I'll ask Uncle Doc."

"He's busy saving a life."

"One of the house servants can go then."

"With the Klan about to storm into Lincolnville? Brad's fate is
in God's hands now. You've done what you could to save him."

In the surgery Luke gave an almost animal bellow. Reen shud-
dered and let herself move into the circle of her brother's arm.

"Take me back to the house," she said. "I'm afraid to go alone."

"Do you think the Selby ghosts are walking?"

"I can almost believe that Brad has joined them."

"Don't trust your powers of divination too far," said Quent cheerfully as they crossed the lawn. "We can do nothing but hope—until
Dan Carroll produces a corpse. This time, it had better be au-
thentic."

She broke free of him on that. "You've no right to think such
things. Much less to say them——"

"Sometimes it's a healthy idea to voice one's deepest wishes," he
said. "Are you *really* sorry I stopped Luke in time?"

Reen did not answer. Glad of the darkness, she stood for a moment on the portico. The sky, which had seemed about to clear,
had grown murky again, with thunderheads massed against the
stars. If the sky was still overcast by moonrise, Brad might ride
through Dan's ambush unharmed. . . .

In the surgery Luke gave a second bellow—but there were no
further sounds from that quarter. During the war years (when there
had been no assistant for Uncle Doc) Reen had helped in similar
emergencies: she could picture the routine clearly. Now that the
vein was tied off, she knew that Yancey had administered an opiate
—strong enough to keep his patient quiet until morning.

In the foyer Quent's voice boomed gaily to rally the frightened servants from the kitchen and order dinner. Reen moved into the lamplight to add her voice to her brother's.

It was incredible that she and Uncle Doc had just stood here at gun point, drained of their last reserve of strength. Now, if she could believe Lieutenant Andrews, the tables were turned. Brad was their only threat—and Brad was riding to his death.

6

Two miles below Brandt's Crossing, where the turnpike forked to meet the river road, the Negro village called Lincolnville slept under a midnight sky that was beginning to show a hint of moonlight as the thunderheads moved on. For the past hour Major Dan Carroll had waited here patiently, his rain-wet hat brim low above his eyes. There was a throb of weariness at his temples as he continued to survey the bottom lands, where the truck gardens of the settlement merged with the swamp.

The night riders had gathered near the crossing: he was sure of that. If the attack was planned for tonight, it must come from that direction. Was it possible that Andrews' feint had failed to deceive them? Had they really withdrawn beyond the river, to fight another day?

Of course, it had been unwise to send word to Reen—but he had wanted her to know the situation was in hand.

Despite his long wait, Dan still believed his plans would bear fruit. The main body of the Klansmen had been ordered to gather at the ford in the hour after sundown, to await the arrival of the Atlanta Kleagle. Thanks to the reports of the deserters, he was sure tonight's raid was a supreme effort. Lieutenant Andrews' simulated attack was meant to suggest he had miscalculated the direction of the strike and its purpose. When the Klansmen had retreated pell-mell across the river, the Army had pulled back, apparently to return to its cantonment. . . . Now, with Lincolnville less than ten miles distant and the dragoons seemingly gone until morning, the Klan's leader must believe he could strike at will. He could never guess he was riding into ambush—unless he had received a last-minute warning.

Carroll dismounted from his restless horse. At his nod the animal was led into the shadows of a thicket where two hundred mounted infantrymen were soothing their mounts with practiced ease. Something about the long waiting (and the nature of the trap) brought back disturbing memories. On surface this was but one of many actions. The stir of memory troubled him, since he could not pin down its origin.

Diagonally across the expanse of the turnpike (its dust well laid by the rain) another dense thicket lifted its tangled mass against the moon. It made a perfect cover for the fifty-odd vigilantes who had ridden into his camp at sundown to offer their services. He had deployed these unexpected allies with care. Most of them were Confederate veterans: he could trust them if the fighting was close.

Not that he expected a battle, in the formal sense—not even the knee-to-knee duel all ex-cavalrymen know by heart. Still, it was good to remember the odds were in his favor. To know that this little group of citizen volunteers was only the vanguard of an alliance that would someday forge a nation's bonds.

Lincolnville lay in a slight hollow, protected from the cold northwest winds by the hills along the river. No lights showed behind the shuttered windows. The occupants of the cabins slept soundly at this hour, unaware of the threat from Indian Ford—and the defense prepared against it.

Dan moved down the line of mounted men to return to his own horse. Here a thicket protected him on all sides. Merely by parting the branches he could look down on that mass of dwellings and study their grouping carefully, by the light of the rising moon.

The village had grown haphazardly at first, along the line of the bottom lands. Today, with Sal as its leader, the settlement had a surprisingly ordered look. Its yards were well raked; many had split-rail fences. Most of the houses were painted. . . . Dan smiled faintly, recalling the outcry that had risen over those white walls. Cray County would have accepted the presence of a Negro shantytown in time. The neatness of Lincolnville, the fact that its better homes compared favorably with the cabins of some poor-white farmers, were insults too great to be borne.

An hour ago, after he had perfected his defenses, Dan had asked himself if he should warn Sal of his peril. But the Negro village would never have remained in this perfect state of repose had word spread that a raid was imminent. When the Klansmen poured down the river road, Lincolnville must seem a sitting target.

Carroll heard a stir in the thicket across the road: a darker shadow detached itself from the ambush. With shoulders hunched, young Captain Keller scuttled among the trees to join his commanding officer. It was the same Keller who had served with the 2nd Pennsylvania Cavalry. Choosing the Army as a career, he had been assigned to this area on request, and now served as Carroll's chief of staff.

"All shipshape, Major—but I wish we had a breeze."

"It's barely midnight. Are the civilians getting restless?"

"Not yet," said Keller. "Don't worry, sir. They'll pull their weight."

"I'm sure of that."

"They're as anxious as we are to see the last of the night riders. Can you believe we've got Johnnies on our side?"

"Tonight we'll use any help we can get," said Carroll. "This is one action that must be decisive, or we've wasted our powder. Remember, we have their leaders' records—all but the Kleagle. They'll be given just ten seconds to surrender. That order includes Colonel Hamilton."

"I understand, sir. Let's hope your warning works."

They rehearsed the strategy for the final time. With the force at his disposal, and the promise of that rising moon, Carroll was positive he could box the enemy in enfilading fire, although they would probably equal his own force in number. Once the last Klansman had ridden into rifle range, he planned to offer these renegades a chance to disarm and surrender. The warning would be shouted by one of his sharpshooters, a leather-lunged sergeant stationed in the crotch of a yellow pine that overhung the road. The signal for this warning would be a shot fired from the command post. If it was disregarded, a second shot (also from the commander's pistol) would be an order to open fire.

"Why d'you think they won't give up?" asked Carroll. "They're bound to see their position's hopeless."

"Nine out of ten of these men are desperadoes, Major. If Army courts here don't want 'em for murder, another state will claim the honor. That sort of outlaw prefers to die in his boots."

"Somehow it was different in the war," said Carroll. "Success in battle was the purpose of all military strategy. It said so in the book, and any dodge was in order. This is an old-style Army trap—with Lincolnville as the bait. It doesn't seem fair to spring it on civilians."

"Don't think these raiders wouldn't ambush *us* if they were smart enough."

Keller had spoken with vehemence: Carroll gave his second-in-command a sharp look. "I gather you're anxious to end your Georgia service, Captain."

"I'm a soldier, sir," said Keller. "I don't enjoy police duty. For that reason alone, I'm eager to see the last of this red clay country. As you know, I've asked for transfer to the West: that's where our real history will be made."

"History's being made in Georgia too, these days," said Carroll. "We'll have a part in the rewriting, if things end well tonight." He held up a white-gloved hand for silence. Far off, where the road was lost in the mossed water oaks of the swamp, a hoot owl had sounded its call in the night. Issued from a human throat, it signaled that the enemy was approaching at last.

"Back to your post, Captain. Cock all carbines. No firing until the second signal—which comes *after* Sergeant Hardy's warning. Is everything clear?"

"Quite, Major."

"One thing more. The first volley will come from this side; we've the greater fire power. When you've answered it, lead the charge. It should help break the enemy's spirit if he sees he's been fired on by Georgians."

"Providing there's a spirit left to break," said Keller. "This should be like the fight at Indian Ford. Remember that ambush, Major— in the fall of '64? We gave 'em no warning *then*. Just between us, I'm against giving one tonight."

Keller was gone before the hoot owl sounded a second signal, to advise Carroll that the enemy was now almost in view. Dan felt his jaw set in a familiar hard line: his chief of staff had jogged his memory alive just in time. . . . The first Klansman rode into view a second later. Tall in the saddle, he seemed to float between earth and sky, thanks to the coal-black charger beneath him.

Carroll sighed—and repeated his order to cock carbines. In the gloom of the copse he heard the order obeyed—staggered by squads, lest the sound carry to the turnpike. History, he reflected, repeated itself less often than the historians claimed—but there was an uncanny parallel between this well-laid trap and the action at the ford. Even in the moonlight the leader of the raid seemed the image of Captain Bradfield Selby.

In another moment, the lone horseman had been joined by a flying wedge of riders. Then, as the raiders poured out of the swamp in full strength, the wedge became a multitude. Each Klansman wore the same ghostly robes—and some of the horses were also caparisoned in white. Only the leader's disguise had a trace of color, a barbaric insignia on the breast that would have been scarlet by daylight. In the uncertain glow of the moon it resembled dried blood.

The Kleagle rode with the easy seat of a cavalryman: in his left hand he held a white lance that served as a guidon for the troop that streamed in his wake. The raiders moved in silence. Save for the beat of their hoofs, they could have passed for monstrous night birds—white cranes, perhaps, or falcons winging from some alien world. Prepared though he was, Carroll felt a prickle of fear down his spine as he lifted his pistol from its holster. Riding at a full gallop, the phantom horde was almost in his line of fire. A second's hesitation could let them burst free of the ambush, with their goal a scant four hundred yards beyond.

On came the dead-white phalanx, rising from a dip in the road-bed to stand out in stark relief against the cloud-flecked sky. It was a sight to stir the heart. Even the ghost robes suited the occasion—since this was, in sober truth, a dash between the jaws of death. . . . A second pistol shot would snap the jaws in earnest. Carroll's finger tightened on the trigger, sending up the signal that would alert Hardy in the pine crotch.

The timing had been perfect. The Kleagle, riding a full two lengths ahead of his wolf pack, was now at the eastern end of the copse, where the trees gave way to meadow. His massed horsemen were dead in the Army's sights. At that pell-mell gait they would be enfiladed before they could grind to a stop. When Hardy bellowed the command to halt, a shiver passed down the line. It was as though the enemy had divined the trap by instinct.

"*You're in a box! Throw down your arms!*"

The warning had been phrased with care. It was a direct appeal to the leader—made on the chance the Kleagle would hesitate to waste his own life along with the others. There was now no doubt that the rank and file behind him understood. With a great sawing of bridles and a brimstone explosion of oaths, the white-sheeted horsemen reared in their saddles, to the last rider. For an instant the Kleagle seemed ready to do likewise as he swung his mount into a suicidal wheel and galloped back, along the flank of his tight-bunched force. Then, as no further sound broke the quiet, he lifted in his stirrups and leveled his white lance at Lincolnville.

"*Yaaaaaaaaaah! On to the Forks!*"

It was a full-throated rebel yell. The Kleagle, Carroll saw, was convinced that the warning had been a ruse. Whatever the cause, there was no time for hesitation. He lifted his pistol and aimed the second shot at the leader's head.

It was the signal to open the action—and Dan's own admission that his warning had been wasted. He had no other choice, now that he had recognized the voice beneath that cone-shaped hood.

Again he had the feeling that history had gone berserk while the first volley smashed home, delivered in unison from two hundred Army carbines. The answer from the road was spatterdashed—and fired at invisible targets. When the vigilantes answered, half the enemy saddles were empty and a score of horses were kicking in the ditches.

There was no need for a third volley before the militia charged from its ambush to fragment the survivors and force their surrender at gun point. Only the Kleagle and two of his lieutenants (who had somehow missed the hail of lead) continued the breakneck charge on Lincolnville.

Carroll's shot had been a clean miss. He fired again before he galloped in pursuit, in a hopeless attempt to head off the madman. One of the lieutenants had already dropped under a rifle crack. The second pitched headlong from his stirrups when his horse went down, and lay beside the ditch with a broken neck. The leader (and this, too, was part of history's repeat performance) rode on, well out of rifle range. A moment later his banshee silhouette was lost among the walls of the Negro village. Then he burst into view, to bear down on the neat white cottage that housed Sal and Florrie.

The headlong approach of the Klansmen (and the double volley that had halted them) had come too fast for conscious timing. Incredible as it seemed, only a literal minute had passed since Dan's warning shot. Riding toward the Forks at his best speed, he could only look on in helpless fury when the torch sputtered into flame on Sal's doorstep.

The cottage, blank-faced like all the others, had not seemed to waken. The shutters were bolted—and seemed, from a quarter mile away, stout enough to withstand assault. A second torch had now been driven into the sandy yard: Carroll noted that both were long-handled flambeaux, with a great ball of pitch at their ends. The rider circled the house one more time, his voice lifted in the rebel yell.

Carroll was unprepared for the double detonation, so close that it seemed almost a single report. It was followed by a sudden spout of flame that seemed to have its origin on one of the window sills—and brought another scream of triumph from the Kleagle. Circling yet again, he plucked both torches from the sand and cast them into the heart of Sal's domain—through the gaping hole the two hand bombs had torn in the clapboard wall.

A single wailing cry had come from the house when the explosives did their work. Carroll recognized Florrie's voice—and shouted to Keller to ride to the left, in a last attempt to cut the Kleagle off. Judging his escape to the second, Brad Selby dared to ride up again to the cottage porch, to check the progress of the fire. Built of pine, the house was already burning like a matchbox.

Brad fired just once, into the massing flames. Then he rode straight for the swamp—bending low in his saddle to avoid the fusillade that followed him and reversing his robes as he went, until horse and rider blended with the night.

Less than five minutes had passed since the action was joined. On the turnpike, hemmed by blue uniforms, the hooded figures were casting down their arms. The fight at the Forks had been a brilliant success—save for the Kleagle's luck. It was already too late to save Sal's home, or its occupants.

Carroll risked his life to ride up on the porch. Florrie, half her face blown away by the explosion, lay dead beside a shattered cradle, where two small brown shapes sprawled like broken dolls. The crumpled form spread-eagled across its foot was Sal. Dan could understand the reason for the Kleagle's shot, and his final howl of joy as he rode on.

Even as Dan stared at that inert tableau, a great blanket of smoke obscured his vision. The house next door had caught, and its owners had begun to tumble into the yard with what belongings they could salvage.

The horse beneath him, an old cavalry mount, had merely whinnied at the smell of death within the cabin. It screamed in real terror as Sal's rooftree collapsed, sending a great burst of sparks across the moon's face. When Carroll rode back to rejoin his command he realized that his tunic was afire and stripped it from his back with seconds to spare.

7

The clock in Sal's cabin, striking midnight in the soothing quiet, had wakened its owner from a profound slumber. For a moment he lay quietly in the comfort of the big double bed while he counted the strokes. He had prayed that the dark would pass without a threat—and could begin to hope the prayer was answered.

True, he had heard persistent rumors that the Klan had massed at the ford—but the air was thick with evil talk these days, and a busy man could hardly pause to listen. . . . Miss Reen's crop was in: when they went over the books in the morning, she would see that her profits had soared to new heights. It was a good thought to take back to slumber as the last strokes died. Saladin Webster let his eyelids droop, and composed his mind for sleep. With a long day ahead at the gin, he would need those hours of repose between midnight and dawn.

Saladin Webster. His dozing brain echoed the words with pride. Like most Negroes, he had assumed a surname to enter on the voters' rolls—when and if the vote became truly universal in this corner of the South. Loyalty to Miss Reen had suggested he take the plantation name, but the memory of Captain Selby made that impossible. In the end Sal had chosen the New England Senator as his sponsor—remembering the history book in the Judge's library, and Webster's immortal plea for the supremacy of the Union.

Only last Sunday he had written his new name in the register of the Negro church at Brandt's Crossing. He had put the name of Florida Webster beside it (his wife could now read well enough, but complete signature was still beyond her). Beneath those bold letters he had inscribed the names of their children—Abraham Lincoln Webster, who was a boy just under two, and Juanita Webster, the six-month-old.

Florrie was not beside him at the moment. He could hear her moving quietly through the room they used as a nursery—and smiled through his drowsiness as he recalled the reason for her absence. Juanita had been suffering from the croup. Two days ago Dr. Yancey had pronounced her cured—and both children now shared the same cradle. But Florrie was a careful mother as well as a loving one. Wakening at midnight, and thinking of the two small sleepers, she could not rest until she made sure they were covered against the chill of morning.

Hearing the creak of the gently rocking cradle, Sal had let his mind drift into dreams again.

The double explosion that smashed the nursery wall did not quite blast him from his bed. But he was up almost instantly, staring wide awake as his nostrils flared to the smoke that filled the room.

Deep in bone-weary slumber, he had not quite heard the hoofbeats on the turnpike, or the shots that had halted some two hundred Klansmen in their tracks. The Kleagle's rebel yell had reached him faintly, in the middle ground between sleep and waking. These sounds in themselves would not have roused him. He had heard other shots in the night, and other rebel yells: it was not the first time the Klan had circled Lincolnville.

The rending crash of the bombs had given his home its death-blow: the house would have burned beyond salvage even without the pine-knot torches the Kleagle had tossed into the nursery. Choking in the roiling smoke, Sal paused to soak a cloth in water and cover his face before he ran down the stairs. Seconds were precious, but the blast of heat would have felled him without some protection.

A glance was enough to confirm his fears. The bomb, exploding less than a yard from the cradle, had killed both children while they slept. As for Florrie, he could not bear to look at the once-lovely body, now reduced to a welter of blood and brains at the cradle's foot.

Her shriek still echoed in Sal's ears when he heard the thunder of hoofs outside and knew the raider was returning for his *coup de grâce*. The wind whipped the smoke away, giving him a clear view of the white-robed figure forcing his horse to mount the porch. Sal crouched beside the cradle, feeling his muscles coil for the spring that would close his fingers on the killer's throat. When he saw the pistol in the Kleagle's hand, an instinct deeper than hate rooted him to the floor.

The muzzle seemed to touch his head, while the rider loomed above him. The sound of the report and the man's insane scream of joy came as one. Hearing the bullet sing past his ear, Sal continued to follow instinct; feigning death, he dropped face down across the cradle and waited breathlessly for his Nemesis to ride off.

He dared not rise at once (though he could feel the flames lick at his ankles) lest the man had lingered outside to make sure of his aim. For a moment there was a sound of another horseman in the yard—and he continued to sprawl across his children's bodies while a second rider mounted the porch. This, too, might be an enemy: he could not risk a look. . . . A little later, when the second horseman had gone, he realized dimly that the roof was about to collapse overhead.

When he staggered into the open, the smoke half blinded him. Until his vision cleared, he moved in a stupor, colliding with other scurrying forms and shaking off the hands that strove to detain him. The same blind force that had saved his life was now urging him into flight—but even now he was moving with purpose. He did not pause for breath until he stood beneath the water oaks that bordered the swamp. Here sanity of a sort returned and he found he could see again.

Of all Lincolnville, only his cottage and the two adjoining houses had suffered real damage. A bucket brigade, working from the river under Army orders, had begun to douse adjoining roofs, to stamp out the brands that still skyrocketed from the three blazing cabins. On the turnpike the surrender of the shattered band of raiders was complete. Sal felt his throat constrict in savage pleasure as he noted the windrows of the dead. It was appropriate that these evil creatures should fall from their saddles, wrapped in ready-made winding sheets.

Unfinished business remained, however: he had no time to rejoice over the destruction of the local Klan. He had come to the swamp for a definite reason: the man who had killed his wife and children (if he made good his escape) would be forced to ride this way. There was a trail to the river road, which led in turn to Selby. . . . Sal had used the weed-grown trace a hundred times as a short cut to the plantation. He could follow it by moonlight, once he was sure of his quarry.

Fumbling his way in the dark, he moved to his first objective, a clearing on a little knoll, a hundred yards from the first house in Lincolnville. His heart leaped when he saw the man's silhouette against the night. Evidently, the Kleagle had paused here for a final check of his handiwork before he followed the trail through the swamp. The night rider had reversed his robe, and now seemed black as the horse he rode. He sat easily in his saddle, with a flask in his hand. Sal's fists curled while the rider drank deep, then flung the empty bottle into the night. . . . Daring to creep closer while his enemy smacked his lips over the brandy, Sal saw that the hood has been tossed back across his shoulders.

With no surprise, he found the Kleagle was Brad Selby. He had half suspected the man's identity when he faced his pistol.

Had he been closer, Sal could have closed the gap in a single leap. But the underbrush was dense with briars; another move might have betrayed his presence, and the pistol in Brad Selby's belt was still a lethal threat. Besides, it did not matter greatly if the Kleagle escaped him at the moment. When Brad cast one more approving glance at the fire in Lincolnville, then swung his horse's head toward the swamp, Sal felt his last doubt vanish.

All roads led to Selby now. He took to the trail in his turn, running with the speed of a homing mastiff.

8

Reen had been the first to notice the glare of flames against the eastern sky.

Too tense to think of sleep, she had forced herself to go through the ritual of dining with her brother and Uncle Doc. When the travesty of that late supper had ended, the trio had settled about a card table, pretending to concentrate on a game of dummy whist. . . . The time had passed, after a fashion. It had been almost a relief to discover a fire had been set in Lincolnville, after all. At least, it proved the Klan's threat had not been an empty gesture.

Uncle Doc spoke first, after they had stood for a moment on the eastern portico. "It isn't too big a blaze."

"A half dozen cabins, at the most," said Quent.

"Does it mean they broke through Dan's ambush?" Reen asked.

"It can't mean much else," said her brother. "If Brad got that far, there must have been heavy fighting."

"I'd best hitch up and head that way," said the plantation doctor. "Dan has only one Army sawbones in his command. He'll need help tonight."

"Take Quent with you," said Reen. "Send him back when you've learned what happened."

She watched them go in a strange, brooding calm—glad that neither of them had put the unspoken question into words. Proof of Brad's rebellion against the future was spelled out now in letters of fire. Until she knew his fate—and Sal's—she could only wait. No matter what that fate might be, she would not betray Brad to Daniel Carroll. If her husband had died in that suicidal onslaught, there would be no need of betrayal.

It had been a bitter choice—but she had found the strength to make it.

Quent and Uncle Doc had left with the waning moon—the plantation doctor with the familiar black bag on the wagon seat, Reen's brother astride her own swift hunter.

Now, a good three hours later, in the blackness before dawn, the fires on the horizon had long since died—and Reen sat unstirring beside her parlor grate. . . . She had dreaded the vigil—and yet, oddly enough, she had found it bearable. When the hoofbeats sounded on the drive she turned up the lamps. Hearing Quent's slow step on the portico, she refused to accept his hesitation as a bad augury. Even when he paused in the foyer to shed his rain cape, she did not go to meet him until she had tossed another pine knot on the embers.

"Dan swept the field," he said. "I suppose you guessed that."

"What about Brad?"

"He led the Klan into the ambush. It's quite possible he was shot down. The count isn't complete——"

"Did Daniel tell you that?"

"There wasn't time. He's unhurt—and will come here as soon as he can. Captain Keller gave me the facts."

"Don't spare me, Quent."

She listened in brooding silence to his report. It was hardly news that Brad had done his best to wipe out Lincolnville—since the Negro settlement was Sal's monument. Now she knew Sal's cabin had been destroyed, she found she could accept the fact without surprise. That, too, was part of the hard story fate had decreed from the beginning.

"You're sure no one escaped before the cabin burned?"

"Dan himself saw the four of them inside," said Quent. "Brad's a dead shot, with a sleeping target. I'm still praying he stopped a bullet later."

"You know he escaped—and so do I."

"Even so, Lorena, you can set your mind at rest. He isn't likely to turn up again."

"Why not? He's accomplished his purpose. Now he can rest on his laurels."

"The attack was a failure."

"It's true the local Klan is smashed. What's that to him? Either he or Sal had to die. Against Brad, Sal never had a chance. The devil fought on Brad's side tonight. He always has."

"Brad can never show his face at Selby now," Quent insisted. "Not with organized vigilantes at Brandt's Crossing—and the Klan destroyed."

"Who knows tonight's Kleagle was Brad? Did you tell Daniel?"

"No, Lorena. I had no chance."

"Colonel Hamilton was probably shot down. Luke will never talk. If Daniel himself suspects, he can't be sure. There's no one to pin the blame where it belongs."

"You'll have to tell Dan the truth now."

Reen hesitated for a long moment. "I can't, Quent."

"Fortunately, I've no such scruples. Nor does Uncle Doc."

"I forbid both of you to speak."

"Let's say Brad did get off with a whole skin. Are you going to take him back? Live out your days with a murderer?"

Knowing there was but one reply, Reen saw she was beaten at last. When her brother put his hand on hers, she let it rest there and bowed her head. She would weep later at the ease of her yielding. At the moment, her eyes were dry, her tired brain empty of responses.

"What can I do?" she whispered.

"First, we'll go to Asheville," said Quent. "We'll get the boy, and start your suit for divorce. If Brad contests it, we've ways to shut him off. No court would grant him custody of Andy."

"It would mean giving up my son's inheritance."

"He'll have precious little to inherit here if Brad's in charge. Get out while there's time, Lorena. I'll hire your lawyers——"

"What can I say to Daniel?"

"Write to him later. You can marry when your divorce is granted."

Reen knew that Quent was right: she should follow his advice. Realizing the depth of her surrender—and all it would mean for the future—she felt peace invade her spirit. Once again there was a joy in yielding to male logic. She spoke quickly, while the impulse held. "Go pack your bags. We'll leave Selby the moment it's light."

She studied her brother closely—a little disappointed that he could accept her yielding with such calm. "We'll take the gig," he said, "and go south to Macon. It'll be daylight in another hour. Hadn't you better start packing too?"

"I'll leave this house as I am," she said. "You'd better hurry before I change my mind."

LORENA

"You won't change this time, my dear. Life won't let you. Not the sort of life Brad plans to lead here."

"Suppose we're mistaken? He could be really dead."

"Selby's yours then. You can always return."

He left her on that note—taking the stairs in quick strides. Once he had gone, she could not quite believe she had uttered the words of capitulation—but even now she had the sense of great weights lifting.

Striving for calm, she let herself drop into the nearest chair. Something beyond her ken swung her eyes to the open french door. The night had begun to lift, though the dawn was no more than a wan promise. Beyond the gate was the Macon turnpike, a train to Asheville, a whole new universe she could explore at will. Yet, like the prisoner who refuses to believe his eyes when his cell door swings wide, she could not accept the proof of freedom.

She saw why, a moment later, when a figure detached itself from the boxwoods and took form against the waning dark. Long before the man stepped into the light, she realized it was her husband.

"So you came back," she said.

"For good, this time. Did you think I wouldn't?" Brad's tone was light, almost pleasant. He tossed his robe aside, unstrapping the pistol at his belt as he did so.

"I've heard what happened at the Forks," she said. "Don't deny your part in it."

Brad folded his robe neatly and tucked it away in a cupboard. Opening the chamber of his pistol, he took out a used shell, tossed it into the fire, and hid the weapon beneath his robe.

"What are you saying, Reen?" he asked. She could almost have sworn his surprise was genuine. "You must remember I returned to Selby at dusk. Since then I haven't stirred from my hearth."

"Will that be your story?"

"*Our* story," he corrected. "Don't blame me if some local raiders tried to burn out colored town tonight—and bungled the job."

"Sal is dead. So are Florrie and the children. You were their murderer."

"It's a wonder someone hasn't killed that uppity Nigra long ago," he said with a shrug. "I won't pretend I'm sorry."

"And you plan to take up here—as if nothing had happened?"

"Why not—until someone else forgets his place? Or should I say *her* place this time?"

"Does that mean me, Brad?"

"Maybe I should teach you right now that I'm master here—in a way you'll remember."

Now that he had traced the pattern of their future, Reen knew she had expected no other. Her impulse to flee with Quent had been purest folly. By the same token, she had expected Brad to return unwounded from all his wars. He would, of course, disavow connection with the Lincolnville raid: as Bradfield Selby, a Southern gentleman, he would keep his status inviolate. The picture was finally in order: like a jigsaw puzzle, each item was in place. . . . Only one piece remained unclassified—the wraith that had dogged Brad's footsteps ever since he had crossed the portico.

She had seen the phantom move from the shadow of the boxwoods. Half aware of its presence, she had watched it mount the portico in turn—then hesitate, just outside the reflection of the parlor lamps, while her husband shed his robes. Now, in round-eyed wonder, she saw that the wraith was Sal.

"You'd better stop posing, Brad," she said. "We have a visitor."

In the act of reaching for a decanter Brad turned sharply. Sal had just stepped into the room. He stood with one hand on a chair back—swaying a little, as though the effort of standing were almost beyond his strength. Reen saw that his clothing was a mass of charred rags, his arms a nightmare of burns. The mark of death was upon him, save for his eyes. They glowed with a consuming fire that made her recoil instinctively, though he seemed to ignore her presence. In all her life she had never seen such hate in a human glance.

"It's me, Cap'n," he said. "Miss Reen's Sal. Doan' yo' know me?"

The fact that Sal's voice had gone back to the singsong of the field hand shocked Reen almost as much as his fire-scarred body. Lucifer emerging from hell could not have been more menacing—and, like that fallen angel, the visitor was here for an accounting.

Brad had reacted instantly to the apparition. For the first time, Reen read fear in his face. She watched his eyes dart toward the cupboard where he had hidden the pistol—and noted the small shrug when he saw he could not reach it in time.

"I killed you, boy," he said. "I shot you between the eyes. Stop haunting me."

"Ah ain't a ghos', Cap'n."

"I burned you out, damn you!"

"Ah doan' die easy, Cap'n Selby. Reckon you'n me's alike thut way."

"For the last time, you black baboon—get out!"

Step by step Brad had inched toward the mantel—and the gun that leaned against it. His eyes were fixed on Sal's right hand—and the bull whip coiled round his wrist like a monster snake. He did not reach his goal: when the whip lashed out, Reen saw the Negro had divined Brad's purpose. The seven-foot rawhide cracked like a pistol at Brad's cheek, just missing the eye. A second crack, and a third, cut Brad's shirt from his back, leaving a bloody cross where the cloth had been. A fourth flick of the rawhide, whipped round Brad's waist like a lariat, tumbled him across the hearth.

"Wait, Sal! That's enough!" It was more scream than coherent protest. Even as she uttered it Reen knew it was beyond anyone's power to stand between this avenger and his prey. Sal noticed her at last, before he lifted the whip again.

"Sorry, Miss Reen," he said thickly. "He gotta pay—fo' whut he done." Each word seemed spaced with a whipcrack, and each blow drew blood as Brad rolled there in the ashes.

"Cain't let yo' die easy, Cap'n. Ah'm fixin' you—lak you fix Black Lolly—"

Black Lolly. Reen closed her eyes on the memory of the huge slave who had once been the Judge's best blacksmith. Lolly had been a broken wreck the year she came to Selby—a pensioner who slept behind the horse barn and dragged his deformed limbs like a sick crab. It was said that a rampaging stallion had maimed him—but gossip insisted it was the aftermath of Brad's beating in one of his drunken rages. . . .

"You broke Lolly's back, Marse Brad," said Sal. "Now Ah aims t'break yo'." He dropped the whip and sprang toward the hearth —just as Brad rolled to his knees and seized the shotgun.

Sal hesitated for the barest fraction. Then, step by step, he bore down upon the hearth, careless of the weapon leveled at his body. The first hammer of the gun clicked on an empty chamber. The roar of the shot, as the second barrel spouted flame, seemed to burst the parlor walls. The heavy charge struck the Negro in the side. Even from where she stood, Reen saw the wound was mortal, that it had torn a literal hole in Sal's body. It did not slow his advance.

Brad flung the gun at his assailant, but the Negro merely dodged. Then, as Sal sprang for the kill, Brad broke into a scuttling run. It was a last effort: one of Sal's hands had already closed on his windpipe. For a moment more both men stood eye to eye while Sal shook his victim as easily as though Brad were a rag doll. Mesmerized by sheer horror, Reen could still marvel at his strength. For that moment, it seemed, Sal was possessed by demons.

Again she cried out a futile protest. This time, it was lost in Brad's bellow as the Negro released his grip on the throat. Brad seemed too weak to struggle when Sal's fist, knotted at his belt, swung him clear of the floor. In the same motion, Sal raised one foot to the arm of the couch. Then, using both hands, he smashed Brad's inert body down, back first, across the upraised knee. There was a fearful cracking sound—and the victim collapsed as neatly as a jackknife.

Sal dropped his broken enemy to the carpet and faced Reen at last.

"Sorry, ma'am," he said in a tone that was both dignified and oddly serene. "He woan' trouble *no* one now." Almost before he could force out the words he had sprawled face down across the hearth.

Reen saw he was dead before she left the wall. She found that she could walk, after a fashion, though she seemed to float in mid-air as she moved to kneel beside her husband.

Minutes later Uncle Doc burst into the room with Dan Carroll a stride behind him. She was still holding Brad's head in her lap and wiping the blood from his eyes as best she could.

9

"Of course he won't walk again," said Yancey. "Not with a broken spine. Paralysis is complete, almost to chest level. But he'll live—for a while, at least. If you can call it living."

"How much time do you give him?" asked Carroll.

"A year, at most. Probably he'll last only a few months. Sal meant to cripple him—so he'd go into old age neither dead nor alive. But he did too good a job. The paralysis is bound to spread."

Dan nodded and walked a few steps down the portico to look up at the brightening day. After the rain the morning was flawless. Yancey breathed deep of the Indian summer air—and settled on the bottom step to let his old bones absorb the sunshine.

It had been a hard night at Lincolnville—and what they found at Selby had been harder still. It was fortunate the Army surgeon had accompanied him in the buckboard, along with an enlisted assistant. They had come to borrow drugs: their help had been invaluable when he had moved Brad to the bed from which he would never rise.

"I still can't believe Captain Selby's in our midst again," said Dan. "Did he really come home to die?"

"Your surgeon endorses my diagnosis." Uncle Doc glanced sharply at Carroll. *You call yourself a philosopher*, he told him silently. *You'll have need of philosophy today.*

"What will Lorena do now? What can she do?"

"We must let her answer that," said the plantation doctor, with his eyes on the garden. Quent Rowley had begun to cross it on weary feet.

"I suppose I already have my answer," said Dan. "Perhaps I'm too stubborn to accept it."

Yancey closed his eyes on the memory of that brightly lighted parlor and the dark avenger sprawled in death at the hearth. He could still hear Lorena's low, crooning wail as she sat close beside Sal's body, with Brad's head in her lap. She had broken off only when the two doctors bent to loosen her hold. Then, refusing all offers of assistance, she had mounted the stairs to her room. Yancey remembered that she had exchanged no word with Carroll. Beyond a silent nod of greeting, she had given no notice of his presence.

"She'll be down directly, Dan," he said. He got to his feet as Quent mounted the portico. Lorena's brother had taken over the disposal of Sal's body.

"Castor and Pollux will make a casket," he said. "We'll lay him to rest—with what's left of Florrie and the children—in the plantation cemetery. The Army chaplain can say a few words. In the circumstances, it's better to move quickly. The truth about last night will spread fast enough."

Carroll spoke with averted eyes. "What's your verdict on Saladin, Doctor?"

So you're making our task easy, thought Yancey. *I rather thought you would.* "Sal was obviously out of his mind," he said. "I still don't see how he lived to—to do what he did to Brad."

"I must put something definite in my report."

"Call it temporary insanity from grief. Won't that do?"

"Well enough, I suppose," said the Yankee major. "Shall I add that Captain Selby killed him in self-defense?"

"What else can you call it?" asked Quent. "Sal was always a little mad. Most men are when they confuse tomorrow with the present."

Silence fell on the portico, broken only by the scratch of Dan Carroll's pencil. "Self-defense it is then," he said. "The label will make things easier for all of us."

"Amen to that," said Yancey.

Carroll took up his hat and side arms. "Will you convey my respects to Lorena—and say I was forced to leave? As you can imagine, I've a long day ahead."

"So have we all," said Uncle Doc. "A long, long day."

An orderly, detaching himself from the group of horsemen on the drive, came forward with the commander's mount. Dan did not speak again until he was in the saddle.

"Will Lorena care for the—the invalid herself?"

"Selby wives have always looked after their husbands when they were ailing," said Uncle Doc. "It's an old Georgia custom."

"If she needs help of any sort, I'm at Four Cedars. Tell her I'll wait. That I'm good at waiting. She'll understand that too."

Warmed by the rising sun, aware that the plantation was spring-
ing to life about him, Yancey realized he had dozed with his back
against a pillar.

Quent had left to unpack his bags a second time. On the lawn a
pair of bluejays were quarreling lustily. They postponed the argument to wing into the branches of the holly tree when a trio of
gardeners (intent on the last autumnal trimming of the boxwoods)
moved up from the rose garden. Beyond the cedar windbreak mat-
tocks swung in rhythm as the hands began to clear another field
for planting, come spring. Even without Sal to marshal them they
had trooped to their work at the first clang of the overseer's bell—
nor did it matter that a darker hand than Luke Jackson's had
sounded that brazen summons.

Selby would endure from this day forward: its course was pre-
dictable as the next sunrise. Brad Selby had given his last order,
and Lorena had come into her own. Was it a hollow victory—and
had she paid too high a price? Such questions must go unanswered
now, thought Uncle Doc. He rose as she came down the stairs, and
entered the house to await her at the parlor door—lifting a detain-
ing palm when she turned toward the study that was now her husband's sickroom.

"Brad will sleep until evening," he said. "I've seen to that."

"Is he resting comfortably?"

"As comfortable as he can ever be. Over the next few days I'll
train three of the girls to serve as nurses—on eight-hour shifts. Caring for him won't be hard, once they learn the routine."

"I want to do my share, Uncle Doc."

"Of course you do. But you've a plantation to run and a boy to
raise. Those jobs come first. Even Brad will see that, now he's
through with interfering."

"Is he really through then?"

"Sal had his revenge," said the plantation doctor quietly. "When
Brad wakens, I doubt if he can speak—much less raise his head. He
may last beyond the New Year—I won't say with luck. He'll be
lucky if he goes sooner."

"You told Daniel that?"

"He has the whole story."

"I saw him ride off," Reen said slowly. "I guessed why."

"He knows you must stay with Brad—to the end."

Uncle Doc studied Reen carefully while she moved to the line of french doors and opened them wide to the new day. She was wearing the homespun dress she called her field clothes. That, too, was as it should be.

"Isn't it strange that a visiting Yankee can know my moves in advance?"

"Not at all, girl. Have you forgotten he loves you?"

She broke under the question, as he had hoped she would, leaning with her back to the french door while her body was shaken by great, racking sobs. He made no move to comfort her. She had needed that release badly.

"I can't wait for happiness forever," she said at last. "It's too much to ask of any woman."

"Not of you, Lorena. Not when you remember your Charleston manners."

It was an old joke between them. Accepting his handkerchief, she wiped the tears from her cheeks, then gave her parlor a glance. The servants had repaired last night's havoc: even the damaged door had a new pane. Only the two shotguns remained where they had fallen. Cautious to the end, the Negroes had not dared to touch them.

Lorena lifted the guns from the carpet and moved to restore them to their place above the mantel. Again Uncle Doc made no move to help. This, too, was an act she needed to perform alone.

"The fighting seems to be over at last," said the mistress of Selby Hall. "I'd best put up the weapons."